THE PRINCE AND THE PLAYER

THE PRINCE PACT BOOK 1

NORA PHOENIX

B

Boldw⚬⚬d

First published in Great Britain in 2025 by Boldwood Books Ltd.

Copyright © Nora Phoenix, 2025

Cover Design by Head Design Ltd.

Cover Images: Shutterstock

The moral right of Nora Phoenix to be identified as the author of this work has been asserted in accordance with the Copyright, Designs and Patents Act 1988.

All rights reserved. No part of this book may be reproduced in any form or by any electronic or mechanical means, including information storage and retrieval systems, without written permission from the author, except for the use of brief quotations in a book review.This book is a work of fiction and, except in the case of historical fact, any resemblance to actual persons, living or dead, is purely coincidental.

Every effort has been made to obtain the necessary permissions with reference to copyright material, both illustrative and quoted. We apologise for any omissions in this respect and will be pleased to make the appropriate acknowledgements in any future edition.

A CIP catalogue record for this book is available from the British Library.

Paperback ISBN 978-1-83656-897-1

Large Print ISBN 978-1-83656-898-8

Hardback ISBN 978-1-83656-896-4

Ebook ISBN 978-1-83656-899-5

Kindle ISBN 978-1-83656-900-8

Audio CD ISBN 978-1-83656-891-9

MP3 CD ISBN 978-1-83656-892-6

Digital audio download ISBN 978-1-83656-895-7

This book is printed on certified sustainable paper. Boldwood Books is dedicated to putting sustainability at the heart of our business. For more information please visit https://www.boldwoodbooks.com/about-us/sustainability/

Boldwood Books Ltd, 23 Bowerdean Street, London, SW6 3TN

www.boldwoodbooks.com

PROLOGUE
TORE

Westminster Abbey was packed to the rafters with the who's who of the royal and rich. The grandeur of the medieval church was on full display with its ornate, stained-glass windows, towering pillars, and intricate details adorning every inch of the cathedral, all polished to perfection.

Princes and queens mingled with pop stars and actresses, and old nobility sat right next to fashion models and even a social media influencer or two. Elegantly dressed guests filled the pews, the women all sporting the most ridiculous hats and their jewels glistening like baubles under the chandeliers.

The air was heavy with the fragrance of fresh flowers carefully arranged throughout the cathedral. Combined with the abundance of expensive perfumes and eau de colognes, it made for an overwhelming attack on the senses.

I'd always been a firm proponent of the "less is more" philosophy, but it wasn't every day that the British crown prince got married, and the royal wedding was the event of the year, if not the decade.

"I give them five years," Floris whispered.

Greg leaned in. "Five? I beg to disagree. It'll take at least ten years."

"What will take ten years?" I asked.

"To pop out an heir, a spare, and an extra." Greg said it as casually as if he were announcing the weather.

I slapped a hand in front of my mouth to hide my laugh. If the press got a picture of me laughing at an inopportune or, worse, an inappropriate time, my mother would kill me, and once she was done, my uncle and aunt would murder me all over again.

"That's your cousin, Greg," Nils chimed in. "Do you think so little of him?"

Greg quirked a well-groomed eyebrow. "Excuse me, but have you met the British royal family? We're not known for our fidelity and long-lasting marriages."

"That's an understatement," Floris mumbled.

"Like you have any right to speak. Your grandfather had two children out of wedlock," Greg fired back.

Floris shrugged. "The difference is that the Dutch don't care, and the Dutch press is only marginally interested."

"God, I wish that were the case here," Greg said with a sigh. "The British tabloids are the absolute worst."

He wouldn't get an argument from me. Being fourth in line to the Norwegian throne wasn't my idea of fun, but things could be so much worse. Like being fourth in line to the British throne, which was the fate of Greg, officially known as Gregory Edward William Mountbatten-Windsor, the future Duke of York.

Then again, at least he wasn't the crown prince, like his cousin Harold, who was promising everlasting love and faithfulness to his bride, Lady Caroline. She was of noble birth, of course, if not an actual princess. Those were in short supply these days, with European royal families all downsizing and no longer granting royal titles to all descendants.

They could take my title today, pretty please and thank you, but alas, I hadn't been that lucky so far. For now, I'd have to be Prince Tore Haakon Anders von Glücksburg, nephew to King Ragnar and Queen Hilda of Norway. At least my chances of ever making it to the throne were slim.

Though that was true for all four of us. Floris was fifth in line for the Dutch throne, and five people had to die before Nils would become the King of Sweden. We were the extras, the expendable princes, the ones who were expected to show up when needed and, above all, behave. Kind of like those fancy poodles at a dog show.

After the church service, we joined the receiving line to offer our congratulations—condolences? Respect? Thoughts and prayers?—to the happy couple. It took for-fucking-ever, and with so many people watching us, we couldn't goof around too much either. Finally, the official part was done, the press was firmly ushered out, and the real party could start.

As usual, at events like this, the four of us hung out together. Weddings, funerals, baptisms, coronations, and the occasional royal visit were the lifelines of our friendship. We'd all known each other since birth. Hell, there was a famous picture of Greg, Floris, and me looking all adorable in full suits as page boys at the wedding of Floris's aunt. I was two, Greg and Floris three. Nils, who was six years older than me, still resented not being asked.

"At least the booze is top quality." Floris leaned back in his chair and took a sip of his no-doubt expensive and old whiskey, then let out a sigh of happiness. The man was a certified whiskey snob.

"Without alcohol, these events would be unbearable," Greg said. He'd opted for some fancy microbrew.

"A couple more years and that will be us," Nils remarked, and that got our attention.

"What do you mean?" I asked.

Nils gestured at the bride, who had changed into her third outfit of the day. "Marriage. Kids. You know that's what they expect of us."

Floris held up his hands. "Not me. Not unless surrogacy is an option."

He'd come out last year as the first openly gay prince, and while it had dominated the news everywhere else, in the Netherlands, it had been accepted with a shrug. You had to hand it to the Dutch, they really didn't care.

"I'm nineteen," Greg said. "Way too young for marriage."

"You'll be first," I said to Nils.

"It's not marriage that scares me," Nils said softly. "It's the feeling that life is passing me by without me truly living it."

I sat up straight. "I'm not following."

He gestured at the party around us. "This isn't real life. This is a privileged, sheltered existence. The ultimate ivory tower. I want to truly live, to experience what normal life is like, away from the spotlight. I don't want to have all these regrets on my death bed of things I never did. I need to know what it's like to live as a... commoner."

As much as we all detested that word, it had no good alternative that conveyed the same meaning.

"How on earth will you pull that off?" Floris asked. "Everyone in Sweden knows you. Hell, all over Europe, people may recognize you."

"America," I said slowly. "Americans may know the crowns but not those further down the line. We don't get much press there."

Nils nodded. "That was my idea as well. Hell, I'd be surprised if they could even locate Sweden on a map."

I snorted. Rude as it was, he wasn't wrong. The American education system didn't seem to prioritize European geography.

I'd met Americans who thought Norway sat right alongside Russia. Finland would like a word about this.

"Did you know about this idea of his?" Greg asked me.

"No, but I was following his line of reasoning and came to the same conclusion. He's not wrong, you know."

"You really think Americans won't recognize you?" Floris asked Nils, looking skeptical.

"Me? No. Greg, maybe, but a disguise should help with that. We'd have to use aliases, of course."

Greg shook his head. "Leave me out of it. I have zero desire to spend time in our ungrateful former colony."

Nils leaned forward. "You could be yourself."

Silence descended as we all processed that. Greg had come out to us as gay right after Floris had made his public statement, but we were the only ones in the know. His secret was safe with us. With the rest of the British royal family and especially the press? Not so much.

Greg orchestrated for himself to be photographed with gorgeous girls all the time, suggesting an endless stream of girl-friends, and so far, no one had even speculated about his sexuality. He'd even gotten the nickname Prince Playboy, which, considering the man was still a virgin, was so ironic that I didn't even know where to start.

"He's right," Floris said softly. "You'd be able to experiment."

Floris, always the levelheaded Dutchman, wasn't known for being emotionally supportive, but he'd been Greg's biggest ally since he'd shared his secret.

"I'm warming to the idea," I said. "I think we should all do it. Spend a year in America and live an ordinary life as commoners." An idea popped into my head. "We could attend university there."

"College," Nils corrected me. "I think they call it college if it's an undergraduate degree."

"Whatever. That's semantics. Though you're a little old for college."

Nils nodded. "I was thinking of applying for a job there. Maybe as a sports coach, since that's what my actual degree is in."

Sports. Oh, there was an idea. I'd played football—soccer, according to the Americans—my entire life and had dreamed of going pro until my father had provided a harsh reality check. Princes did not become pro football players, no matter how good they were. But I'd continued playing at a high level, so maybe football could be my way in? American colleges were big on sports, so surely there had to be one that was interested in an international student who excelled at football. Soccer. Whatever.

"I wouldn't mind studying in the US for a year," Floris said, "but I'm not sure I'd want or need to go undercover. I can see the reason or even the necessity for you guys, but most people in the Netherlands don't even recognize me. And if they do, they don't care."

"The British press would care very much, trust me. For me, an alias and even some disguise would be crucial," Greg said, but then let out a long sigh. "Who am I kidding? The king will never allow it."

After too many scandals, King Edward—Greg's uncle—had tightened the rules, warning everyone in the family that he wanted no more salacious headlines. I feared Greg was correct that he'd be fighting an uphill battle here.

As for me, I could probably convince Uncle Ragnar and Aunt Hilda, the king and queen, to let me go, providing I built a solid case. Nils shouldn't have an issue either, and Floris had the most freedom out of all of us, so he'd be fine. But Greg? Greg was in for one hell of a fight.

"Let's make a pact," Nils said, shifting to the edge of his seat. "Let's promise each other to do whatever we can to spend a year outside the bubble of our privileged existence and see if we have what it takes to make it in the real world."

He held out his hand, and I was the first to place my hand on top of his. "I'm in."

After a brief hesitation, Floris joined us. "Me too. It sounds like fun."

We all looked at Greg, who bit his lip and then sighed as he slowly placed his hand on top of ours. "I'll do my very best to convince the powers that be to let me go."

We all grinned at each other.

"Let's meet two years from now and share our experiences," I suggested. "I can't wait to hear all of your stories."

Everyone agreed, and we let go of each other's hands. I leaned back in my chair. Where should I go? Somewhere exciting. I didn't want to be stuck in the middle of nowhere, like Kansas or Oklahoma or something. Maybe a big city like New York City? Not LA. I'd been there and hadn't seen the appeal. Boston was nice. Very European in its atmosphere.

Wait, I needed a college with a campus. I wanted to live on campus, in a dorm like in all the movies and TV series. And it needed to be a college with a good soccer team.

I rubbed my hands together. This was going to be so much fun.

1

FARRON

I stepped into the locker room, the scent of antiseptic and lingering sweat a familiar balm to my senses. No matter how often they cleaned this place, that odor never truly left. Not that I minded it. This was what home smelled like to me, and I inhaled deeply, a grin breaking free.

Lockers stood in silent rows, dented from years of jostling and jubilant cheers, their blue paint chipped away to reveal a history of victories and defeats. Most of the team was already there—I had stopped by Coach's office first—and a cacophony of chatter filled the air, interspersed with the echo of cleats on concrete and the rattle of metal doors swinging open and closed.

Thank fuck summer break was over. I couldn't wait to get back on the field with my team, the Hawley Hawks, for my second year —and last, since I was a senior—as team captain.

"Hey, Farron!"

My teammates welcomed me back and we exchanged hugs, slaps on the back, and brief summaries of what we'd done in the summer. Mine was super short, as always. I'd worked and I'd played soccer. That was it. Well, I'd hung out with my three siblings too, but that wasn't any more exciting than the other two activities. My life might be boring, but I was fine with that. One more year, and I would have my degree... and hopefully play for a club.

I slapped my rusty locker, number fourteen, with fondness. "Hello, old friend. Let's hope you'll bring me luck once more."

We'd come far last season, and I had high hopes for this year. We had a great team and the best coach on the planet. All we needed to do was lock in and get it done, and we'd make it all the way to the championship and maybe even nationals.

I was settling in, lacing up my worn-out cleats that needed to hold out just a little longer, when the door to the locker room opened and a tall, lean guy with meticulously styled blond hair stepped in, an easy smile on his face. "I've found the football team, yes?"

I snorted as I took in his designer jeans and shirt that probably cost more than I made at my job in a year. I might not give two shits about clothes, but that didn't mean I'd never heard of brands like Balenciaga. The kid had money. Also, football? Was he serious? They'd squash him like a goddamn bug. "Football is on the other side of the campus, near the, you know, football fields. This is soccer."

He chuckled. "My apologies. I haven't fully grown accustomed to the appropriate terminology. I'm from Europe, where we call it football... like the rest of the world."

Arrogant asshole. Oh, fuck. I knew who he was. "You're that international student from Norway. Tore something." I pronounced it the way it was spelled, like the past tense of tear.

"It's pronounced Tor-ay, and yes, that's me." He walked toward me and offered me his hand. "Tore Haakon. It's a pleasure to make your acquaintance."

Faint snickers came from the rest of the team. *Make your*

acquaintance? What kind of old-fashioned expression was that? "Farron Carey, team captain."

His blue eyes lit up. "Oh, it's a pleasure. I'm looking forward to playing with you and the team this year."

I couldn't exactly say the same. Coach had only told me about him joining the team fifteen minutes ago, and to say I wasn't happy about it was an understatement. Sure, I trusted Coach when he said the kid was good—good enough that he could've made it to the big leagues if he'd tried, Coach had assured me— but that didn't mean I liked having a freshman join the team as a first-string player. Especially not one who would hog the spotlight, and this kid looked like you couldn't drag him away from it if you tried.

"Locker twenty-nine is yours," I said. "Hurry the fuck up with changing because we're starting in two minutes, and Coach doesn't tolerate tardiness. And neither do I."

His smile didn't falter. "Perfect."

I kept an eye on him as he changed, not missing the way his eyes lit up when he saw his jersey with his name on it. At least he was properly impressed with the honor of playing for Hawley College. But then I spotted his cleats and my mouth tightened. Holy shit, he was wearing the latest Nike cleats, the ones that cost, like, nine hundred bucks. His parents had to be fucking loaded.

The locker room chatter died down as Coach Gold made his entrance, an imposing figure whose authority was as much a part of him as the whistle around his neck. "All right, Hawks!" he bellowed. "Circle up."

We shuffled into a tight group, each player casting curious glances at the others, sizing up both friends and new competition. Coach clapped his hands together once, commanding silence as his gaze swept over us. "We have some new faces. Let's get to know the team. Name, position, and if you want, a fun fact. Keep it quick."

We went around the circle, some guys boasting hometown glory while others offered up trivia ranging from weird pet—a pig? Seriously?—to even weirder hobbies. I kept my arms folded across my chest, my stance firm.

When it was Tore's turn, he had an easy smile. "Hey, I'm Tore," he began, his accent a clear giveaway of his European roots. "I'm a center midfielder, and I'm from Norway, which is known for its fjords. It's also one of the happiest countries in the world."

That explained his perpetual smile, then. Didn't make it less annoying. And what the hell were fjords?

"I'm excited about playing for Hawley College this year and giving it my all."

When my turn came, I kept it brief. "Farron Carey, center-back and team captain. I'm here to play soccer, win games, and lead this team to victory."

I wasn't gonna share anything personal. Let them judge me by my game, not some contrived tidbit meant to endear me to them.

Coach nodded, satisfied with my no-nonsense approach, and I retreated, my glare lingering on Tore for a split second longer than necessary. His eyes met mine, unflinching, and for a brief moment, I saw the challenge reflected back at me. Hmm, maybe he had more of a backbone than I'd initially thought.

But then he flashed me a toothy smile. Nah, he wasn't a threat.

"To the field, Hawks!" Coach barked, and we were moving, a disjointed stream of blue jerseys flowing out of the locker room and into the open air.

I jogged out, feeling the familiar thrill that always surged through me at the start of a new season. The sun beat down on the soccer field, turning the air thick with midday heat. August in Ohio was usually muggy to the point of unbearable, though I'd gotten used to it, having grown up only a hundred miles from Hawley.

As my cleats hit the grass, I felt solid, grounded, despite the fact Tore effortlessly sidled up beside me, his blond hair reflecting the sunlight like some kind of halo. I spared him a glance, my jaw clenched tight, and his eyes flickered toward me. I turned away sharply, focusing on the green expanse before us as I took the lead in our warm-up. Three full turns around the soccer field, then five minutes of exercises to warm up and loosen each major muscle group.

"We're starting with the basics," Coach said when we were done with the warm-up. "Team up for passing drills."

I paired up with Jake, another senior and one of our strikers, and we fell into an easy rhythm forged over three years of playing together. We jogged up the field, passing the ball back and forth in a steady cadence, never missing a beat. And when we'd reached the end of the field, we turned right back around and made our way back, keeping it tight to give everyone else space.

Tore had found a partner in Colin, my roommate for the second consecutive year and our goalie. I'd known Tore was tall, but seeing him next to Colin made that even clearer. Colin was the tallest on the team at six foot five, and Tore was only an inch or so shorter.

He and Colin ran parallel to Jake and me, so it was easy for me to observe him. He moved with an effortless grace that made it impossible not to watch. His passes were crisp and precise, the ball landing directly in front of Colin's feet. At least he had technical skills, then. That fancy footwork didn't mean he'd do well in a game, but it was a start.

"Let's run defensive drills. Carey and Tore, pair up."

Had Coach picked up on my feelings toward Tore? Or was this because I hadn't exactly been subtle about my annoyance over this addition to the team? Either way, I'd have to suck it up. Great. Just fucking great.

I strode over to the designated spot, with Tore following close behind. I could feel his eyes on my back, probably sizing me up or trying to get under my skin. But I wouldn't let him; I couldn't afford to.

The concept of these drills was simple. The attacker, Tore in this case, had the ball, and my job as the defender was to separate him from it. We took to the field in positions opposite each other. Tore didn't say anything as I created some distance between us, then started his dribble forward. I'd expected him to make an evasive maneuver, to try and outflank me, but he came straight at me, his eyes trained on me.

I came at him, my right foot shooting out toward the ball... which wasn't there anymore. He'd moved it from one foot to the other so fast that I lost track for a second. Fuck, he was quick on his feet. I tried again, but he did a lightning-fast roll and stopover, stopping the ball with his back foot and tapping it lightly to move it to the side.

"Fuck," I muttered under my breath, unable to shake the sense of awe that crept up my spine. His footwork was impeccable, a delicate balance of finesse and power, and he outplayed me with an ease that was as impressive as it was annoying. Dammit, he was good. But so was I, and I wasn't about to let him show me up on my own turf.

I forgot about everything else as I focused on the ball. Hell if I was gonna let a freshman get the better of me. "Again," I snapped.

We swapped roles with him trying to take the ball from me. He was taller than me, but I was bulkier, and I used that to my advantage, shoving him aside. Well, that had been the plan, but he stood his ground, not budging.

I blasted the ball downfield, my gaze fixed on the net when

Tore slid into my periphery, intercepting with a deft touch that sent a ripple of irritation coursing through me. "Nice block," I grunted, more an acknowledgment of his presence than genuine praise.

"Thank you, Farron," he replied, his accent smooth yet grating. "Your pass was quite impressive too."

"Save it." Did he really think I wanted his approval? I brushed past him to reclaim my position.

But in the end, I had to admit he was good. Really, really good. Still didn't mean he'd be able to replicate those skills in an actual game, but he'd outsmarted me seven out of ten times. I'd have to step up my game if I wanted to beat him.

"Watch and learn, Farron," Jake teased when we were done with the defensive drills, elbowing me lightly in the ribs. "Maybe you'll pick up a thing or two."

"Shut it."

Admiration was a bitter pill to swallow, especially when directed at someone like Tore, whose life had probably been handed to him on a silver platter. This was my field, my dominion, and I'd be damned if I let Tore's European charm and flair outshine my own hard-earned skills.

With renewed determination, I charged into the fray for our next drill. My passes were sharp and calculated, and my movements, though not as fluid as Tore's, were effective.

"Nice hustle!" someone shouted, and the gazes of my teammates followed me, their respect something tangible that I thrived on.

As practice wore on, sweat clung to my skin like a second jersey, my breaths coming in heavy torrents. But I didn't let up, not even for a second. By the time Coach blew the whistle, signaling the end of practice, my legs were shot, but my spirit soared. I'd set out to prove myself, and if the burning in my lungs and the ache in my muscles were any indications, I'd done just that.

"Good work today, team," Coach said. "We're shaping up nicely. Keep this intensity, and we'll have a hell of a season."

Damn straight. If Tore was as good in games as he was in practice, he'd be an asset, even if he was an ass. All I had to do was work hard, set a good example, maintain momentum, and lead the team to victory.

And as for Tore... Well, he'd have to get used to sharing the spotlight.

2
TORE

The late summer warmth hung like a suffocating blanket over the campus as Luke and I, clad in our dark-blue practice uniforms, walked to football practice. Strike that. Soccer practice. How long would it take me to get that right? Probably as long as it would be until my British English made way for an American twang. Which wasn't bloody likely, seeing as how I'd spent a year in the UK for an exchange program in secondary school.

Luke was my roommate and a fellow freshman, a blond, sturdy farmer's boy from rural Ohio. He played center-back, like Farron, but unlike our team captain, Luke was easy to like. He called his mom daily, which I thought was adorable, and he constantly wolfed down food like a man after a week's fast. We had two classes together, though he planned to major in agricultural science, whereas I was focused on political science.

"Seriously, though," I grumbled, adjusting the strap of my soccer bag on my shoulder. "Keller assigned *War and Peace* like it's some kind of breezy beach read."

Luke chuckled. "You think that's bad? My philosophy assignment might as well be written in Ancient Greek. It took me an hour to read four pages yesterday."

"Maybe we can swap," I offered with a grin, knowing full well neither of us would fare better in the other's shoes. "I'd rather ponder the meaning of life than try to keep track of Tolstoy's characters."

"Tempting, but no. Pretty sure your study load also comes with learning details about historic battles I couldn't possibly care less about."

We rounded the corner of the Arts building, the Gothic architecture giving way to the open expanse of the soccer fields, our sanctuary from academic tribulations. But even here, a shadow lurked: a dark-haired enigma with the build of a defensive wall and the warmth of an ice bath.

"Speaking of battles..." I lowered my voice as I watched Farron leading a few early birds in stretching exercises. "Have you ever seen him crack a smile?"

"Who? Farron?" Luke glanced over, his eyebrows raised ever so slightly. "Nah, that guy's got resting brood face. Why?"

"Resting brood face, that's hilarious." I'd never heard that expression before, but it fit Farron perfectly. "He doesn't seem to like me, and I can't fathom why. I haven't crossed him, have I?"

"You?" Luke looked genuinely perplexed, as if the idea of anyone not getting along with me was beyond the realm of possibility. "Tore, you're the friendliest guy I've ever met. You probably greet spiders before you escort them outside."

"That's called Norwegian hospitality."

"Maybe it's not personal." Luke held open the door to the locker room. "Farron takes this all super seriously."

"Perhaps." I wasn't convinced, though. It felt personal to me. Very personal. I suspected there was something more to it, something I was missing. Farron didn't know my real identity, so that couldn't be it, though it would've been a plausible explanation. What other reason could he have to not like me?

"Have you considered that Farron might see you as a distraction?" Luke asked. His tone was casual, but the implication was heavy enough to weigh down my next step.

"A distraction?"

"Look, from what I understand, Farron's gunning for the pro leagues. He doesn't have time for—no offense—charming Norwegian imports who might not bleed soccer as much as he does."

"None taken." I masked the sting with a grin. But truthfully, it felt like a cleat had dug into my pride. We were at the end of week two, and from day one, I'd thrown myself into every practice. Wasn't that enough? "I'll have to convince him I'm as serious about football as he is."

Luke clamped a hand on my shoulder. "You may wanna start with calling it soccer."

Crap.

"Soccer. One of these days, I'll get it right."

"In the meantime, let me share a little bit of wisdom with you that my high school coach always said. Focus on the ball, not the bullshit. Don't let Farron rob you of your joy in the game."

Wise words, and they resonated with me. *Focus on the ball, not the bullshit.* I liked that. "Thanks."

We dropped our backpacks at the edge of the field, then joined the rest of the team in running warm-up laps, Farron leading the way, of course. What could I do to make him see I wasn't a distraction, that I wanted this team to succeed as much as he did?

Having to prove how much this sport meant to me wasn't new. I'd gone a hundred rounds with my parents over the years, especially once it became clear that I had real talent—and the discipline and dedication to go far. But in the end, my heritage had won, like it always had and always would. Princes did not become professional football players, no matter how good they were.

Seeing my dream crushed like that had been a blow, but I'd gotten over it. Maybe that was why it hurt that Farron didn't take me seriously? Hmm, I might have to consider taking a psychology course if I wanted to figure that one out.

"All right, Hawks, let's get moving!" Coach Gold's voice boomed across the pitch, and I fell in line with my teammates. The group's energy was palpable, a collective pulse that quickened with every pass and shot. I focused on the rhythm of the ball at my feet, the feel of the grass beneath my cleats, the scent of freshly churned earth rising with each stride. This—this was where I belonged, where titles and heritage faded into nothingness, and only the game mattered.

I chased down balls, intercepted plays, and sent passes slicing through the defense like a hot knife through butter. Sweat beaded on my brow, my breath coming in short bursts, but I welcomed the fatigue.

It didn't matter that Farron glared daggers at me every time I outmaneuvered him. I wouldn't let his disdain slow me down. I played harder, faster, letting my performance speak for itself.

"Nice work, Tore!" Coach Gold bellowed from the sidelines, his praise ringing in my ears like a victory chant. He used last names for everyone but had apparently decided my first name was easier to pronounce than Haakon. I couldn't blame him.

The practice wore on and I didn't let up, not even when my lungs screamed for mercy and my muscles trembled with exertion. I tackled each scrimmage as though it was a championship game, pushing myself to be faster, stronger, better. Some of my teammates threw admiring glances my way, and a few of the other newbies studied me closely, trying to emulate my movements. Yet my eyes kept seeking out Farron, looking for any sign of approval.

By the time Coach Gold blew the final whistle, signaling the end of practice, my muscles cramped and my chest heaved. But underneath the exhaustion was a sense of satisfaction so profound, it bordered on euphoria.

"Good work, team. Hit the showers," Coach Gold commanded, and we dispersed, a flock of spent Hawks grateful for the reprieve. I lingered on the field for a moment longer, taking in deep gulps of air, and allowed myself a small smile of pride. I'd given everything out there. Whether it was enough to win over my toughest critic was yet to be seen, but for now, I had the respect of my team, and that was victory enough.

Despite Farron's coldness, a sense of accomplishment thrummed through me. Sweat dripped from my brow as I jogged over to where Farron was packing up his gear, his back turned to me, the sharp angles of his shoulders tense beneath the fabric of his jersey. He'd been like a wall on the field, immovable and imposing, but I was determined not to let his gruff exterior deter me.

"Hey, Farron." I mustered the cheeriest tone I could despite being exhausted. "That was some solid defending today."

He glanced over his shoulder, dark eyes flicking to meet mine for an instant before returning to his task. "Thanks."

"It's impressive how you anticipate the play."

"Part of the job." He shoved his cleats into his bag with more force than necessary.

This conversation was like dribbling a ball through an obstacle course. Each response from him was a hurdle I had to navigate. But I wasn't one to forfeit the game so easily. "It's a skill, though. One I hope to learn from watching you."

"Watch all you want." His tone bordered on dismissive, but I didn't miss the briefest hitch in his movements—a pause that suggested my words might have landed somewhere soft inside him.

"Will do." I smiled, undeterred by the walls he put up. My mother always said kindness was a language anyone could understand, and I intended to be fluent in it.

I caught his eye again as we walked out of the locker room at the same time, offering him a smile that I hoped conveyed more than words could—my respect, my earnest desire to be part of the team, to be seen as an equal.

For a heartbeat, I thought I saw a crack in his armor, a softening around the edges of his hardened gaze. But then, just as quickly, it was gone, replaced by an icy veneer that felt like a gust of winter wind. His expression hardened into something unreadable, and he looked away, leaving me with a hollow feeling in my chest. I must've imagined it.

"See you tomorrow, Farron," I called after him, my voice buoyant even as doubt crept into the corners of my mind.

"Sure," he threw over his shoulder, the word devoid of warmth.

I watched him go, his figure retreating until it merged with the shadows, and I was left standing there alone.

"Thanks for waiting," Luke said, finally done showering and changing. He wasn't the fastest when it came to personal hygiene, I'd already discovered. But it would be rude not to wait for him, considering we were both heading back to our dorm.

"No problem."

"Man, you were on fire today." Luke bumped shoulders with me in a friendly nudge. "If you keep playing like that, Farron's gotta come around."

"Thanks." The compliment warmed me, but my mind was still churning over Farron's cold dismissal. "I don't get it. It's like he's determined not to like me."

"Give it time. I doubt that guy warms up quickly to anyone. You've got talent and drive. Plus, you have that whole Viking thing going on," Luke teased, nudging me again, but softer this time.

"Well, I won't be raiding any shores or pillaging villages any time soon. All I want is to play football and…"

"Win over the grumpy captain?" Luke finished for me, a knowing look in his eye.

"Exactly." I sighed, feeling the weight of my task settle on my shoulders. "No matter what it takes. He's important to the team, and I need him to see that I am too."

Luke stopped and turned to face me, sincerity etched into his features. "You don't have to prove anything. You belong here. Farron will see it eventually."

"Maybe, but I can't shake the feeling that it's going to take more than scoring goals to win him over."

"He can't overlook genuine effort forever. And hey, if it doesn't work out, you've still got the rest of the team on board. I think everyone's already convinced you're one hell of a midfielder."

"Thanks, Luke," I said, grateful for his unwavering support.

I wasn't giving up this easily, but dammit, breaking through Farron's defenses might be the toughest challenge I'd ever faced on or off the field.

3

FARRON

I had a twist in my gut as I pushed open the front door to the Sigma Phi house, the place already buzzing with the thump of bass and the chatter of too many conversations. Parties weren't my scene, but a promise was a promise, especially when it was to your co-captain and buddy who could throw a guilt trip like nobody's business.

"Come on, Farron, it'll be fun!" RJ had said. "We'll hang out and get drunk together."

Clearly, he and I had very different definitions of the word fun.

I wasn't in the best of moods to begin with after working all day and being forced to pick up half an extra shift because of a coworker's no-show. After a day like that, a frat party was the last thing I wanted, but if I didn't show, RJ would be on my ass for weeks, and that was even less appealing.

The air inside was thick with cologne and the sweet tang of spilled beer. Multicolored strobe lights pulsed over the sea of bodies who danced, flirted, and laughed, some lounging on the tattered couches while others hovered around a makeshift bar manned by a guy wearing sunglasses despite the lack of sunlight.

I scanned the room for RJ or any of the soccer team, hoping for a familiar face to latch onto until I could decently make my escape. That's when Tore walked in, looking like he'd stepped out of a European fashion magazine instead of a frat party. Even here, I couldn't escape him.

He wore a designer jacket that probably cost more than I made in a year at Walmart, tailored to perfection over his lean frame. He walked through the crowd, all relaxed and confident despite probably not knowing anyone. And even the fact that people stared at him was apparently not bothering him at all.

"Who's that?" I heard a girl ask her friend, her voice rising above the music.

"I dunno, but he's hot," her friend replied.

I watched, leaning against a wall, as he started chatting with a group of guys from the lacrosse team. Within minutes, they clapped him on the back, offered him drinks, and he was laughing along with them, his smile easy and infectious. It was something about the way he carried himself, how people were drawn to him like he had his own gravitational pull.

How did he do that: slide into any situation like he belonged there?

I felt an unwelcome prickle of... What? Envy? Annoyance? It was hard to tell. All I knew was that watching Tore effortlessly charm his way through a crowd made me want to punch something. Or maybe someone.

"Hey!" A hand clapped my shoulder, and I turned to see RJ, a grin splitting his face. "You made it!"

"Didn't have much choice, did I?" I forced a half-smile.

"Lighten up, man. Have some fun for once!" He shoved a red plastic cup into my hand before disappearing into the throng. So much for hanging out together—not that I had expected anything else. Like Tore, RJ was a social butterfly.

Fun, right. I took a sip, the beer cheap and bitter, just like my mood. A group of sorority girls had joined the guys from the lacrosse team, all focused on Tore like he was holding court. His laugh, bright and clear, cut through the noise, and it made me clench my jaw tighter.

He'd slipped into this party, into this world—*my* world—as easily as he did into those expensive clothes that whispered wealth and privilege. It was as if he emitted some sort of silent siren call that drew people to him. Arms reached out to touch him, the guys bumped his shoulder, and a ripple of giggles followed his every word.

Envy stabbed me, not for what he had, but for how effortlessly he navigated this sea of social niceties. He was a freshman, new to this college and even to the country, so how could he so easily fit in when I was still wondering where I belonged other than on the soccer field?

Tore shifted positions, his eyes scanning the room until he spotted me. He froze for a moment, and somehow, that small moment of breaking his composure felt like a triumph. But then he excused himself and headed toward me. I straightened up, bracing myself as if I were about to take a hit on the soccer field.

"Good evening, Farron," Tore said as he approached, his accent lending an unintentional formality to his greeting.

"Hey."

"I wasn't expecting to see you here."

What was that supposed to mean? "Well, I'm here anyway."

"Are you enjoying yourself?" His gaze was direct, and there was a sincerity in his question that I didn't want to acknowledge.

"Not particularly, but I'll live."

His forehead creased slightly. "Why are you here if you don't enjoy it?"

"Because I made a promise."

"Ah, okay. We could step outside if that would be better?"

"Thanks, but I'm good here." My voice was sharper than I'd intended, and he raised an eyebrow, a small frown tugging at the corners of his lips as if he couldn't quite grasp the edge in my tone.

"Suit yourself," he replied with a shrug that was too graceful to be anything but annoying. "If you need something—"

"I won't," I cut him off, my words slicing through the space between us. There was a twinge of guilt somewhere in my chest for being such an ass to him, but I shoved it down. Nothing Tore had done had made him deserve my attitude, yet that only seemed to irritate me more.

I didn't say anything else, and when the silence lasted, his shoulders hunched. "I'll see you later then," he finally said.

"Or not," I muttered as he walked away, slipping back into the crowd as effortlessly as he'd emerged. His departure left me oddly unmoored. I took a deep swig from the cup, letting the bitterness wash over my tongue.

It wasn't fair how he could charm everyone without even trying, while I stood there gripping my Solo cup like a lifeline. I drained the rest of my drink, the liquid doing nothing to quell the growing annoyance at Tore's effortless sociability. How long did I have to stay before I could leave? At least another hour. Sigh.

Three drinks later, my head was buzzing, a rare sensation since I usually steered clear of drinking too much. But tonight, with Tore parading around like he owned the place, I needed something to take the edge off. Not that it was working, as I couldn't seem to take my eyes off him.

Wait, someone had handed him a red cup, and he was slamming it back. Was he drinking alcohol?

Before I'd thought it through, I stalked toward him and shoved my finger against his chest. "Are you drinking?"

"Excuse me?"

"Are. You. Drinking?"

He raised his cup in a mock salute. "Why yes, I am."

"You're an idiot. You're under twenty-one."

He shrugged. "It's legal in Norway, you know?"

"You're not in Norway."

"Thank you, I hadn't noticed."

Fucker. "It's illegal here."

He gestured at the room. "Then why is it okay that everyone else is drinking? Or are you merely objecting to my consumption?"

I gritted my teeth. He wasn't wrong, but hell if I was admitting that. "It could cost you your scholarship."

"I don't have a scholarship."

Of course he didn't. At least I could stop him from drinking more. I snatched the red cup from his hand before he could react, sniffing it. It was soda, the carbonation tickling my nose. "What the fuck? You think you're funny?"

"You asked if I was drinking. You never specified what."

Around us, laughter arose, and my cheeks heated. "You damn well knew what I meant."

"I apologize if my imperfect command of the English language resulted in a misunderstanding."

Imperfect command, my ass. He might have an accent, but he understood everything perfectly. Not that I could say that without looking like a dick to his gaggle of admirers. Which he knew all too well, considering his little smirk.

"I was trying to look out for you and make sure you weren't

getting kicked off the team or losing your scholarship, but I shouldn't have bothered. Privileged, spoiled, rich kids like you always get away with everything," I blurted out, the words fueled by more than the alcohol. "No idea what it's like to have actual obligations."

His blue eyes flared with something I hadn't seen before—anger. It should've felt satisfying, watching Mr. Perfect lose his cool, but instead, a pang of regret twisted in my gut.

"Privileged? Yes. Spoiled? Maybe." Tore stepped closer. "But don't you dare presume to know me or my life."

"Whatever." I turned away to disguise the sudden tightness in my chest. This wasn't how I wanted things to go down, yet I had no one to blame but myself. Not my finest moment.

"Way to kill the mood, bro," one of the lacrosse guys said, and I took that as my cue to leave before things got out of hand.

"I'll see you at training," I said to Tore, and it sounded fake and hypocritical even to my own ears.

He didn't say anything, and I spun on my heels and stalked out.

"Leaving already?" RJ stopped me when I'd almost reached the front door.

"Yeah, not feeling great." Technically, not a lie.

"Ah, gotcha. See you at practice, dude."

I waved, then headed out. Once outside, I took a deep breath, my head clearing from the slight buzz. Fuck, what a disaster. I shouldn't have let him get under my skin. As much as I hated to admit it, this was all on me.

Shaking my head at my own stupidity, I headed toward my dorm. In front of me was a couple, the guy supporting the girl as she wavered and tripped over her own feet, falling onto her knees on the grass. "Sorry," she giggled. "I'm a little drunk."

He hauled her to her feet again. "That's okay, baby. We can still have fun."

Fuck. I didn't like the sound of that at all. They hadn't spotted me yet, so I slowed down, wanting to see what was happening. Were they an actual couple, or had he picked her up at the party?

"My, you're such a gentleman. What's your name again?" she asked in a Southern drawl.

Well, I had my answer. Shit. I didn't have much of a choice now, did I?

I caught up to them in a few quick steps. "Did you guys have a good time at the party?" I asked jovially.

His head whipped around. He looked familiar, and it only took me a few seconds to place him. "Ben Jones, right? You play football?"

His face tightened. "Yeah, why?"

"Nothing, man. Just recognized you."

"I'm Elise." The girl almost tripped again as she extended her hand to me.

I took it, forcing a smile. "Hey, Elise. I'm Farron, captain of the soccer team."

"Ooh, I like soccer." She blinked a few times, and I had to hold her up by her hand. Jesus, she was drunk off her ass. "Y'all have such great abs."

I could barely hold back a snort. "Thank you. We work hard for those."

"I'm a little drunk," she said again, this time addressing me.

"More than a little, I would say."

"And..." She sighed as she turned to Ben. "I forgot your name again."

"Ben," I supplied helpfully. "His name's Ben."

"Ben was gonna take me to his room."

"Was he now?" I shot him a dark look and he cowered a little.

"Just making sure she got home safely," he mumbled.

Yeah, right. "I'm sure you were."

"I would never..."

"...take advantage of a drunk girl? Of course not. Your entire team is known for being such chivalrous white knights."

"Chi... Civil... I can't say it." Elise giggled again.

"Chivalrous. It means honorable, gallant, noble," I said. "Which Ben is. Aren't you?"

His look would've made lesser men pee their pants, but I shrugged it off. I'd caught him red-handed, and we both knew it.

"Of course," he said through clenched teeth.

I stepped closer to him, bringing my mouth to his ear. "I'm gonna check on her in the morning, and if I even so much as suspect you kissed her, I'll raise hell, you got me?"

After the longest pause on the planet, he tersely nodded. Message received.

"Sleep well," I told Elise. "And put some ibuprofen by your bed. You're gonna need them tomorrow morning."

With a last glare at Ben, I took off, confident he wouldn't try anything.

I'd made it a habit not to get involved in anything on campus, especially not frat fights or rivalries between sports teams, but in this case, I hadn't had much of a choice. While some people would've argued she shouldn't have gotten drunk, my viewpoint was always that drunk people couldn't consent and were automatically off-limits.

It wasn't like it would be fun to fuck someone who was only half-conscious. Honestly, I didn't get the appeal. And Ben Jones was popular enough that he could easily score, so why was he resorting to sleazy tactics like this? It made zero sense to me.

Knowing that I had at least prevented something bad from happening to Elise made me feel a little better, but it didn't take away the bitter taste my exchange with Tore had left in my mouth. Had I taken it too far?

Fuck, I hated that dude.

4

TORE

The piercing whistle cut through the air.

"Tore!" Coach's voice boomed across the field, his eyes zeroing in on me. "Stick to your position, goddammit. You're all over the place."

"Sorry, Coach!"

Fuck, I was doing it again. Stupid Americans and their rigid-position football. I had been trained according to the concept of total football, where each player had flexibility on the field and could fluidly move when and where needed. Another player would simply take over. The originally Dutch approach had now found favor with many coaches worldwide, but not Coach Gold.

Playing with rigid positions felt like a straitjacket, but Coach Gold had made his tactics clear, and I knew better than to argue mid-session. I wasn't gonna change his mind, but god, I really needed a way to remember to not move around on the field as much.

The drills continued, each pass and play sharpening our skills, but I couldn't shake off the sensation of being watched. Out of the corner of my eye, I caught Farron's piercing gaze, his dark brows furrowed. Even from a distance, the disdain was palpable, like an electric current charging the space between us.

He'd been such a dick to me at the party last week, and he'd truly hurt me with his accusation I was a rich, spoiled kid. Well, technically, he wasn't wrong. I was rich and I had been spoiled in many ways. I wasn't disputing that.

No, it had been his statement that I had no idea what obligations were that had hit home. My whole life was nothing but obligations. I'd given up my dream because of obligations and duties to my family, my country. In fact, this year was the first time in my entire life that I was doing something for myself—and I'd had to fight tooth and nail for it.

What was Farron's problem? I'd never done anything to him, yet he constantly treated me as if I'd pissed in his Cheerios—which was an amazing expression, by the way. Luke had taught me that one yesterday, and I loved it.

But back to Farron, I had no clue what to do to make him like me. Hell, at this point, I'd even settle for him to stop hating me and plain ignore me. But how? What had I done to earn his instant disapproval and judgment?

A ball swished by me. Crap, I needed to stop thinking about Farron and get my head in the game. I pushed down everything else and locked in. This was my time, and hell if I was gonna let Farron ruin it for me.

When another ball hurtled toward me, I pivoted on my heel, sending it flying down the wing with a deft touch. Simon sprinted forward and spun by Farron, who'd been too focused on me. I took off in an Olympic-record dash and was in the perfect position for Simon's pass back. With a little flourish, I sent it into the upper right corner of the net. Goal!

"Epic goal!" Simon hugged me to celebrate.

"Thank you! Your pass was perfect. Right in front of my feet."

When he let me go, I turned to see Farron striding over, his face set hard. My stomach dropped. What had I done now?

"Stick to your damn position, Tore," he spat out, the words like bullets. "You can't just switch wings because you see an opportunity to score. This is not the Tore Haakon show."

He was drawing stares from the other players who'd skidded to a halt, their attention snatched away from the scrimmage.

"Ease up, Farron," one of them called out, a note of caution in his voice. But it was like waving a red flag at a bull.

"Stay out of this, Colin," Farron snapped, eyes never leaving mine. His eyes were fierce, the intensity of his anger burning there like molten steel. The air between us crackled with animosity.

"But I—"

"Save it." He jabbed a finger at my chest. "You screw up our formation and get everyone confused. Stick to your position or get off the goddamned field."

I'd never been more grateful for my years of training to keep my composure in public, no matter what vitriol was slung at me. "My eagerness sometimes gets the better of my judgment. I'll endeavor to keep to my assigned role."

"He did score," Simon said, and I admired his balls to speak up when Farron looked like he was about to clock me out cold.

Farron shot him a look that had Simon take a step back. "It's not about scoring. It's about playing as a team."

I crossed my arms. "And here I thought goals were what got us wins. Or do Americans give trophies for team spirit?"

Suppressed sniggers rang out around me, and Farron's face darkened even more. "You think this is funny?"

"The team spirit comment was funny, cap," RJ said. "Come on, Farron, lighten up. The kid is playing well and trying to win, like everyone else on the team."

Oh, this was not what I had intended. People were now

choosing my side against Farron's, which would only make him hate me even more. But what choice did I have? Was I supposed to stand there and take whatever verbal garbage he was throwing at me?

I had to salvage what I could. "I'll try harder to stick to my assigned position, but you have to understand that I—"

"I don't have to understand anything except that you're a midfielder who should do what he's told."

I could feel the eyes of my teammates, heavy with a mix of curiosity and discomfort, watching the drama unfold. My hands clenched into fists. I had never lost my temper in public, and I sure wasn't about to start now. "If you'll allow me to explain. I was trained—"

"Newsflash, you self-centered little shit. No one cares."

"Carey!" Coach shouted. "A word, please."

Farron froze for a moment, then spun on his heels and jogged toward Coach, who did not look happy. Had he overheard Farron's remark? On the one hand, I hoped Coach would dress him down for speaking to a fellow teammate like that, but on the other, it would only make things worse.

RJ put his hand on my shoulder. "Don't let him get to you. For some reason, he's even grumpier than usual, and he's taking it out on you. He'll come around. Just keep scoring goals."

"Thanks. I sure hope so. It was never my intention to cause discord."

RJ grinned. "The way you talk cracks me up, dude. You sound like some British prince or something. So fucking formal."

My cheeks heated. If only he knew. "My apologies. I'm still adapting to the American vernacular as I was raised with British English."

"Nah, don't bother. It's all part of your Eurocharm," RJ joked.

"And the chicks totally dig it. You were quite the sensation at the party."

Was he serious? I'd only tried to make some friends and I'd been elated to have succeeded. Well, with Farron as the notable exception, of course. "I had fun."

Farron came running back, his face tight. "Back to work."

He didn't look at me, but I had no doubt he blamed me for everything. How had things escalated this quickly? My intention had never been to disrupt or cause strife, only to add flair and create room for myself to shine and elevate the team with me. Was Farron right? Was that selfish?

The question kept running through my head during the rest of the practice. What could I do to avoid further tensions with Farron? How could I teach myself to stop moving out of my position? Maybe I could write a reminder on my hand or arm so that I'd see it while playing? We had our first game in a few days, and if I forgot then, things could get ugly.

I had to figure out something, but for now, I'd better focus on the next scrimmage, where Farron and I had been put on the same team. Maybe Coach hoped it would solve the tension between us? I highly doubted it would be effective, considering Farron's glares in my direction.

"Tore! On your right!" The call snapped me back into action, my legs pumping as I sprinted toward the edge of the field. I swerved past a defender, feeling the muscles in my thighs tighten, power propelling me forward. With a deft maneuver, I crossed the ball toward the penalty area, setting up a teammate for a shot at goal. He missed, but it had been a nice play.

The ball rolled at a feverish pace, pursued by the determined thuds of cleats against the grass. My focus was absolute, every fiber of my being attuned to the rhythm of the game. Yes, this was why I was here. Not for glory, not for accolades, but for the sheer, unadulterated joy of the sport.

"Nice one, Tore!" someone shouted as I intercepted a pass, the adrenaline surging through my veins. I allowed myself a flash of pride—a reminder that I belonged here, among the pulse of the game and the camaraderie of teammates who judged me solely on my merit and mettle.

Farron kicked it up the field with a bit of a sloppy pass, too far away from anyone but me to intercept it, so I sprinted forward and managed to catch it against my chest, then bring it down to my feet. With a smooth heel flick, I passed Joey, who was playing defense for the other team, and with a rocket-like shot, I sent it into the net.

Before I could celebrate, Farron's shadow loomed over me. "Dammit, Tore, what did I tell you?"

"I was the only one in position to accept that pass," I protested. "No one else was even close."

"Are you criticizing my pass?"

I was so over this. "You know what? I am. That was a sloppy pass, and you bloody well know it. Yes, I was out of position, but no one else would've been able to intercept but me, and if that means going out of my box, then so be it. If you don't want me to do that, then fucking pass where I don't have to."

His face grew red, but I stood my ground, refusing to back down. I'd had enough of his verbal abuse for the day. I'd tried to stay kind and friendly and even to explain myself, but if he was determined to find fault with me no matter what, it wouldn't make a difference. I might as well keep my pride and stand up for myself.

Without saying another word, he spun around and stalked off. As I watched him walk away, something within me wilted. It wasn't the weight of unaccepted apologies or the burden of proving myself. It was the realization that no matter how hard I tried, some battles couldn't be won by sheer determination alone, and this was one of them.

"Hey, ignore him," Daniel whispered, clapping a hand on my shoulder. But the comfort fell flat. I nodded, dredging up a small smile. I'd never be able to bridge the divide between Farron and me. And it hurt more than I had expected it to... and more than it should.

As the whistle signaled the end of practice, I took a deep breath, letting the tension roll off my shoulders like sweat as I headed to the locker rooms with everyone else.

"Hey, Tore, nice footwork out there!" Ethan called out as we entered the locker rooms. I shot him a grateful smile, appreciating the camaraderie that seemed to come so easily with everyone but Farron.

"Thanks, mate. Just trying to keep up with you lot."

The interaction was brief, but it fortified something within me. I didn't need Farron's approval to succeed here at Hawley College. My own abilities spoke for themselves, and the nods of respect from the others were a testament.

As I peeled off my sweat-soaked jersey, tossing it into my bag, a sense of clarity washed over me—a bright, unwavering certainty that was as refreshing as the cold shower I was about to take.

This was my year undercover, away from the weighty expectations of my lineage, and I was determined to make every moment count, with or without Farron Carey's approval.

And it would have to be without. I would never win him over, so I had to stop wasting energy on it.

"Focus on the ball, not the bullshit," I repeated Luke's advice. I'd make that my new mantra.

I was determined to excel, to show everyone, including myself, that I was more than a prince, even if they didn't know who I really was. This was my year, and I would make the most of it, come what may. It was liberating, this newfound independence from seeking validation from someone who had already decided not to like me.

I glanced briefly at Farron, who was behind me, avoiding my gaze. Let Farron stew in his hostility. I would rise above, untethered from the desire to win over someone whose opinion could not alter my course.

Or, as my teammates would say, fuck him.

Of course, that conviction only lasted about a day.

5

FARRON

Nerves battled with excitement as I laced up my cleats. We were about to play our homecoming game, which also happened to be our first game of the season, and we'd be facing our archrival, Connor College. The rivalry dated back decades and was ingrained in our culture. Few things mattered more than beating the Connor Condors.

Yes, condors were literally twice as big as hawks—I'd looked it up in my freshman year—and we were the underdogs for sure. We hadn't bested them in fourteen games, and that needed to change. Today. Unfortunately, our first game of this season would be against them, which wasn't ideal as we'd barely played together as a team. But it would have to do.

"Listen up!" My voice carried through the locker room with confidence despite the riot of nerves beneath my skin. "Today, we end this damned losing streak!"

Heads lifted, eyes locked on me with the fierce hunger that only comes when you've tasted defeat more times than victory. "Connor College thinks they've got this in the bag. They think that because they've won the last fourteen games, we're gonna roll over and let 'em take it. Hell no! We're the Hawks, and we fight with everything we've got!"

I paused, letting the silence hang heavy for a moment. My gaze swept the circle of my teammates, everyone's expression showing a determination mirroring my own. Tore's face shone with excitement. Fuck, that kid had better stick to the plan. If I caught him drifting out of position again, I'd bench him myself. Though I'd have to be careful. Coach hadn't liked it when I'd called Tore a self-centered little shit, and he'd given me a warning.

"Let's show them what we're made of. Play hard, play fair, but above all"—I clenched my jaw, the growl in my tone rising like a battle cry—"play to win!"

A chorus of shouts met my final words, the team erupting into a cacophony of warlike whoops and hollers.

"Bring it in," I commanded, and they surged forward, hands stacking atop one another at the center of our huddle. Blue-and-yellow jerseys blurred into a singular force of will.

"ONE TEAM!" I bellowed.

"ONE DREAM!" they responded, voices melding into a thunderous promise of the battle to come.

"LET'S GO TAKE WHAT'S OURS!"

As one, we thrust our hands skyward, a unified gesture of defiance and hope. It was more than a game—it was redemption, it was pride, it was us against the world. No one believed in us, but we did. I did. No matter how this ended, we would leave every drop of sweat and blood out there on that field because that was what Hawks did: we soared higher, we dug deeper, and we never, ever gave up. At least, that was what I told myself and what I wanted the team to believe.

The whistle's sharp tweet unleashed us onto the field, a flurry of determination as we clashed with our rivals from the get-go. The first five minutes were the usual chaotic back and forth as we battled for dominance and control of the game—a battle Connor College won.

Their defense was weak, but they had fantastic midfielders and wingers, and rumors were that Devin McGregor, their star striker, was in negotiations with a European club. I hated his guts, of course, but I couldn't deny he was brilliant. And above all, fast. On the counter, he could out-sprint anyone and everyone, and I saw far more of him on my end of the field than I wanted to.

Fuck, here he came again, charging up the field, always smart enough to not be offside. He could afford to with his speed. Tore was chasing him, but he couldn't catch up, having been too far forward again. Fucker.

I braced myself, my eyes focused on the ball. When McGregor came close, I saw my chance and slid between his legs, managing to get the ball away from him. It rolled over the goal line. Corner for the Condors. It sucked, but it was better than the alternative because there had not been a single player between McGregor and our goalie other than me.

We took up positions. "Little to the left," Colin shouted at Tore, who was apparently blocking his view. No wonder. The kid was tall.

The Condors player hit the ball perfectly, and a wave of players jumped up to attempt to head it. RJ managed to hit it, aiming it sideways and away from the goal. Fuck! He dropped it right in front of McGregor, who didn't hesitate and tapped it straight into the goal with a little flick of his foot. No offside, of course, so that was a goal against us.

"Keep pressing, Hawks!" I shouted as we jogged back to our starting positions from the center line, my shouts partly to encourage, partly to drown out the growing voice of dread in my gut. We were playing hard, but it wasn't enough. It never seemed to be.

Adam passed the ball to Tore, who took it forward in a blur of motion, zigzagging past the Condors' defense. *Pass it, pass it, fucking pass it!* I was chanting it inside my head, but Tore kept the ball, deftly outmaneuvering all defenders. He was good. I might hate his guts, but he had better technical skills than any of us.

Out of nowhere, a Condors defender tackled Tore, aiming for his ankles and sending him flying to the ground, rolling a few times before his body came to a stop.

"What the fuck!" I yelled, but the ref was already on it, whistling sharply and immediately reaching for a yellow card.

The fucker had done it on purpose, of course, just like I'd taken yellow cards if I saw no other way to prevent a goal. But I usually waited with dirty tactics like that until things were dire. They were ahead, so why had he done it so early in the game?

Tore was still on the ground, clutching his ankle, and I jogged over, pushing everyone who was in my way aside. "You okay?"

"Not sure," he said between gritted teeth.

I immediately waved at Becca Leigh, the team's athletic trainer who also worked as an EMT, and she came running, carrying her bag. Coach jogged over as well.

As Becca knelt next to Tore, immediately icing his ankle, the team huddled around Coach and me. The Condors had retreated, giving us some space, and while Tore was being treated, we might as well use the time for some strategy.

"Farron and Adam, I want you two on that McGregor kid like fleas on a dog. Daniel, you gotta speed up your passes. The extra touches are costing ya." Coach continued to give a whirlwind of instructions until Tore was back on his feet, still wincing slightly when he put his full weight on his ankle.

"You good to play?" the ref checked.

Tore nodded. "Yes, Ref."

Coach and Becca jogged off the field as everyone got back into position. "Good huddle?" Tore asked, winking at me.

Why the fuck was he...? My eyes traveled to his ankle, which suddenly seemed fine as he jumped a few times, landing without wincing. Had he faked the whole thing to give us some time? The tackle had been real and should've been yellow under any circumstances, but maybe he hadn't been as badly hurt as he let on.

We had needed it. A hard reset like that could make all the difference, and I owed him for that. "Yes. Thanks."

The game resumed, and a renewed vigor pulsed through the team, fueled by Coach's instructions or maybe by the shared desperation to not let our dreams slip through our fingers. It was only the first half, but still.

I charged, slid, blocked, and tackled, my brow slick with effort as our opponents matched us stride for stride. Fuck, they were relentless, battering our defense like a proverbial ram, looking for our weak spot.

And they found it.

Luke, my fellow center-back, tripped as he attempted to block an attack, this time from the left flank, by their other striker. Probably because Adam and I hadn't given McGregor even an inch of space. And now their striker sailed past Adam and, with a bullet from outside the penalty box, hit the net. Fuck.

Zero-two. We were behind, and the taste of looming defeat was bitter on my tongue.

"Focus!" I barked at the team as we regrouped. "We can't let them walk all over us! We need to amp it up!"

But we played like the air had been let out of our tires. The halftime whistle blew, signaling a temporary reprieve from the relentless pace of the game. I bent over, hands on knees, sucking in air like it was my last lifeline until my lungs stopped hurting.

We trudged into the locker rooms, where I immediately guzzled down a Gatorade. My whole body hurt as I peeled off my sweat-soaked shirt and dropped it in the laundry basket. I needed to keep moving, albeit at a snail's pace, and so I slowly walked around the room as I wolfed down two energy gel packs and a dark-chocolate-and-sea-salt bar. Bananas were almost everyone's favorite for a quick energy boost, but they gave me horrible heartburn unless I ate them with yogurt. My body was funny that way.

"Listen up!" The room quieted immediately when Coach spoke up. "We're playing well, but it's not enough. They're still outrunning us, outpacing us, and outsmarting us." He turned to me. "You and Adam did a good job guarding McGregor, but it left the other flank too vulnerable."

"I know. That's how they scored the second time."

"So Adam will have to go back to his old position, and you'll have to do it by yourself, Farron."

"Yes, Coach."

Coach addressed the whole team again. "Their defense is weak. It's their offense that's strong, but if we can create an opportunity for a fast counter, we could break through their defense and score."

I agreed, but how could we do that when we were constantly playing defense? Coach didn't seem to have any concrete ideas either, though he did sub in Simon for Ethan so we had an extra midfielder. But would that be enough?

"Coach, can I make a suggestion?"

That was Tore, of course, and I gritted my teeth.

"What's on your mind?" Coach asked him.

"Now that we have an extra midfielder, is it possible for me to have a bit more flexibility in my position? You know I'm fast. We haven't been able to get the ball forward far enough for our strikers, but we've had plenty of possession in the midfield. If you'll allow me to move up the lines more, I can take it and make a run for it."

"By yourself, of course," I snapped before Coach could say anything.

"Well, yes, because passing it would mean risking it being intercepted. Plus, I'm the fastest. No one can keep up with me."

The fact that he wasn't wrong only pissed me off more.

Coach scratched his beard. "I'm not usually a fan of experiments in the middle of a game, but we're two down with little to lose at this point, so if you see an opportunity, go for it."

"Thank you, Coach. I won't let you down."

Tore was motivated to win, that much I had to give him. And I didn't have time for anything else as we needed to get back onto the field, so I quickly put on a fresh compression tank and a clean jersey, then led the team out.

We took our positions on the other side of the field, and the whistle shrieked, signaling the start of the second half. I could feel the energy thrumming through the team, an electric current that seemed to jumpstart a renewed sense of purpose. We were back in the fight, and fight we did, repelling wave after wave of attack, even breaking out a few times ourselves.

I intercepted a pass to McGregor and, with a kick fueled by desperation, sent it up the field. Like a bolt from the blue, Tore came alive. He seized the ball from a tangle of legs and burst forward, a streak of blue and yellow weaving through defenders with an ease that left me breathless. There was an artistry to his movements that was undeniable—step, feint, twist, turn.

Our sidelines erupted as he broke free and shot forward in a sprint that left everyone in his dust until he was one-on-one with the goalkeeper. Time slowed, every heartbeat a drumroll, but then, with a precision that felt almost surgical, he slotted the ball into the back of the net.

"YESSS!" The cheer ripped from my throat, raw and triumphant. Around me, the team surged forward, a wave of elation crashing over me as they mobbed Tore, lifting him on their shoulders, his face alight with the thrill of success.

But as they set him down, a cold seed of resentment lodged itself in my gut. It was ludicrous. I should be ecstatic. We were back in the game, but inside me was this insidious whisper, reminding me it was Tore who'd turned the tide. Not me.

The match resumed with a fervor that bordered on frenzy. And Tore, damn him, remained the eye of the storm. When the ball found him again, it was like watching poetry in motion—a dance of such fluidity that even I couldn't help but admire it. With a grace that belied his towering frame, he dispatched another shot past the goalie, the net billowing like a flag of surrender from Connor College.

"TORE! TORE! TORE!" The chant rose, but I couldn't make myself join in. My emotions churned like a roiling sea of pride for my team with a bitter undercurrent of envy.

"Nice shot," I managed to grind out when Tore trotted past, sweat slicking his blond hair to his forehead, eyes shining with triumph.

"Thank you, Farron." His accent wrapped around my name, and he clapped me on the shoulder, a gesture of camaraderie that should've warmed me. Instead, the heat of jealousy singed my insides.

"Keep it up." I turned away, unable to bear the sight of his smile any longer. What was wrong with me? This wasn't the time for pettiness or rivalry. This was what we had worked so hard for. Hell, this was the stuff of legends. We were tied against our archrival, all thanks to Tore, yet I was angry.

As I tore down the field, mud splattering up my shins, I could feel it: the divide between me and the rest of the Hawks. The cheers for Tore vibrated through the air, yet they seemed to bypass me as though I were a ghost among them. My teammates clapped each other on the backs, their faces flushed with the thrill of the chase, but their eyes... Their eyes kept darting to him. To Tore.

They'd chosen him over me. My dislike of him had not been a secret, and now I'd lost my team. The camaraderie that had once included me now felt like a private club where my membership had expired. I was the captain, dammit. But somehow, Tore's easy charm and those ridiculous goals had made him the sun, and I'd become just another planet in a forced orbit around him. The fact that he deserved it made it burn even more.

The final whistle blew with us tying with Connor College for the first time in fourteen games. As our team converged in celebration, I hung back. The slap of hands, the exuberant yells—it all felt distant, like watching a scene from someone else's life.

The air in the locker room was thick with the scent of sweat and victory—yes, we all counted tying as a victory—but it did nothing to mask the sense of isolation wrapping around me like a shroud. Laughter bounced off the walls, and every pat on the back felt like a reminder of a divide that kept widening.

"Good game," Tore said, his bright-blue gaze finding mine. There was kindness there, maybe even a plea for acceptance. But something within me had shifted—and I seemed helpless to stop it.

"Thanks to you." I had to force the words past my tight throat and turned away from him. I wouldn't let him see me crumble. When I looked over my shoulder, he was walking away, his shoulders hunched.

Tore's success on the field—those two goals that had everyone chanting his name—had ignited something unexpected: an undercurrent of rivalry... or was it envy? The emotions were too tangled to decipher, and I didn't have the luxury of time to untie the knots.

"Good work out there, Carey. You held the line," Coach's gruff voice cut through the noise, bringing a semblance of normalcy.

"Thanks, Coach," I said, trying to shake off the unease. "We pulled together when it counted. In the end, teamwork won."

"Indeed." His eyes flickered past me for a moment before returning with a knowing look. "But remember, teamwork doesn't mean everyone is equal. It can also mean being selfless and giving stars room to shine."

I absorbed his words, the implication clear. Tore was the comet streaking across our sky, and I...

Maybe I was a star that had already died, its light fading until nothing was left.

Fuck my life.

No, fuck Tore.

6

TORE

Tidying wasn't my favorite thing to do, but this time, I was grinning as I began straightening the array of textbooks and soccer gear strewn across our dorm room. Luke was studying in the library and wouldn't be back for hours, giving me plenty of time to prep for a FaceTime call with Floris, Greg, and Nils. Not exactly something I could do when Luke was here, considering our identities.

"Ew," I muttered under my breath as I chucked Luke's dirty laundry into a basket. I wanted everything to look spotless, a visual reassurance that I was managing fine in this new American college chapter. Besides, I'd always been tidy and didn't function well in chaos. A psychologist would probably have a field day tying that to my neat and structured upbringing I was expected to rebel against.

After a last visual check, I perched on the edge of my neatly made bed and pulled out my phone. My fingers couldn't move quickly enough as I tapped Greg's, Floris's, and Nils's smiling thumbnails on the screen, initiating the FaceTime call. I bounced my knee, the energy within me too much to contain.

The very second their faces popped into view, a quadruple grid of princely features, my grin widened, and something warm unfurled inside me. "Hi!"

"Say that again," Greg urged me.

"Hi?"

He laughed. "You already sound American."

"Fuck you too, asshole," I said in my best American accent, and that had us all laughing.

"All right, spill it," I said. "How's life in your corners of the world? What's new? Who's pregnant, who broke up, and what's the latest scandal? I feel so out of the loop."

"Margarethe is pregnant," Nils offered. Margarethe was his older sister, married to some absurdly handsome commoner determined to make her happiness his life goal. Nils really liked him, and because of that, so did we.

"Right on schedule," Greg said. "She's been married two years, right?"

Nils nodded. "Yup."

"Congrats, soon-to-be uncle Nils," I said. "How far along is she?"

"Four months, so out of the danger zone... according to her. Not that I know anything about it. She showed me a printout from the ultrasound, and it looks like a shrimp-shaped blob. Not that I was stupid enough to tell her that. I ooh'd and aah'd appropriately."

Of course he did. All of us had been trained to respond properly in any and every situation.

"And with you, Greg?" I asked.

"Everything's rather mundane here." Greg chuckled, lounging back in what looked like an antique chaise-longue. "So please, dazzle us with tales of American splendor."

"Did you really eat deep-fried Oreos?" Floris asked, his eyes crinkling with amusement. He was in his dorm room, which looked much neater than I had expected, using his computer to FaceTime.

"Ah, yes, the culinary chaos of the American cuisine." I flopped back onto my bed with a dramatic sigh. "Where gluttony dresses up in gourmet clothing. It's not just Oreos. They'll happily drown candy bars, pickles, and even ice cream in batter too. It's like watching a mad scientist at work, only with more grease and less concern for arteries."

Nils snorted. "You really know how to make it sound delicious."

I rolled my eyes at him. "I tried one of those abominations and felt like I'd swallowed a pickle coated in oil." I paused, grinning. "But on the bright side, there's this extraordinary thing they call "tailgating." Imagine a festival devoted to sports fervor. People camp out with their trucks, feasting and drinking as if preparing for battle before a match. Seriously, they bring barbecue pits, massive coolers, and heaps of food to a football game."

"Or a soccer game, in your case," Floris interjected. "Speaking of which, how's the season going?"

"Splendid. We've tied twice and won all our other games. Coach is very happy. And at our games," I continued, suddenly animated, "the mascot—a giant hawk named Hawkeye—does these ridiculous dance moves that have half the crowd in stitches. At first, I thought it was some sort of majestic bird display, but no. It's pure comedic gold."

"Are you sure you're not describing your own victory dance, Tore?" Nils teased, and laughter erupted from each corner of our virtual gathering.

"As if I'd ever lower myself to that level," I protested, but the smile tugging at my lips betrayed my mock indignation. "For your information, my victory dance is elegant and refined."

"Of course, how could we forget? The epitome of royal grace," Greg joked.

"Speaking of elegance," I said, steering the conversation away from my questionable dance skills, "you should've seen the homecoming parade. Floats and banners as far as the eye could see, and me, trying not to look utterly bewildered amidst a sea of blue-and-yellow streamers."

"Did you wave like the prince you are?" Floris asked, his smirk visible even through the digital divide.

"More like a tentative hand flutter." I demonstrated a half-hearted royal wave. "I didn't want to betray my experience with waving and outshine everyone else."

"Your modesty knows no bounds," Nils observed drolly.

"International incident averted," Greg said, nodding sagely. "Well done, Tore."

"Every day is an adventure here. Speaking of which, I've heard a rumor that you will finally be joining Floris and me in the land of the free, Nils. Is it true? Are you really coming to the States?"

"Guilty as charged." Nils's smile broadened over the screen. He was practically radiating enthusiasm, so much so that I could almost feel it through my phone. "I have permission. Now all I need to do is find a job as an assistant coach since I'm a little too old to pass for a student."

"You'll love it." Floris's grin matched Nils's. "I'm having an absolute blast here in Massachusetts... though I'm not sure how I'll feel once winter hits."

"If you find a spot somewhere on our side of the country too, Nils, we should try to hang out sometime." I frowned as something occurred to me. "Or do you think that would be too much of a risk? Do you think someone would be more likely to recognize us if we're all together and Floris is out?"

"Out as what? Gay or royalty?" Nils teased.

I flipped him the middle finger. "The latter, asshole. As if I could possibly care about his sexuality."

"I'm not sure where I'll end up yet, but I have to admit the Midwest sounds good to me," Nils said. "It seems so quintessentially American, you know? Plus, I'm not one to spend a year in or near a big city like LA or New York or something. I'd go mad."

"Ah, but not all of us can partake in this American dream," Greg's voice cut through our excitement, and I saw his wistful expression. His disappointment was a stark contrast to our enthusiasm.

"Still wrestling with the powers that be?" I asked sympathetically, sitting up straighter with concern for my friend.

"Indeed." Greg sighed. "The king is adamantly opposed so far, citing security issues. But I'm working on it, so don't count me out yet. In the meantime, I'll live vicariously through your escapades. Make sure to send daily updates, okay? And don't be skimpy on the details, including pictures."

"We're all keeping our fingers crossed for you," Nils said.

"In Dutch, we say 'thumbing.' As in, we'll be thumbing for you," Floris commented.

"I'll take all your fingers, thumbs included," Greg said with a small chuckle, though his eyes held an unspoken yearning. "Until then, I'll send you all the strength I can muster. Or, as us Brits say, keep calm and carry on."

"Chin up, Greg. If anyone can charm their way across the Atlantic, it's you," I said, trying to bolster his spirits.

"Keep making waves stateside, and maybe they'll realize I need to join to keep you out of trouble," he replied, the corner of his mouth lifting in a half-smile.

"Trouble? Me?" I feigned innocence before laughing along with them.

"Until then, stay safe, stay scandal-free, and for heaven's sake, try not to fall prey to any more deep-fried absurdities," Greg warned.

"It's not scandals I'm worried about. Or deep-fried culinary craziness, for that matter. I have a much bigger challenge here. It's Farron who's been driving me up the bloody wall."

"Who?" Floris squinted at me through the screen, his brow furrowed in concern.

"Farron Carey, that bloke on the football team I told you guys about. Fuck, I meant soccer team." My voice took on an edge, recounting our latest encounter. "He's the captain and he's got this inexplicable vendetta against me, and for the life of me, I cannot figure out why. We're like oil and water, fire and ice—whatever metaphor suits your fancy."

"Have you tried talking to him?" Nils suggested, leaning forward with genuine interest.

"Talk to him?" I scoffed, throwing my hands up in exasperation. "He won't even let me finish my sentences. Every time I try to explain myself to him, he cuts me off. It's like we're jousting, except with words."

"Maybe he's jealous? You are quite the talented player," Greg chimed in, though his tone didn't sound entirely convinced by his own theory.

"I suspect jealousy is a part of it, but it's deeper than that. He accused me of being a spoiled rich kid."

Floris held up a hand. "No offense, but you are. We all are."

"Sure, but then he accused me of not knowing what having obligations is like, and that one hurt."

"He doesn't know you're a prince, so I'm sure he thinks your life is carefree. You have to admit, for most rich people, this would be true." Nils was, as usual, the peacemaker. He always saw solutions to conflicts, the perfect diplomat.

"Maybe, but why wouldn't he ask? Why is he assuming he knows anything about me?"

"Oh, he's hot," Floris said in an appreciative tone.

"He's what now?"

Floris held up his phone to the camera. "I googled him and plenty of pictures came up. He's hot. Broad-shouldered, perfect six-pack, thighs that could squeeze me any day, not to mention his soulful eyes. The man is undeniably hot."

"Excuse me, and I'm not?" I asked, a little offended by Floris's extensive praise of my archenemy.

"You know you are, but you're not my type."

"I'm everyone's type," I muttered, still not entirely appeased. "He's just... He's exhausting. He's always looking at me, always keeping an eye on me, always watching me."

"You do realize those three mean the same thing, right?" Greg checked, repressing a smile.

"Yes, but he really can't take his eyes off me. I always feel the weight of his stare. And each interaction is a battle, each glance a silent challenge. It's tiresome."

"Perhaps it's not disdain," Floris said, a mischievous glint lighting his eyes. "Maybe all this animosity is a form of foreplay."

"Foreplay?" I nearly choked on air. The very notion was ludicrous. "That's... That's preposterous! You know I'm straight, and I'm fairly sure he is too. But even if we weren't, I'd sooner kiss a frog."

"Stranger things have happened." Floris was clearly enjoying the flush that crept up my cheeks.

"Let's not add fairy-tale twists to my already complicated collegiate narrative, thank you very much," I retorted, desperately trying to steer away from the absurdity of the suggestion.

"All right, all right." Floris was still smirking. "But keep an open mind, Tore. The line between love and hate is sometimes thinner than one might think."

"Thin lines be damned." I made my voice as stern as I could, yet somewhere deep down, an unsettling curiosity stirred. "Let's agree to disagree on the matter and never speak of it again."

"Agreed," they all said in unison, but their knowing looks spoke volumes more than their words.

I exhaled, realizing that the hour had flown by and night had crept along the edges of my dorm window. "I should probably say goodnight. I have an early training session tomorrow, and Coach has been relentless. Plus, I've got reading to catch up on, and clearly, some bizarre theories to forcibly forget."

"Good luck with your American adventures," Greg said warmly. "I truly hope you'll have the experience of a lifetime. And about Farron, keep us in the loop, yeah? We want all the juicy updates on your nemesis."

"Enemy, not nemesis," I corrected him, my hands gesturing dismissively, brushing off the weight of the word. "But yes, I'll keep you posted. Though I sincerely hope there won't be anything worth reporting."

I ended the call with a mix of relief and lingering disquiet. I couldn't shake Floris's words, and for some reason, now I kept seeing the image of Farron's intense brown eyes that seemed to burn into mine with every heated exchange.

And why had Floris felt the need to point out how attractive Farron was? I might not be into men, but I wasn't blind. He did have a near-perfect body—aside from the permanent scowl on his face, obviously. His chest was rather broad, and Floris hadn't exaggerated about the man's perfect six-pack. The thought of Farron's abs sent a shiver down my spine, one that had nothing to do with the chill in the air-conditioned dormitory.

Shaking my head, I willed those thoughts away. It was another of Floris's jests, nothing more.

"Focus, Tore," I murmured to myself, opening a textbook to distract myself with academia, pushing aside thoughts of Farron Carey and his perplexing animosity. He'd taken up far too much space in my head already.

7

FARRON

Mom's text had been short but clear.

> Call your brother.

Funny enough, she hadn't indicated which one, as I had two, but I didn't even need to ask. Rowan never got into trouble. Nope, that was always Caspian, now a senior in high school and my mom's biggest worry.

I jabbed at my phone screen, initiating the FaceTime call with a sense of dread clawing at my chest. What had he done now? It rang twice before Caspian's face filled the frame, his eyes shadowed and defensive. "Yo."

"Why did Mom text me to call you?"

He scowled at me. "Why does she always get you involved?"

"Because you don't listen to her and she's hoping I can get through to you. What happened?"

Caspian's gaze flickered away. "She's overreacting."

"How about you let me be the judge of that? Tell me what's going on."

It took a moment—seconds that stretched into an eternity of silence—before Caspian's walls crumbled. His mouth opened, then closed, a silent war waged behind his eyes. "I got into a fight at school and now I'm suspended for two days."

"Suspended? You got suspended? It's only the second week of school, bro. What the fuck happened?" My voice rose despite my attempt to keep cool. I leaned forward, making sure my presence filled his small screen.

"The principal screwed me over. That's what happened."

"Start at the beginning."

Another deep sigh. "There's this new kid, Chandler Rodham III."

I couldn't hold back a snort. "For real? That's his name?"

"I know, right? Totally pretentious, which fits him because he's a stuck-up rich kid. His family moved into the Rollins House."

The Rollins House was an old mansion in my hometown that was on some historical list for reasons that eluded me. It had been for sale for a while since, first of all, not many buyers in our area had one point five million to spare, and second, no one wanted to carry the burden of the strictly regulated upkeep. You couldn't even paint the damn house without permission.

"So that finally sold, huh? What does his dad do?"

"He owns, like, half of Dealership Row."

All the car dealerships were concentrated in one area of town everyone called Dealership Row. "That'll do it. Anyway, what's up with this Chandler kid?"

"He took offense to my clothes." His voice was laced with embarrassment and anger.

I blinked. "He did what now?"

"Off-brand junk, he called it. Said even thrift stores wouldn't take 'em."

I nodded, absorbing the half-truths and reading between the

lines. We never had much, and it stung more than either of us liked to admit. "You stood up for yourself."

"I showed him that I might be wearing cheap-ass shit but that I could still kick his ass. But of course, his dad complained to the principal and that got me a suspension. I mean, what would you have done?"

I would've beat the shit out of that kid as well, and Caspian knew it. The defiance in his eyes was mirrored in my own—Carey pride mixed with a healthy dose of Carey temper. "Who threw the first punch?"

"I did, and I don't regret it. What the fuck am I supposed to do when he's mocking me and he won't stop?"

"Did anyone hear him say this shit?"

"Fuck, yeah. All my friends did. Plus Mr. Summers, my math teacher. He told Chandler to stop. Which he did... until that class was over."

"Okay, I'll call the principal and see what I can do, okay? You can't have a suspension on your record during your senior year. That'll kill your chances of getting a full ride."

"Coach threatened to kick me off varsity."

Oh, hell no. Like me, Caspian excelled in soccer, and it would be his ticket out of there. He had college scouts interested in him already. No way was some little rich punk gonna mess that up. "The fact that he didn't already tells you how much he values you as a player."

"How much he needs me, you mean. They don't stand a chance of winning State without me, and he knows it."

Caspian's confidence in his abilities bordered on arrogance, but was it wrong when we both knew he spoke the truth? He had a solid team, but he was the star player, and everyone knew it.

"I'll talk to Coach as well, okay? I'll do my best to sort this out.

But Cas, you can't get into any more fights. You gotta keep your cool, man."

His shoulders hunched. "I know. I was so angry, you know?"

I knew what it felt like, the sting of humiliation when you couldn't measure up to everyone else's standards. "He's a spoiled, rich kid, and he's an idiot, Cas. He has no idea what honest work looks like. You need to learn to ignore people like him."

"Easy for you to say. You don't have to deal with them every day," he shot back, tinged with a bitterness that seemed too harsh for someone his age. "For once, I'd like to wear what everyone else is wearing, you know? And I'm not even talking about some five-hundred-dollar sneakers or some shit. Just a pair of decent jeans would be great."

"Look, Mom's working her ass off." I raked a hand through my hair, the frustration clear in my voice. "And I'm sending back money when I can. But with everything getting more expensive, it's tough to keep up."

"I could get a job again."

I firmly shook my head. "Not in your senior year. You need to focus. Keep your eyes on the ball, dude. You're almost there. You can do this. I have so much faith in you." I softened my tone, tried to smooth the edge of command into something more resembling support. He needed to know I was here for him, not merely laying down the law.

"I'm just so…"

"Angry," I finished softly. "I know."

"Not at you or Mom. I know you're doing what you can, but it feels so unfair that we're always struggling. We can never catch a break."

"If you wanna be mad at someone, be pissed off at Dad's family. They're the ones who let us down after Dad died. They're loaded and they could've helped us, but they chose not to because they didn't think Mom was good enough for Dad. They'd been married for fourteen years when he died, but they still held a grudge."

"I don't understand why. What was wrong with Mom?"

I shrugged. "Wrong side of town. White trailer trash, they called her. When she got pregnant with me, they accused her of doing it deliberately to trap him."

"Did she?"

I firmly shook my head. "They were so in love, Cas. I know you don't remember much of that, but I was thirteen when he died, and I remember so many moments where I could see how much they were in love. Don't ever question that, okay? He chose her because he loved her."

I had to fight to keep the bitterness out of my voice. Not only was I old enough to remember my father's death; I'd been in the car with him when we'd been hit. I had walked away with minor injuries, but the drunk driver had hit the driver's side, and my dad never stood a chance. My only consolation was that his last words had been that he loved me and that he was sorry.

Which made the betrayal of his family all the worse. I'd always felt the arctic cold from my dad's parents but had never fully understood why. After Dad died, Mom had no choice but to explain the situation to me because we quickly ran out of money and I was forced to get a job.

"How do you deal with that anger?"

"You learn from it. The lesson is that we can't trust those rich pricks. They're all about themselves, their own image. They'll step on anyone to stay on top, and they don't give a damn who they hurt along the way."

Caspian's eyes narrowed, the blue of them darkening with the shadows. "So, what? We let them walk all over us?"

"No." I shook my head with force, the movement so vigorous I felt my neck crack. "We play smarter, not harder. You've got brains, Cas. Use 'em."

"Easy for you to say."

"Damn right it is," I said, leaning close to the camera. "Because I'm doing it, aren't I? Here at Hawley, on the soccer team, busting my ass day and night. And the only reason I'm here is because I got that scholarship."

He tilted his head, and I could see he was listening.

"Listen, Cas," I said, shifting to sit on the edge of my bed, the phone propped up against my knee. "You've got every right to be pissed. Life dealt us a crappy hand. But remember, it's not about the labels on your clothes. It's what you do that counts."

"I know, but..."

"Listen to me." I squashed my own frustration. "We're stronger than them. We don't need their damn money. We've got something they'll never have."

"Which is?" His tone was skeptical, but underneath it was a plea for something to hold onto.

"Each other," I said simply. "We've got each other's backs as a family, Cas. Always. We'd never treat each other the way they treat us."

He nodded slowly, the tension easing from his shoulders as he let out a long breath. "Yeah. Yeah, you're right."

"Damn straight, I am." I flashed him a half-smile, trying to lift the mood. "Now, wipe that scowl off your face. You're gonna get wrinkles before you even hit twenty."

A reluctant grin tugged at the corners of his mouth. "Shut up, Farron."

"And how will you make me?" The familiar warmth of sibling banter eased the heavy atmosphere.

"Thanks," he said after a moment, his voice softer. "For being here, even when you're not."

"Always. Remember that."

He slowly nodded.

"Promise me you'll focus on what matters? Your education, soccer, the future you've worked so hard for?" I held his gaze, willing him to see the conviction in mine.

"I promise."

"All right, time for me to hit the books," I said, pushing off the wall and preparing to dive back into my own set of responsibilities. "Remember what I said. Stay strong," I urged him, wiping a smudge off the phone screen absentmindedly, as if I could clear away the obstacles in his path just as easily. "You've got me in your corner."

"Thanks, Farron," he replied, his voice steady but with an undercurrent of emotion that made me want to reach through the damn screen and give him a noogie. Instead, I settled for a firm nod.

Leaning back against my desk, I let out a long breath, feeling it ripple through me. Frustration knotted in my gut because he deserved better than this crap, but there was determination too, hot and fierce, lighting a fire within me.

The weight of responsibility for my siblings was heavy, but it was mine to bear, and I wouldn't have it any other way. We'd been dealt a crappy hand, sure, but we were Careys. We played to win, no matter the odds. And I'd be damned if I didn't do everything in my power to give them a life where brand names on their backs weren't a measure of worth.

8

TORE

I'd never been much of a party animal. Being a prince meant getting invited to lots of events, some formal and some firmly falling into the wild and unhinged category. The first were an obligation, one I dutifully executed to various degrees of actual fun, depending on who else was there. Anything Floris, Greg, or Nils were invited to as well was guaranteed a good time.

But the second category was the kind that landed you in the tabloids with fabricated stories and manipulated pictures. And for obvious reasons, no royal family wanted that kind of publicity. It was the worst for Greg, purely because the British press were bloodhounds with the morals of rats. But they didn't limit themselves to the British royal family alone, so we had learned to steer clear of them.

I rarely accepted invitations to parties I suspected could get out of hand. My presence at the frat party where I'd run into Farron had been a careful exploration of American frat life, but I'd stayed away from alcohol and left as soon as things got too rowdy for me. Sure, those present might not know I was a prince, but at some point, they would, and I didn't want any embarrassing stories or footage out there.

So when I'd heard that the Alphas—the biggest fraternity on the campus and the name itself too cringey to be appealing to me—were throwing their famous Fall Fest, a yearly party that apparently was notorious, it had been the easiest decision ever not to go. Luke had shown me the flyer and a quick Google search had resulted in pictures that would give my uncle a heart attack, so nope, I'd stayed home.

Luke had still gone, and around four, he'd stumbled into our dorm, knocking over a chair before falling headfirst onto his bed. I'd done a quick check to ensure he was breathing, had tilted his head to the side in case he vomited, and then gone back to sleep.

When our alarms went off for training, he'd fallen right back asleep. If he wanted to piss off Coach, that was his prerogative, so I'd left him by himself.

I stepped onto the soccer field, the early-morning dew soaking through my cleats. The familiar scent of freshly cut grass filled my nostrils, and I took a deep breath. I'd always been a morning person. What was more inspiring than a new day?

But then I noticed my teammates staggering out onto the grass, their movements slow and uncoordinated, shadows of the disciplined players I knew them to be. Oh, bollocks. Apparently, they'd all partied hard and were now paying the price for it. Only a few of them looked normal. What would Coach say when he saw them?

I felt a presence beside me and turned to see Farron, his dark eyes narrowed as he surveyed the pitiful scene before us. Our gazes met, and his expression mirrored my own frustration.

"Look at this mess," he said, his eyes sweeping across the hungover bunch with undisguised disgust.

"They look like zombies."

"Looks like there's only a handful of guys, including us, who didn't attend last night's rager."

Something unspoken passed between us—a mutual understanding of what dedication should look like. It was an odd moment of solidarity, given our history. "Indeed. It appears our teammates have confused hydration with inebriation."

Farron snorted, a hint of amusement breaking through his scowl. "Big words this early in the morning. But yeah, these idiots are gonna regret it when Coach sees them."

"I'm well-versed in the art of the hangover, but I prefer to save such indulgences for after we've secured victory."

"You and me both," Farron agreed, his muscular arms crossed over his chest.

Jake, our usually energetic striker, tripped over his own feet and face-planted into the grass. He didn't even bother getting up, instead choosing to roll onto his back with a groan.

My jaw clenched. This was unacceptable. We had a championship to win, and here they were, barely able to walk, let alone play soccer.

Farron blew a furious come-here whistle on his fingers, and the team gathered around us. Most sported guilty expressions.

"Seriously, guys?" Farron's voice sliced through the morning haze. He stood at the center of the field, his broad shoulders squared and his hands planted firmly on his hips. His face was contorted with anger, his jaw clenched tight. I stood beside him, my arms crossed, silently backing his words.

"Look at yourselves..." His eyes, dark with reproach, locked onto each of our hungover teammates in turn. "Is this what we're about? Showing up half-dead to training? What the hell were you thinking last night? We've got a real chance at winning the conference and maybe even nationals, and you idiots decide to get wasted? We're supposed to be a team, but right now, you're letting everyone down. Yourselves, Coach, the college, and every damn person who believes in the Hawley Hawks."

I nodded in agreement, my own frustration building. These were my teammates, and some of them had become my friends, but their lack of commitment was infuriating.

"I hope your one night of fun was worth it. If you think I'm mad, wait till Coach gets here. We're starting warm-up now, and you'd better keep up."

Farron broke into a jog, and I was on his heels as we began our first lap around the field. The rest of the team fell in line. The ones who hadn't partied were right behind us and the rest followed at a much slower pace.

As we ran laps, I studied Farron from the corner of my eye. Despite our differences, we seemed to be on the same page when it came to our dedication to the sport. Hopefully, he'd see that too.

I caught sight of Coach approaching, his face like a thundercloud ready to burst. Apparently, he'd already found out about the unfortunate turn of events. I braced myself for the storm to come, ready to prove that not everyone on this team had forgotten what it meant to strive for victory. Farron had spotted him too, and he led the team back to the middle of the field.

"What in the name of all that is holy is going on here?" Coach bellowed, his eyes scanning the disheveled group before settling on Farron and me. Farron opened his mouth to respond, but Coach held up a hand, silencing him. "On second thought, I don't want to hear it. I can smell the poor decisions from here." His eyes narrowed as he took each of us in. "And I can also see who had their priorities straight."

Coach paced back and forth, his anger palpable. When he spoke again, his voice was low and dangerous. "Every time you choose to party instead of prepare, every time you pick a hangover over hard work, you're spitting in the face of everything this team stands for. You're not just letting yourselves, your teammates, and your coaches and staff down. You're disappointing every player who's ever worn the Hawley Hawks jersey."

Coach's words hung heavy in the air, and my teammates' shoulders slumped. The gravity of their actions seemed to hit them all at once. Jake, our usually cocky striker, looked like he might actually cry.

As Coach's tirade continued, I glanced at Farron. His face was set in grim determination. Who would have thought that a bunch of hungover teammates would be the thing to bridge the gap between us?

Coach's face was still flushed with anger as he barked, "All right, boys! Since you all seem to think you're invincible, let's put that to the test. Hope you're ready for the workout of your lives. Line up!"

A collective groan rippled through the team, but nobody dared to protest. As we shuffled into position, I caught Farron's eye. There was a fire there that matched my own feelings. Whatever hell Coach was about to put us through, hopefully, it would help everyone else get their priorities straight.

He blew his whistle, and we were off, sprinting across the field. The hungover guys were already panting, their faces a sickly shade of green. I pushed myself harder, feeling the burn in my legs.

"Faster!" Coach yelled. "My grandmother could outrun you lot, and she's been dead for ten years!"

As we transitioned into burpees, I heard retching sounds behind me, but I had no compassion. Instead, I sped up, pushing myself to my limits. Next to me, Farron did the same.

"Great work, Tore!" Coach called out, and pride surged inside me. "That's the kind of dedication I want to see!"

I lost track of time as we moved from one punishing exercise to the next. Suicides, mountain climbers, squat jumps—Coach threw everything at us. My muscles screamed in protest, but I refused to give in.

"This... is... bullshit," Jake gasped between push-ups.

I gritted my teeth, pushing through the pain. "Should've thought of that before you decided to get wasted."

"Water break!" Coach Gold bellowed. "Two minutes, then we're back at it!"

I groaned internally but forced myself to my feet and trudged toward the water cooler. When I grabbed a paper cup and filled it with cool water, my hands were shaking slightly, proof of how hard I'd been pushing myself. As exhausted as I was—and we weren't even done yet—it felt amazing.

"Break's over!" Coach's voice cut through the air. "We're doing suicide sprints until I see some real effort!"

I tossed my empty cup aside and jogged back to the starting line, ignoring the burning in my legs. Farron fell into place beside me.

As Coach's whistle blew, we exploded into action. My legs felt like lead, but I pushed through the pain, focusing on the rhythm of my breathing and the pounding of my heart. One sprint, then another, and another. I lost count of how many times we raced back and forth across the field.

Around us, our teammates were dropping like flies. Some collapsed mid-sprint, while others staggered to the sidelines, faces pale and sweaty. But Farron and I kept going, matching each other stride for stride.

I don't know how long we continued like that, existing in a world of discipline and determination over pain and protesting bodies. All I knew was that I refused to let Farron outpace me, and he seemed equally unwilling to fall behind.

Finally, mercifully, Coach's whistle pierced the air. I stumbled to a stop, hands on my knees as I gasped for air. Farron stood nearby, equally winded but still upright.

Coach surveyed the massacre. "All right, that's enough! Hit the showers."

I collapsed onto the grass, chest heaving, every muscle in my body screaming. Pushing myself up onto my elbows, I surveyed the carnage around me. Half the team was still sprawled on the ground, while others were hunched over, dry heaving.

But something had changed. The team looked broken, but there was a newfound respect in their eyes as they glanced between Farron and me. The air felt charged with possibility, tinged with hope.

I caught snippets of awed whispers from our teammates.

"Did you see that?" Jayden whispered. "Tore and Farron, working together like they don't hate each other's guts?"

Ethan chuckled. "Man, I never thought I'd see the day. It's like... What do they call it? A sign of the apocalypse?"

I rolled my eyes but couldn't completely suppress a smile. Farron and I had never seen eye to eye, but today had felt different. For once, Farron and I were united in something other than our mutual dislike. Something had shifted between us. It wasn't friendship—I wasn't that naïve—but it was... something.

And as I glanced at him, I felt a strange flutter in my chest that had nothing to do with exertion. I quickly looked away, chalking it up to oxygen deprivation and Floris getting into my head with his crazy suggestion of foreplay. Running suicide sprints was not foreplay. And anyone who said it was, was seriously fucked up.

We stumbled to the locker room, where I lowered myself onto a bench with a groan. Farron pulled off his sweat-soaked jersey, revealing toned muscles and sun-kissed skin. I quickly averted my gaze from his muscular form, focusing instead on unlacing my cleats. My heart was racing, and I wasn't sure if it was from the intense workout or something else entirely.

I wiped the sweat from my brow, stealing another glance at Farron. Our eyes met, and for a moment, something beyond the usual disdain showed—a flicker of respect, perhaps even admiration. My cheeks heated.

Coach's booming voice interrupted my confused thoughts. "All right, listen up. Today sucked, but it will be nothing compared to what will happen if you show up for practice like this again. That's a promise, not a threat." His gaze swept across the locker room before settling on Farron and me. "The one good thing was to see you two give it your all and go all out. Good work, boys."

A rush of warmth filled me at his words, coupled with an unexpected surge of something else I couldn't pinpoint—this warm feeling inside me, mixed with anticipation and adrenaline. Almost like... butterflies? I risked a glance at Farron, who stood there, shirtless and glistening with sweat, a look of quiet satisfaction on his face.

"Thanks, Coach," Farron said.

I nodded in agreement, not trusting myself to speak.

"The rest of you could learn a thing or two from these guys," Coach said to the team. "This is the kind of dedication that wins championships. Remember that."

As Coach left, a buzz of conversation filled the locker room. I caught snippets of surprised comments and speculation about Farron and me.

"Did you see them out there?"

"Never thought I'd see those two working together."

"Think this means they've buried the hatchet?"

I wondered the same thing. Had we? Had this training finally broken whatever grudge he held against me? I glanced at Farron again, catching his eye. He gave me a small nod, the ghost of a smile playing on his lips. My stomach did a little flip, and I quickly looked away, confused by my body's reactions.

Walking out of the locker room, I overheard two of my teammates talking in hushed tones.

"You think this changes anything?" one asked.

"I don't know, man," the other replied. "But if those two can work together like that... maybe we've got a real shot at the championship after all."

I smiled to myself, a mix of pride and uncertainty swirling in my chest. As I pushed open the door to leave, I nearly collided with Farron.

"Watch where you're going," he grunted, but there was no real heat behind his words.

"My apologies," I replied, my voice coming out huskier than I had intended. "I'll be more careful next time."

Our eyes met, and for a moment, neither of us moved. The air between us crackled with energy. Then Farron cleared his throat and stepped aside, allowing me to pass.

As I walked away, I could feel his gaze on my back. Was he as affected by our newfound dynamic as I was? One thing was certain: things were never going to be the same again.

9

FARRON

As much as I hated it, that hangover-from-hell training, as everyone, including Coach, now collectively referred to it, had been good for the team. I wasn't sure if it had been the brutal punishment for the hangover or seeing Tore and me compete against each other, but somehow, it had created a bond between us.

The team, I meant, not Tore and me. We coexisted, maybe with a little less hate than before, but we weren't friends or anything.

Okay, so I did respect him for not attending that party—which I'd totally expected him to, by the way—and for pushing himself so hard during that training. I still thought he was an arrogant, spoiled jackass, but at least he had his priorities straight.

And he could play. We'd won three more games and held the top spot in our conference, tied with Connor College. We really stood a chance at the championships. Tore had played a huge role in all three victories. As soon as Coach let him out of the box of his position, Tore seized the opportunity and managed to either score or pass to someone else to score.

But our next game was a crucial one. Butler College was a formidable opponent, and playing against them would be a good test of our abilities. We didn't have the rivalry with them like we did with Connor College, but I still wanted to go all out and beat them. Even if it meant letting Tore play outside his assigned position.

And why the hell was I so focused on him? Our team was bigger than him and me, yet all I kept seeing was his annoying face and that mop of blond hair that stood out even from across the soccer fields. Oh, and his eyes, which were a peculiar shade of blue. Lighter than most people's and, of course, they stood out because he was so tanned. They were as flashy as the rest of him.

"You good, Cap?" Ethan called from across the locker room, probably because I'd been staring into space.

I forced my features into neutrality. "Yeah, I'm fine. Just thinking about some shit."

As I headed out to the field, cleats crunching on gravel, I shook off the confusing tangle of emotions. The crisp autumn air helped clear my thoughts. I needed to get my head in the game, not waste energy on Tore.

But as we started warm-ups, my eyes kept scanning the sidelines. Where the hell was he? Tore was annoyingly punctual, always one of the first ones out here.

"All right, boys, pair up for passing drills," Coach called out.

I jogged over to him. "Hey Coach, where's Tore?"

Coach glanced up from his clipboard. "Oh, he had to head home to Norway for a few days. Some family thing came up."

I stood there, frozen, as the rest of the team paired up around me. Norway. Fucking Norway. The audacity of it hit me like a punch to the gut. Who hopped on a plane to another continent just like that?

"He left in the middle of the season?" I tried to keep the irritation out of my voice.

"He'll be back Thursday, so he won't miss a game. Now focus, please." Coach's voice was sharp, snapping me back to reality.

I nodded stiffly and turned away, my jaw clenched. Of course. Tore could apparently jet off whenever he felt like it, consequences be damned. I shook my head, trying to clear the fog of anger and something else I couldn't quite name.

As Coach directed the team through defensive maneuvers, my gaze kept drifting to Tore's empty spot on the field, irrationally irritated at his absence. Why did I care so much that he wasn't here? I should be relieved for the break from his insufferable presence. But instead, I felt unsettled. Off-balance.

I threw myself into the drills with extra intensity, desperate to burn off this restless energy. But no matter how hard I pushed myself, I couldn't shake the nagging awareness of Tore's absence. Which, obviously, pissed me off even more.

After practice, I stormed back to my dorm to make sense of this roiling mess inside me. Without thinking, I grabbed my phone and dialed Wesley, my best friend from high school, who was attending Ohio State.

His familiar face popped up on the screen, grinning. "Yo, what's up, man?"

"You won't believe this shit," I burst out immediately, not bothering with pleasantries. "That pompous asshole Tore just up and flew to Norway. For a family thing. In the middle of the fucking season!"

Wesley's eyebrows shot up. "Damn, that's cold. Coach okay with that?"

"Apparently. It's like the rules don't apply to Mr. Fancy Cleats, you know? He does whatever the hell he wants."

"Sounds like you're pretty worked up about this," Wesley

observed, his tone cautious. "I mean, I get it, but why does it bother you so much?"

I paused, caught off guard by the question. "He's part of the team, you know? He can't bail whenever he feels like it."

But even as I said the words, I knew there was more to it. If it had been anyone else, Coach would've never let him leave, but for Tore, he was making an exception? He was being treated different, and that pissed me off. And underneath that anger was something else, something that felt dangerously close to... disappointment?

"You sure that's all it is?"

I felt heat creep up my neck. "What the hell is that supposed to mean?"

Wesley held up his hands defensively. "Nothing, man. But you're always talking about this Tore guy. Seems like you're letting him live rent-free in your head is all."

I snorted, flopping down on my bed. The springs creaked in protest. "Yeah, 'cause he's a spoiled, rich kid who doesn't know what real life is like."

My voice trailed off as I struggled to put my feelings into words. Images of Tore flashed through my mind: his perfectly styled hair, those designer clothes that probably cost more than my entire wardrobe, the way he effortlessly charmed everyone around him. It made my stomach churn. "I don't get it, Wes. Every time I see him, it's like... I don't know, like my skin's crawling or something. He walks around campus like he owns the place, and it drives me crazy."

Wesley raised an eyebrow. "Sounds like he's really getting under your skin, man."

"That's an understatement," I muttered, absently picking at a loose thread on my worn T-shirt. "I can't figure out why he bothers me so much. It's not like he's openly bragging or anything, but there's something about him..."

"Maybe it's because he represents everything you've fought against," Wesley suggested, his voice thoughtful. "You know, the whole silver-spoon thing."

"You should see the shit he wears. Designer everything, brand-new cleats that cost almost a thousand bucks. Meanwhile, I'm rocking my Walmart specials."

Wesley nodded, his expression softening. "I hear you. Must be nice to jet off to Norway on a whim. Remember when we thought a trip to Cedar Point was living large?"

We'd saved for months, scraping together every penny from our part-time jobs. And here was Tore, flying to Norway just like that. Did he even realize how privileged he was?

"Exactly," I said, my voice thick with frustration. "He has no idea what it's like to struggle. To wonder if there's enough food in the fridge or if the electricity's gonna get shut off."

"Word."

Why would someone like Tore choose Hawley? There had to be a reason. And despite my best efforts, I found myself curious to know what it was. "Seriously though, Wes, how did he end up at Hawley College when he's got that kind of money? He's smart, and with his money and connections, he could buy his way into any school he wants."

"Maybe he's looking for the 'authentic' college experience," Wesley suggested, but I could tell he wasn't buying it either. "Or he's hiding from something or someone."

"Or he's slumming it. You know, playing at being one of us commoners for kicks before he goes back to his castle or whatever."

"Castle, dude? Are you sure you're not secretly writing a fantasy novel?"

"Feels like it sometimes with this guy." I ran a hand through my hair, trying to grasp something solid in all this speculation.

"But seriously, it doesn't add up. There's gotta be a reason. Nobody would give up a cushy life to come to Hawley without a reason."

"Have you considered that maybe he's not as bad as you think? I mean, you haven't really given him a chance, have you?"

I scoffed. "What's there to give a chance to? He's probably never worked a day in his life."

But even as I said it, doubt filled me. Was it really that black-and-white? Did I know enough about his life to judge?

Wesley was quiet for a moment, weighing his words carefully. "Look, Far, I get where you're coming from. We both know what it's like to struggle. But maybe you're letting your prejudice cloud your judgment a bit?"

His words stung, but I couldn't entirely dismiss them. Was I being unfair? The thought made me uncomfortable, and I pushed it away. "I don't know, man." I sighed, feeling suddenly drained. "I can't shake this feeling about him. It's driving me crazy."

"Dude, you're obsessed with this guy."

"Shut up," I grumbled, but the seed of truth in Wesley's words took root despite my resistance. Why was I so fixated on Tore? "Anyway," I said, changing the subject. "Practice was brutal today without him. The team felt off."

"Sounds like you missed him on the field."

"Missed kicking his ass during drills, maybe." My retort lacked conviction. The thought of Tore's swift footwork and the way he moved with the ball entered my mind unbidden, and I shoved it away.

"Whatever you say," Wesley replied, amusement clear in his voice. "I gotta go. Football practice starts in half an hour, and I need to get ready. I'll catch you later, all right? Don't let Prince Charming get to you too much."

"Ha ha," I said dryly, ending the call.

I yanked open the mini fridge and grabbed a water bottle,

taking a long gulp before tossing it onto the desk. My reflection in the small mirror caught my eye: dark hair sticking up wildly, eyes blazing with an emotion I couldn't name.

My mind was whirling, replaying our conversation and everything I knew about Tore. The more I thought about it, the more my dislike for him intensified, mingling with a confusing curiosity that I couldn't quite shake.

Lying back on my bed, I stared at the ceiling, my thoughts a chaotic mess. Who the hell flew to Norway for a family event? The sheer extravagance of it made my stomach churn. We'd never even been able to afford a vacation out of state. The contrast was stark, infuriating.

But beneath the anger, there was something else. A nagging desire to understand. What was Tore's game? Why would someone with his kind of money and connections choose Hawley of all places?

I rolled onto my side, punching my pillow in frustration. "Fucking Tore," I muttered, the words tasting bitter on my tongue. But even as I said it, I felt a strange flutter in my chest, a feeling I couldn't quite place. Why did he have to be so... everything? So annoyingly positive, polite to a fault, and stubborn as hell on the field. And why did my chest tighten whenever he was around?

My mind drifted to the way he moved on the field, all grace and speed. The way his accent made even the most mundane things sound somehow interesting. I groaned, pressing the heels of my hands into my eyes.

Tore was thousands of miles away, yet somehow, he was everywhere. In the empty space on the soccer field. In the silence of my dorm room. And above all, in the restless thoughts that I couldn't seem to shake.

10

TORE

So far, I'd been content to ride along with Luke or other teammates to anything off campus. But I'd quickly discovered that America was not a world that could be conquered without a vehicle, as the distances were vast, even within towns, and public transport was nonexistent.

That had convinced me to purchase a car. My father, who was quite the car aficionado and the owner of several British classic cars, would have a fit if he saw my humble Subaru Crosstrek, but it fit in nicely with the other vehicles on campus. I needed something with four-wheel drive to be able to drive in the snow, according to Luke, who would know, having grown up in Ohio. And I'd wanted to avoid standing out by getting a car no other student could afford.

Did I miss the sleek BMW i8 that was, for now, parked inside our garage back home? Absolutely, though I could only drive it a few months out of the year in Norway as well. But for now, I was content with this dependable car. At least the color, a flashy orange, stood out.

Now that I had my own transportation, it was time to do some more exploring. I'd hoped to do that sooner, but I'd had to fly back home for a few days. My parents had celebrated their twenty-fifth wedding anniversary, and I had been expected to attend. It had been lovely to see my two younger siblings and sneak in a quick visit to my best friend, Andor, but at the same time, being home had felt strange.

Had I truly gotten accustomed to living in the US that quickly? Even in those three days, I'd missed having a roommate, soccer training, and camaraderie. And it had been weird not thinking as much about Farron. That should have been a relief, but it had left me feeling strangely unmoored. Not something I wanted to spend too much time figuring out.

Anyway, I was back, and it was time to venture out on my own. I'd always been curious about the fabled Walmart, its mythical status solidified by endless scrolling through the *People of Walmart* social media account. The photographs of shoppers in outlandish attire were the sort of spectacle that, in my mind, couldn't possibly live up to reality. Only one way to find out, right? Luckily, Hawley had a Walmart Supercenter right outside of town, so I didn't have to drive far.

The sliding doors parted with a whoosh, and I was hit by a blast of air-conditioned air. The moment I crossed the threshold, the hum of fluorescent lights and a cacophony of sounds embraced me. My eyes widened as I took in the sheer vastness of the space before me.

To my left, a tower of discount DVDs teetered precariously—an eclectic mix of B-movie horror flicks and forgotten romantic comedies. Straight ahead, a kaleidoscope of cereal boxes painted the aisle in vibrant hues, boasting every combination of sugar and grain imaginable. Rows upon rows of shelves stretched as far as I could see, stocked with everything from toilet paper to televisions.

"Bloody hell," I muttered under my breath, earning a strange look from a woman pushing a trolley—cart, I mentally corrected myself—past me.

As I turned down the cereal aisle, my eyes were assaulted by a riot of colors and cartoon characters. I picked up a box adorned with a grinning leprechaun. "Lucky Charms," I read aloud, bemused. "Magically delicious? I highly doubt that."

I tossed the box into my cart, along with a few other curiosities from other aisles. Something called Twinkies, a jar of marshmallow fluff—What on earth was that?—and a disturbingly large container of cheese puffs.

I wandered past an endcap adorned with an army of plastic blenders, the price so low, it made me wonder if they'd simply blend themselves apart upon first use. Nearby, a gentleman heaped his cart with enough toilet paper to survive an apocalypse —or perhaps a particularly dodgy takeaway.

As I weaved between families and solitary shoppers, my gaze fell upon a stack of flannel shirts, their patterns loud enough to startle any wildlife within a ten-mile radius. And then there were the gadgets: aisles dedicated to electronic devices that promised to simplify life, all for prices lower than I'd ever seen. Norway was relatively expensive, but this was insane.

I kept scanning the other shoppers, half-expecting to see someone in a bathrobe or dressed as a superhero. But aside from a few questionable fashion choices—Was that man really wearing socks with sandals?—everyone looked normal. People might not be as weirdly dressed as I had anticipated, but Walmart was everything I'd expected and nothing like I'd imagined all at once. It was too much, excessive, yet strangely compelling. A microcosm of America itself, perhaps.

It was all at once overwhelming and fascinating, a consumerist carnival where every possible need—or want masquerading as need—could be met under one massive roof.

I turned around the corner of yet another aisle, one with endless rows of bottled water, and came to a full stop. There, methodically scanning items with a handheld device and putting them in a cart that held several shopping baskets, was Farron.

My heart skipped a beat. What on earth was he doing here? I hesitated, unsure if I should approach him. But curiosity got the better of me, and I pushed my cart toward him.

"Farron?" I called out, my voice a mix of surprise and confusion. "I didn't expect to see you here."

He looked up, his eyes widening slightly before his expression settled into something more neutral. "What are you doing here?"

I felt a flush creep up my neck. "Oh, exploring, I suppose. But do you work here?"

Farron's jaw tightened almost imperceptibly. "Yeah, I do. So?"

I blinked, taken aback by his defensive tone. "I didn't know you had a job outside of school and football."

"Soccer, you mean."

I winced. "Yes, soccer."

"Not all of us can afford not to work," he said, his voice clipped.

I felt a twinge of discomfort, suddenly very aware of the stark differences in our backgrounds. "That must be challenging, balancing work with your studies and soccer."

Farron shrugged, turning back to his task. "You do what you have to do."

I watched him for a moment, feeling a strange mix of admiration and guilt. Here I was, treating Walmart like some exotic adventure while Farron was here out of necessity. "I thought you had a full scholarship. I heard someone say that," I added quickly when he shot me a look that could curdle milk.

"Yeah, and that pays for school. Doesn't put food on the table or keep the lights on at home, does it?" He shoved a six-pack of water bottles into the shopping cart with more force than necessary. "I've got a family to support."

His words struck me with an unexpected force. Surely, he didn't mean he had kids, did he? "A family?"

"My mom works two jobs. I've got three younger siblings who need stuff like school supplies, clothes, food." He gestured around the store. "So here I am, picking groceries for rich folks who can't be bothered to do their own shopping."

He didn't mention a dad, and I was afraid to ask. Technically, it was none of my business.

"My dad died when I was thirteen," Farron said with a sigh. Maybe he'd seen the question on my face anyway. "He was driving me home after soccer practice when a drunk driver hit our car."

"Oh, Farron, I'm so sorry. That's awfully young to lose your dad. How old were your siblings?"

He looked at me for a few seconds as if gauging if my empathy was genuine. "Caspian was nine, Rowan five, and Calista only three. The youngest two have no memories of him, which sucks because he was a great dad."

"That's so young. I'm sure you've been sharing your memories with them, keeping him alive that way." He stared at me with a frown, so I plowed on. "The ancient Greeks stated that as long as someone was alive in people's memories, they weren't truly gone. So your dad is still with you and your siblings when you share your stories with them."

"That's..." He swallowed. "I like that thought. And yeah, I've done my best to tell them about him. He was always supportive of my dreams to become a pro soccer player. Drove me to every training, every clinic, every game. Never complained."

My father hadn't been quite so understanding. When I'd been little, he'd been fine with it, but the older I got, the more he protested football was taking up too much of my time. And in the end, he'd been the one who'd axed my dreams. "I envy you for that."

"You envy me?"

I nodded. "My father forbade me to accept an offer from a European club."

His eyes widened. "You had an offer from a club?"

"Ajax, a Dutch club."

"I know Ajax."

"I was accepted into their youth program, but my father put his foot down."

"Why?" Farron seemed stunned.

"Family obligations that were more important. He didn't want me to move to the Netherlands, even though I had friends there." Floris's family had been more than willing to take me in, even providing extra security if needed, but my father had still said no.

"Dude, that sucks."

It was the first time that Farron had expressed any kind of sympathy for me, and the rush of it cruised through my veins. "It did, and I still resent him for it."

"Yeah, no shit. I mean, what kind of family obligation could be more important than a chance to play professional soccer at that level?"

I opened my mouth, then closed it again. As much as I wanted to tell Farron the truth, I couldn't. Not only because I wasn't sure how he would react but also because of the security risks it could create. Right now, no one knew who I was, but once word got out, I wouldn't be able to live in the anonymity I enjoyed now. "He gave me no choice."

"I'm sorry," Farron said.

Never had those words meant more to me.

"Thank you. And thank you for sharing your story with me," I said, and even I could hear how oddly formal that sounded, like a phrase I'd been taught to say—which I had been. "It must be quite the balancing act with all your responsibilities."

"Balancing act?" He snorted. "More like a damn circus, and I'm juggling flaming torches while riding a unicycle." The image conjured a brief, unexpected smile from both of us before his expression shuttered again.

"Still, it takes a remarkable amount of strength to manage all that. I admire your dedication."

Farron shot me a piercing look, discomfort flashing across his features. "Don't," he said flatly. "It's not a choice. It's a necessity."

The honesty in his tone struck a chord within me. I'd never considered the relentless pressure of such responsibilities. My own worries felt embarrassingly trivial by comparison. "And what of your dreams, Farron? Outside of soccer?"

He paused for a moment, the flicker of vulnerability in his eyes gone as quickly as it appeared. "To make sure those three have more options than I did. That's all that matters."

I nodded, understanding that drive all too well. In my own way, I was also bound by duty and expectation, though the chains that tethered me were golden, not iron. "That's admirable."

Farron's cheeks reddened slightly, and he busied himself with his scanning device. "Yeah, well... Thanks, I guess. But I don't need your pity or your praise, all right?"

I bit my lip, unsure of how to respond to that. If he didn't want me to admire, praise, or pity him, what was left? "Anyway, thank you for sharing. It was eye-opening."

He nodded curtly, not looking up from his device. As I turned to go, I couldn't shake the feeling that I'd somehow managed to offend him, though I wasn't quite sure how. I pushed my cart away, my earlier excitement about Walmart fading, replaced by a nagging sense of unease.

After everything I had seen and learned in my education, my

travels, and in my role as representative of the Norwegian royal family, I'd thought I understood the breadth of the world, with its myriad struggles and joys. In truth, I'd only skimmed the surface. Farron had unwittingly held up a mirror, revealing my ignorance and privilege in stark relief. It hurt, yet I was grateful he'd shared a little bit of his personal life with me. I'd have to try harder to understand him since, clearly, there was much more to him than his gruff surface.

11

FARRON

The hotel lobby buzzed with excitement as we piled in, a sea of blue-and-yellow jerseys flooding the polished marble floor, each of us buzzing with the kind of electric excitement that only came before a big game. I breathed in the crisp, air-conditioned atmosphere, a welcome respite from the stuffy three-hour bus ride to Butler College.

"All right, Hawks!" I called out, clapping my hands to get everyone's attention. "Listen up for room assignments. Remember, lights out at 10 p.m. sharp. We've got a big game tomorrow."

My teammates gathered around, their eager faces a mix of anticipation and nervous energy. I felt it, too, that familiar pre-game jitter in my gut. As I read off the list Coach had handed me before we got off the bus, pairing up my fellow players, Tore hung back, his perfectly styled blond hair setting him apart from the rest of us.

When I got to the end of the list, my stomach dropped. "Tore, you're with me."

Coach crossed his arms, his gaze on me unwavering. "You two need to learn to work together. I thought we fixed that shit in the hangover-from-hell training, but you're back to glaring at each other. If we want to win, we need you two to get your act together, so you're rooming together until you figure it out."

Fuuuck. I didn't dare protest, knowing he was right.

Tore's blue eyes widened slightly, his Adam's apple bobbing as he swallowed. "Right-o," he said, his accent crisp. "Shall we, then?"

I gritted my teeth, shouldering my worn duffel bag. "Yeah, let's go."

As we walked to the elevator, the tension crackled between us like static electricity. Tore's cologne—probably some fancy European shit—wafted over, making my nostrils flare. I jabbed the elevator button harder than necessary.

"According to Luke, I don't snore," Tore said. "So you won't have to worry about me keeping you up all night."

I grunted in response, not in the mood for his small talk. The elevator dinged, and we stepped inside. Why did I have to share a room with this privileged pretty boy? Coach had done me dirty. All I wanted was to focus on the game, not deal with whatever the hell this uncomfortable energy between us was.

"Everything okay?" Tore asked, his tone light, almost cautious. He seemed to sense the tension radiating off me like heat from asphalt on a hot summer day.

"Fine," I grunted, not trusting myself to say more. I was annoyed by how much mental real estate this guy had taken up without paying rent—his image, his voice, all of it crowding my thoughts. "Stick to your side of the room, okay? I need to be on top of my game tomorrow."

Tore's face fell slightly, but he quickly masked it with a polite smile. "Of course. I shall endeavor to be as unobtrusive as possible."

I rolled my eyes at his flowery language. Couldn't he talk like a normal person?

I tossed my duffel onto the bed nearest the window, claiming my territory. Tore followed suit, carefully placing his brand-new bag on the other bed. His long fingers gracefully handled the zippers, and I quickly averted my gaze, annoyed at myself for even noticing.

We unpacked in silence. At least Tore was as tidy as I was. That was quite the improvement on Colin, who was the world's biggest slob.

The air was thick with unspoken words as I flopped down on the bed, my body sinking into the mattress. I was tired—tired of fighting, tired of thinking, tired of trying to figure out whatever this thing was that twisted inside me every time Tore was near.

"So, Farron," Tore said after we'd both unpacked, his voice tentative. "I was wondering if you might share some insights about tomorrow's match. You've played against Butler before, and I'm keen to hear any suggestions or tips."

I sighed. Part of me wanted to tell him to fuck off, but the captain in me couldn't ignore a teammate asking for advice. "What do you want to know?"

As Tore's face lit up with genuine enthusiasm, I felt a weird flutter in my stomach. Damn, why did he have to look so...?

No. I squashed that thought immediately. This was about soccer, nothing else.

"Well, I've watched some of their games, and they have a midfielder who seems to play very rough, Ian Sharp," Tore explained, gesturing with those elegant hands of his. "I'm a little apprehensive of him injuring me. What would be the best strategy for me to deal with him?"

I nodded. "Yeah, I've noticed that. Look, you've got speed on your side, but you need to anticipate the play better to avoid him surprising you. Watch his body language..."

As I delved into a tactical explanation, Tore hung on my every word, his blue eyes fixed on me with rapt attention. It was unsettling, how intensely he listened. And even more unsettling was how much I enjoyed it.

Tore reached out to grab a notepad from the nightstand, his hand accidentally brushing against mine. A jolt of electricity shot through me, and I jerked back as if I'd been burned. What the fuck was that?

"Oh, sorry," Tore said, his cheeks flushing slightly.

"It's fine." My skin still tingled where he'd touched me, and I hated how much it affected me. I needed to get a grip.

Tore nodded, looking flustered as he jotted down some notes. I tried to continue my explanation, but my mind kept wandering to how soft his hand had felt against mine. Fuck, what was wrong with me?

"I need to use the loo real quick," Tore said, interrupting my thoughts. "I'll be right back to finish our discussion."

I grunted in acknowledgment, grateful for the brief reprieve. As soon as the bathroom door closed, I flopped back on my bed, scrubbing my hands over my face. This was getting ridiculous. I needed to focus on the game, not on my annoying roommate's stupidly perfect hands. Also, what the fuck kind of weird word was *loo*? Couldn't he say bathroom, like a normal person?

A crash from the bathroom jolted me upright. "Shit!"

I was on my feet in an instant, striding to the bathroom door. "What happened?"

The door opened, revealing a wide-eyed Tore and the unmistakable scent of my cologne. My stomach dropped as I saw the shattered remains of my bottle of Spicebomb on the tile floor.

"I'm dreadfully sorry," Tore stammered. "I was reaching for a towel and accidentally knocked over your cologne. I'll replace it, of course—"

"Replace it?" I wasn't sure what pissed me off more: the fact that he knew I wouldn't be able to afford simply buying a new one... or the fact that he could.

"Obviously. I broke it, so I should buy you a new one."

I let out a harsh laugh. "Just like that, huh? Must be nice to throw money around without a second thought."

Tore's brow furrowed. "That's not... I simply want to make amends. It's the right thing to do."

His earnestness was infuriating. I wanted to stay angry, to keep hating him and everything he represented. "That shit costs, like, a hundred bucks."

Realization dawned in his eyes. "You're upset because I can afford to replace it."

How could this spoiled, rich kid possibly understand what it meant to save up for something? To work your ass off for a simple luxury? "Would it hurt you to realize that not everyone has your money?"

"Would you prefer I not replace it?"

I glared at Tore, my fists clenching at my sides. His blue eyes were wide with genuine remorse, and I hated how it made my anger waver. I couldn't take it anymore. The tension in the room was suffocating, and Tore's constant apologetic glances were driving me insane.

"Will you stop looking at me like that?" I snapped, shoving Tore's shoulder hard enough to make him stumble back a step.

His blue eyes widened in shock, hurt flashing across his face. "I... I'm sorry, I didn't realize I was—"

"You're always sorry, aren't you?" I advanced on him again. "Sorry for breaking my stuff, sorry for existing in my space. Well, maybe I'm sick of your sorries!"

"Farron," he breathed, the hurt in his voice slicing through my rage, giving me pause. My chest heaved as I realized what I'd done; I'd crossed a line, let my anger morph into physical force.

I saw the moment something shifted in Tore's expression. The hurt was replaced by a steely determination I'd never seen before. He squared his shoulders, standing tall. "That's quite enough, Farron," he said, his voice low and firm. "I understand you're upset, but that doesn't give you the right to put your hands on me."

I blinked, taken aback by his sudden change in demeanor. Even in defense, he carried himself with a strange grace, commanding respect without demanding it. Not that I was ready to surrender that easily, my temper still brewing.

"What, you can't handle a little shoving? I thought you were tougher than that, pretty boy."

Tore's jaw clenched. "My ability to handle your aggression is not the point. Your behavior is unacceptable."

He was right, but my anger was still boiling over, and I couldn't help myself. "Oh yeah? What are you gonna do about it?"

"I'm going to remind you that we're teammates," Tore said, his accent more pronounced in his agitation. "And that regardless of our personal feelings, we have a responsibility to work together. I've apologized and offered to make amends. If that's not enough for you, then perhaps we should speak to Coach about alternative rooming arrangements."

I stared at Tore, my heart pounding. The air between us crackled with tension, and suddenly, I was hyperaware of every detail—the slight flush on his cheeks, the way his chest rose and fell with each breath, the intensity in those blue eyes. Something shifted, and before I could think, I grabbed the front of his shirt and yanked him toward me.

Our lips crashed together, hard and desperate. It wasn't gentle or romantic. It was all teeth and tongue, fueled by anger and frustration and something else I couldn't name. Tore made a surprised sound against my mouth, but he didn't pull away. Instead, his hands came up to grip my shoulders, his fingers digging in.

The world spun. All the anger and frustration melted into a blaze of something wild and desperate. Our mouths moved together with a raw urgency, tongues clashing, teeth grazing.

I gripped his shoulders, pulling him closer, needing more, needing everything he was willing to give. It was as if we were both starved, devouring the kiss with a hunger that bordered on madness.

I pushed him back against the wall, pressing my body against his. The heat of him seeped through our clothes, and I groaned, deepening the kiss. Tore responded with equal fervor, one hand sliding up to tangle in my hair, tugging gently, tilting my head back to deepen the kiss. Every nerve ending screamed to life under his touch, and I groaned against him, the sound swallowed by the fervor of our connection.

When we finally broke apart, we were both panting. I stared at Tore, my mind reeling. What the fuck had just happened? His lips were red and swollen, his hair mussed where I'd run my fingers through it. He looked as shocked as I felt.

"Farron," he breathed. "What was that?"

I shook my head, taking a step back, unable to fully comprehend the seismic shift that had just occurred. My brain scrambled to catch up with the aftershocks rippling through my body. "I don't know. I... Shit. I don't know."

Tore ran a hand through his hair, looking lost. "I thought... Aren't you straight?"

"Yeah," I said automatically, but the word felt hollow. "I mean, I thought I was. Fuck."

"So did I."

I frowned. "Wait, what?"

"I thought I was straight."

"Oh."

We stood there in awkward silence, neither of us knowing what to say. The anger from earlier had dissipated, replaced by confusion and a lingering desire that I didn't want to examine too closely. The lingering desire was palpable, either a tantalizing promise or a terrifying threat—I couldn't decide which.

What the hell came next after kissing your soccer teammate like your life depended on it?

"Perhaps we should take some time to process this." Tore's voice was unsteady.

I nodded, grateful for the out. "Yeah. Yeah, good idea. I'm gonna go for a walk or something."

As I headed for the door, I caught a glimpse of Tore in the mirror. He was touching his lips, a bewildered expression on his face. I hurried out of the room, my head spinning.

What the hell had I done? And, more importantly, why did I want to do it again?

12

TORE

I stared at my reflection in the hotel room mirror, my fingers ghosting over my lips. They still tingled from Farron's kiss, sending sparks through my body at the mere memory. What in the bloody hell had just happened?

My heart raced as I replayed the moment: the scorching heat of Farron's body, the intoxicating scent of his cologne, the slick slide of his tongue against mine, the way his strong hands had gripped my waist. It was unlike anything I'd ever experienced before.

But what did this mean? I finally dragged myself away from the mirror and flopped down on my bed, staring at the ceiling. Had Floris been right? Had all of the sparks between Farron and me been foreplay? I didn't even care that Floris had called it, though usually I would've been irritated he'd gotten one over on me, but I couldn't figure it out.

If you kissed another guy and liked it, that meant you weren't straight, right? As confused as I was about the whole thing, one thing I knew with absolute clarity: I had loved that kiss. Every second of it. Which meant I was attracted to Farron, which in turn explained a whole lot about the last few weeks.

So that was a first conclusion, something to cling to. I was attracted to him, which meant... Labels meant little to me, but I'd never expected to have to change my identity from straight to bisexual, but here we were.

Not that it bothered me. A label was mostly useful for others. I didn't have an issue with being attracted to another guy. My issue was with it being Farron, who had been nothing but a jerk to me, and now I wanted him to kiss me again? What did that say about me?

I'd had relationships before—with girls, obviously—but never anything serious. Some had come from a royal or noble background, while others were classmates. None had been problematic, and certainly none had hated me, which I was fairly sure Farron did. How could he both hate me and kiss me like that?

The silence in the room was oppressive, filled only by the sound of my accelerated breathing and the occasional whisper of traffic from the streets below. I closed my eyes, willing myself to make sense of it all, but the image of Farron—dark hair tousled, brown eyes burning with an intensity that threatened to consume us both—kept replaying like a relentless loop in my mind.

A key card clicked at the door, the electronic beep shattering the stillness. I sat up, apprehension tightening my chest as the door swung open. Farron strode in, his presence immediately filling the room with palpable tension. His walk must've done little to quell the storm raging within him, evident in the clench of his jaw and the purposeful way he avoided my gaze.

"Hey," he grunted, tossing his room key on the nightstand.

"Hello, Farron." I winced at how formal I sounded. Bloody hell, why couldn't I act normal around him anymore?

Farron grabbed a water bottle from the mini fridge, gulping it down. I watched him, tracing the outline of his broad shoulders down to the defined muscles that tapered to his waist. I stared at the strong column of his throat as he swallowed. Heat rushed to my cheeks, and I quickly averted my gaze.

"Good walk?" I asked, desperate to break the awkward silence.

He shrugged. "It was fine."

More silence stretched between us. I fidgeted with the hem of my shirt, searching for something else to say. But my usually eloquent tongue felt like lead in my mouth.

"Look, Farron, about earlier—" I started, only to stop when he held up a hand, silencing me.

"Save it, Tore. I don't wanna talk right now."

My heart sank. Did he regret kissing me? Was I reading too much into it?

But the kiss—no, the kisses—they were real. They happened. And they meant something. At least, they did to me. My heart raced at the thought of his lips on mine, the way his stubble had felt against my skin, the undeniable strength in his embrace.

I opened my mouth to press further, but the words died on my lips as Farron yanked off his sweaty T-shirt. My eyes roamed over his muscled torso of their own accord, drinking in the sight of his tanned skin and defined abs.

Good lord, I was in trouble.

I took a deep breath, steeling myself. "I think we should talk about what happened."

He turned to me, his dark eyes flashing with irritation. "What's there to talk about? We kissed. It happened. No need to dissect it to death."

"But don't you think we should discuss what it means? For us, for the team—"

"Christ, Tore," Farron cut me off, exasperation clear in his voice. "Not everything needs a fucking committee meeting. Sometimes, things just happen, all right?"

I flinched at his harsh tone, feeling foolish for even bringing it up. Of course someone like Farron wouldn't want to analyze every little thing. He was a man of action, not words.

Farron's expression softened slightly. He ran a hand through his messy hair, sighing. "Look, I didn't mean to snap. I'm not good at talking, to begin with, and this... I don't know what this is, okay? And until I do, I don't wanna risk saying the wrong thing."

I nodded, not trusting myself to speak. My mind was a whirlwind of conflicting thoughts and emotions. Part of me wanted to keep pushing until I understood what was happening between us. But another part, a growing part, wanted to feel his rough lips on mine again.

His dismissal stung but also fanned the flames of something reckless within me. I rose from the bed, driven by a newfound resolve to explore this uncharted territory between us. Farron's eyes widened as I stepped close to him.

"Tore..."

"Fine," I said, the word barely above a whisper, "then let's not talk."

I bridged the gap between us, capturing his lips with mine, and it was like throwing gas onto a fire. The fire that had burned so brightly between us immediately flared up again. The kiss was a collision of need and confusion, our tensions igniting a fervor that consumed any lingering doubt. His hands threaded my hair, angling my head back as if searching for something deeper, something more profound than the mere meeting of mouths.

Our tongues touched, tangled, sending sparks throughout my body. If I'd harbored any doubt about my attraction to him, the fact that my cock grew hard as iron sealed the deal. On instinct, I rubbed myself against him, and my erection met his. We both froze and then Farron broke off the kiss.

I was still catching my breath when Farron's guarded eyes met mine, a silent challenge in their depths. The unspoken questions danced between us like shadows, and I couldn't let the moment pass without trying to capture it, to make sense of the chaos.

"I don't like you," Farron said.

I snorted at his timing. "Trust me, I'm well aware."

"But for some reason, I do like kissing you."

How pathetic was I that I savored that little crumb of praise? "Thank you."

He tilted his head, studying me from alarmingly close. "You're not gonna say it back?"

"I would've thought my body's reaction was sufficient proof of how much I enjoyed it."

"Christ, the way you express yourself, even now. Do you ever lose your composure?"

No, because that was a luxury I didn't have. I'd been trained to always keep my cool. The fact that my temper was naturally slow to ignite had made it easier, but I'd still struggled sometimes as a child. Now, it was rare for me to act impulsively. "Seldomly."

"You do realize that's a challenge for me now, right? Making you lose your grip on yourself?"

"Not a challenge I set intentionally, I promise."

"Like that would make a difference to me." He brushed his thumb along my lips, still wet and throbbing from his kisses. "I think it's because we have this strange energy between us."

"Attraction."

He hesitated. "I would've said sexual energy or chemistry, even, but it's nothing like I've ever felt before."

"Same."

"We need to work through it."

I frowned. What did that mean? "I'm not sure I understand."

"It's burning too hot to be more than a fluke, so if we let it run its course, it'll fade."

"Run its course?" I still had no clue what he meant.

"Oh for fuck's sake." With a low growl, he yanked me forward again.

His lips found mine, more urgent this time. I tangled my fingers in his dark, damp hair, marveling at how soft it felt. Farron's tongue teased the seam of my lips, and I opened for him without hesitation. The taste of him was intoxicating, like mint and something uniquely Farron.

The passion between us was an answer in itself, a truth that needed no articulation, only to be felt, to be lived. And in that heated moment, I let go of everything else—the expectations, the labels, the fear—and surrendered to the intensity of what was unfolding between us. Every thought vanished from my brain, leaving only need.

A need for him.

"I wanna touch you," Farron growled, and suddenly, I understood what he had meant by letting it run its course. He wanted to give in to the sexual chemistry between us so it would disappear. Who was I to tell him that I highly doubted it would work that way?

"Same."

Our eyes met, and we nodded in mutual agreement.

Possessed by a weird kind of urgency, we fumbled with sweatpants and underwear until we both stood with them around our ankles. Our breaths mingled and became ragged as skin met skin, the air around us charged with the electricity of first contact.

With an unfamiliar boldness, I wrapped my hand around him—the first time I was touching another man's cock. He was soft as silk and hard as steel at the same time, hot and throbbing in my hand. I gave an experimental tug.

"Ah fuck..." Fallon groaned, the low timbre of his voice sending shivers down my spine. I couldn't help but smile at the profanity, so very Farron, so very real amidst the surreal whirlwind of sensation.

But then he touched me, and the smile was wiped off my face.

"You're uncut," he said with a measure of wonder.

"It's common in Europe. Few men are circumcised other than for religious reasons."

"I've never seen one." Then he blushed, and it was the most peculiar sight.

Suddenly, Farron let go of me and pulled away. The loss of contact was jarring, leaving me dazed and confused.

"I can't do this," he mumbled, not meeting my eyes. "I'm gonna shower."

Before I could form a coherent response, Farron had dragged up his pants and headed for the bathroom. The door shut behind him with a soft click, followed by the sound of running water.

I stood there, trying to catch my breath and process what had happened. My body still thrummed with unfulfilled desire, but my mind was reeling. What did this mean? Did Farron regret what we'd done?

The sound of the shower seemed to mock me as I stared into the distance, replaying every touch, every kiss in my mind. It had felt so right in the moment, but now doubt crept in.

After what felt like an eternity, I made a decision. I couldn't let things end like this, with so much left unsaid. I fixed my clothes and walked to the bathroom door. My hand hovered over the knob for a moment before I steeled my nerves and turned it.

The bathroom was filled with steam, Farron's silhouette

visible through the frosted glass of the shower door. I hesitated, suddenly unsure of what to say or do.

"Farron?" I called out, my voice barely audible over the sound of the water.

He didn't respond, but his body tensed. Taking a deep breath, I stripped off my clothes and stepped into the shower behind him. We stood there, the hot water cascading over us, not touching, not speaking. The silence between us was deafening, filled with all the things we weren't saying.

I watched the water run down Farron's muscular back, tracing the contours of his body. My fingers itched to reach out and touch him, but I held back, unsure of where we stood.

Finally, Farron turned to face me, his dark eyes unreadable. "Tore," he said, his voice low and husky. "We shouldn't..."

But he didn't finish the sentence. Instead, he reached for me, pulling me close. Our lips crashed together, the kiss desperate and hungry. I melted into him, my hands exploring the wet planes of his chest and shoulders.

He was still hard, and when I touched him, he didn't protest. I wrapped my hand around him firmly, waiting for him to stop me, but he didn't. The water alone wasn't slick enough, so I squeezed some conditioner from the hotel into my hand. Hmm, what if I...?

I used both my hands and brought our cocks together. The slick slide was as erotic as anything I'd ever felt, and Farron's low groan told me he liked it too. He rested his forehead on my shoulder as I began jacking us off together, awkward at first but then with better coordination and more confidence.

I quickly discovered that he was less sensitive than I was. When I accidentally squeezed his tip a bit harder, he moaned in appreciation where I would've winced at the pain. I used that knowledge to my advantage, putting pressure on his tip with my thumb.

"Feel good?" I checked.

"So fucking good."

His rare praise filled me with a pride that only intensified the pleasure. "I've never done this before, so you'll need to tell me if I'm doing something wrong."

His response was a mere grunt, but he moved closer to me, and I reveled in his nearness.

It didn't take long for me to reach the point of no return. But Farron's breathing had sped up as well, and his muscles were tensing. "Are you…?"

"Don't fucking stop. Please."

That last added word did it for me. I didn't think I'd ever heard him utter it, not to me, at least. I sped up, our cocks sliding against each other like slick steel. Farron grunted, and his whole body froze. Seconds later, his cock erupted, jerking against mine. It was enough to set me off as well, and I clenched my eyes shut as I came so hard, I was dizzy for a moment. Bloody hell, that had been the most intense orgasm of my life.

Panting, chests heaving in unison, Farron and I clung to each other, the air around us thick with the electricity of our release. Would he walk away again?

Then Farron inched back, his softening dick slipping from my grip, and I had my answer.

"Thank you," he said, avoiding my eyes.

Without waiting for a reply, he stepped out, wrapping a towel around his waist. My shoulders dropped as I washed the cum off my hands and my spent cock, now soft and retreating again.

I turned off the shower, my mind a whirlwind of confusion and desire. As we dried off and dressed for bed, the silence between us grew heavier and more oppressive. I wanted to say something, anything, to break the tension, but the words wouldn't come.

We climbed into our separate beds, the distance between us a chasm the size of the Grand Canyon. I stared at Farron's back, willing him to turn around, to acknowledge what had happened between us. But he remained still, his breathing eventually evening out into sleep.

I lay awake for a long time, my thoughts racing. What did this mean for us? For me? I'd never felt this way about another man before, and the intensity of it scared me. But as sleep finally claimed me, one thought won.

I wanted more.

13

FARRON

The locker room was the usual craziness of motion and noise, but amid the chaos, my gaze drifted to Tore. He sat across from me, lacing his cleats with meticulous care, the kind that came from being raised with standards higher than the rafters above us. The weight of our last encounter hung between us like a heavy fog, thick and unspoken.

We'd barely exchanged a word since yesterday evening. Getting up this morning had been a silent storm of avoidance and awkwardness, interspersed with only the most necessary communications. When Coach had spotted us coming down for breakfast, his look of disappointment had hit hard. He was counting on me to fix this, and instead, I'd only made things worse.

The locker room buzzed with pre-game energy, but all I could focus on was Tore across the room. My palms were sweaty, and it wasn't from the upcoming game against Butler College. Games like that only fired me up.

No, it was him sitting there. His golden hair caught the fluorescent light as he put on his jersey, muscles flexing, and my stomach did a weird flip.

In the mirror's reflection, I watched him stand, muscles moving under the fabric of his jersey in a way that shouldn't have been distracting. But it was. Everything about him was distracting, and I hated it.

Shit. This wasn't supposed to happen. Getting each other off was supposed to solve this, not make it worse. I tore my eyes away.

"Everyone ready?" I called out, forcing myself into captain mode. "Let's show Butler what we're made of!"

A chorus of cheers went up. I risked a glance at Tore. He met my eyes for a split second before looking away, a flush creeping up his neck. Dammit. This awkwardness between us was going to fuck up our game.

"All right, Hawks, hands in!" I said, gathering the team. We huddled up, and I found myself right next to Tore. The heat of his body radiated against my side. I swallowed hard, trying to focus. "ONE TEAM!"

"ONE DREAM!" everyone else shouted. As we broke apart, Tore's hand brushed against mine. A jolt went through me. What the hell was happening to me?

We jogged out onto the field to the roar of the crowd. The crisp fall air hit my face, helping to clear my head. I had better fucking focus. We had a game to win.

The whistle blew and we were off. I lost myself in the rhythm of the game—the pounding of feet on grass, shouts echoing across the field, puffs of breath steaming from my lungs, muscles operating on pure memory. For a while, I managed to forget about Tore.

Then it happened. Tore got the ball, weaving through Butler's defense like it was nothing. A perfect pass to Jake, who sent it sailing back to Tore right in front of the goal. With a powerful kick, Tore sent the ball flying past the goalie.

The crowd erupted. Before I knew what I was doing, I was

running toward Tore. He turned, beaming, arms outstretched. Instinct took over, and my arms wrapped around him in a brief, fierce hug—an embrace meant to be purely congratulatory. For a moment, everything else faded. All I could feel was the solid warmth of him, his rapid heartbeat against my chest. But as our bodies pressed close, the line between camaraderie and something more blurred dangerously.

Then reality came crashing back. We jerked apart like we'd been burned. Tore's eyes were wide, a mix of elation and panic. My own pulse was racing, and not from the exertion.

"Good... good job," I managed to get out, awkwardly patting his shoulder.

We stood there for a moment, neither sure what to do. Then Jake came barreling over, tackling Tore in a hug. I used the distraction to retreat, my mind reeling.

What the fuck was I doing? I couldn't be feeling this... whatever it was... for Tore. It would ruin everything: the team dynamic, my focus, my whole damn life plan. But as I glanced back at him, surrounded by our cheering teammates, my heart clenched.

I was so screwed.

As the match continued, I played harder, ran faster, desperate to prove to myself that nothing had changed. Yet the truth was etched into every stolen look, every accidental brush of our hands. Somehow, Tore had gotten under my skin, and kissing him had only made it worse.

Butler scored in the last minute before halftime, which was always tough timing. Heading into the break when you were ahead in the game was so much easier. But we were playing well, and Coach only had encouragement and praise for us, which was rare.

Then he turned to Tore. "You have free rein," he told him. "Have at 'em."

"Unleash the Tore!" Jake yelled, which had everyone in stitches, and even I chuckled. Something told me that phrase would stick.

We started the second half feeling good about our chances. My eyes followed Tore as he navigated the pitch with the grace of a dancer and the precision of a predator. The Butler defense had clued into the danger Tore created, and he had two men on him at all times. That left Ethan open, who saw his chance. He took the shot, and the ball curved through the air like it had been fired from a cannon. But the goalie was on it, managing to block it with outstretched fists. Still, it had been a solid attempt.

We kept pushing, kept pressuring, and time and again, Tore tried to break free, but to no avail. His frustration was palpable, but he stayed calm. Time passed, and no matter what we did, we couldn't break through again.

Then, in the last minute of regular play time, Tore received a perfect cross from Daniel, and the roar of the crowd swelled as he broke away from his defenders, sprinting at full speed. I held my breath as he pivoted gracefully, his lean body a blur of motion. With a precision that seemed almost superhuman, he connected with the ball, sending it sailing past the goalkeeper's outstretched hands. Goal!

This time, I held back, letting the others swarm him first. Our teammates slapped his back and ruffled his perfectly styled hair. His laughter, bright and genuine, cut through the pandemonium, reaching me even as I stood rooted to my spot. His face was flushed, hair tousled, eyes bright with exhilaration. He looked... breathtaking.

Across the field, our eyes met and held. His grin was broad, and for a moment, it felt like we were the only two people on the field. I raised my hand in a silent acknowledgment of what he'd done for us. He nodded. It somehow cost me to break eye contact and resume playing.

The final whistle blew a few minutes later, cementing our victory. As captain, I gathered the team for our post-game huddle, trying to ignore how my skin prickled when Tore's shoulder brushed against mine.

"Great job out there, everyone," I said. "Especially you, Tore. Those were some damn fine goals."

I ignored the shocked gasps of my teammates and focused on Tore, who ducked his head, a pleased smile playing on his lips. "Thank you, but it was a team effort. I couldn't have done it without everyone's support."

I cleared my throat, wrapping up the huddle quickly before heading to the locker room.

Back in the locker room, the adrenaline was still palpable, echoing off the walls along with all the laughter and chatter. I slumped onto the bench, allowing myself a moment to breathe, to try and sort through the jumbled thoughts colliding in my head.

The celebratory atmosphere continued as we changed. I tried to keep my eyes to myself. I really did. But they kept drifting to Tore like a compass finding true north. He was peeling off his sweat-soaked jersey, revealing smooth, pale skin. A bead of perspiration trickled down his spine, and I found myself wondering what it would taste like if I licked—

"Earth to Farron!" Colin's voice snapped me back to reality. "You good, man? You're looking a little out of it."

"Yeah. Coming down from the adrenaline, you know?"

Colin nodded, but he wasn't entirely convinced. I forced myself to relax, to act normal.

I waited until most of the guys had left before standing, keeping my eyes fixed on my locker as I undressed. My hand shook slightly as I unbuttoned my shirt, and I frowned at my own reaction.

"Hey, you okay?" Tore's voice, too close for comfort, made me stiffen.

"Yeah, fine," I grunted without turning to face him. "Tired."

"Me too."

I could feel his gaze on me, heavy and unsettling. "Good game," I added because what else could I say?

"Thank you, Farron," he said softly, and something in his tone had my heart beating faster, betraying the disinterest I tried so hard to project. Fuck, I loved the way he said my name with that posh accent.

"Shower's waiting for you," I said in a lame attempt to redirect the conversation as I stepped past him.

"Right," he murmured, and as I walked away, I didn't dare look back.

***

The bus rumbled beneath me as we returned to Hawley College. I stared out the window, not really seeing the trees and buildings streaking by. My mind was a fucking mess.

I thought getting each other off would solve this... whatever it was. A one-and-done kind of deal. But now, every glance, every accidental brush of skin, set my nerves on fire. It defied logic, clashed with everything I thought I knew about myself. If anything, it had only made it worse. Every time I closed my eyes, I saw Tore's face, flushed and wanton. I felt the ghost of his touch on my skin.

I leaned my head against the cool window, watching the blur of passing streetlights cast intermittent shadows across Tore's face. He sat across the aisle, lost in his own world, his eyes closed and a faint smile playing on his lips.

I clenched my jaw. Why him? Why a spoiled, rich-as-fuck guy who never had to work for a damn thing in his life? It went against everything I stood for.

But then I remembered the determination in his eyes during practice, the way he pushed himself harder than anyone else on the field. How he'd kept pace with me during the hangover-from-hell practice. The genuine happiness when he scored goals, not for himself, but for the team. How he'd kept fighting to score today, even with two defenders on him. Was that not grit, discipline, determination?

"Fuck," I muttered, rubbing my temples.

When we finally got back to campus, I hung back as everyone filed off the bus. "Tore," I called out, keeping my voice low. "Stay behind and help me with the equipment, yeah?"

He blinked, those impossibly blue eyes widening slightly. "Of course."

We made our way to the locker room in silence. As soon as we were inside, the air thickened with tension. Our movements around each other in the locker room were hesitant like two magnets repelling and attracting at the same time. I busied myself with unloading gear, hyperaware of Tore's presence behind me.

"That was quite the game," Tore said, his voice soft. "I still can't quite believe it."

I turned to face him, my breath catching at how close he was. "You played amazing. Those goals were beautiful."

A pleased flush spread across Tore's cheeks. "Thank you. Though I couldn't have done it without the support of the whole team."

He reached past me to grab a bag, his arm brushing against mine. Even that slight contact sent a jolt through my body. I inhaled sharply, catching a whiff of his cologne—something woodsy and expensive that made my head spin.

"Sorry," he mumbled. His closeness was a live wire, sparking against every nerve I had.

"Stop apologizing." My heart hammered against my ribcage like it was trying to escape, betraying my cool exterior.

"Then stop making me feel like I need to," he countered.

He was right there, so close I could see the darker flecks in his blue eyes, the faintest sheen of sweat on his brow. It was intoxicating.

The air between us crackled with electricity. I should step back, put some distance between us. But my body had other ideas, gravitating toward him like a moth to a flame.

I couldn't resist any longer. With a low growl, I grabbed Tore's jersey and pulled him against me, crashing our lips together. He responded immediately, his hands tangling in my hair as he kissed me back with equal fervor. He tasted like victory, his mouth forcing mine open with a demand I met willingly.

The kiss was hot, desperate, and messy, just like our first encounter. Our need hadn't diminished, and there was no hesitation, only raw desire coursing through us both. We were lips locking, bodies brushing, hands threading hair and grasping at fabric.

I backed Tore up against the lockers, pressing my body flush against his. He gasped into my mouth, the sound sending shivers down my spine.

"Fuck," I breathed, breaking away to trail kisses along his jaw. "What are you doing to me?"

Tore's laugh was breathless. "That bewilderment is quite mutual, Captain."

His accent, thicker now with arousal, drove me wild. I captured his lips again, sliding my tongue into his mouth. Tore met me stroke for stroke, his hands roaming down my back to grip my ass.

"Fuck," I gasped when his teeth nipped at my lower lip, drawing a thin line of pain that shot straight to my dick. My hands roamed over his back, feeling the play of muscles beneath his shirt, wanting more, needing everything.

"Here?" Tore panted against my neck, and the word was a question and an invitation.

"Fuck yeah." I didn't care where we were. All that mattered was the heat of his body, the way he fit against me, the sheer relief of giving in to this craving.

Our shirts came off, our hands slipped under our pants, and we were lost in the moment, the sound of our ragged breathing and the sensation of skin against skin making everything else disappear. It was raw and real and nothing like I've ever felt before.

A sudden click of the door handle pierced through the haze of desire. We sprang apart, panic flooding my system. My heart pounded as I frantically tried to straighten my disheveled appearance, dragging my shirt over my head so roughly, my ear got caught, and I stifled a curse.

"Hello?" Becca called out. "Anyone still in here?"

I exchanged a wide-eyed look with Tore, both of us frozen in place. If we were caught like this... One look at us and she'd know what we'd been up to. I cleared my throat. "Just me," I shouted. "I'll be out in a minute."

"Okay. Make sure to lock up, Farron, okay?"

"Will do!"

The door closed again, but I still waited until I was certain Becca had left. Then, I let out a deep exhale. "Fuck, that was close."

Only moments ago, Tore's lips had been on mine, heat and

urgency pressing us together. Now, stark fear replaced that warmth like a cold shock to the system, a brutal reminder that what was happening between us wasn't merely complicated; it was impossible, a risk that could change everything, that could affect the entire team.

My mind raced with all the potential fallout, the criticism, the gossip... But even in the midst of the fear, there was a defiant part of me that didn't want to let go. Not yet. Not until I knew what this was.

"We can't," I said, squashing my needs down. "It's irresponsible toward the team."

"Agreed," Tore said quickly, too quickly.

"Okay, then we're on the same page." I finally risked meeting his eyes and regretted it immediately. How was I supposed to walk away when he looked so forlorn?

I spun on my heels, forcing myself to step away. "Go home. I'll finish up here."

I didn't look up until he'd left.

14

TORE

Norwegians are known for being pretty levelheaded, like most northern European countries. Our tempers tend to run cool and our patience long, which comes in handy with our endless dark winters. In parts of Norway, the sun barely shines in the winter and days only have a few hours of light. The landscape is brutally beautiful, desolate and devoid of human interference, but I couldn't survive there, unlike the Sámi people, who have made that area their home for well over two thousand years.

That was why it was so baffling to me that I couldn't stop thinking about Farron. Not only that, but my thoughts focused on him with an intensity that was new to me. I'd had crushes before and had even considered myself in love with a girl once, but this was a whole different level. Why was I so obsessed with Farron?

After our kiss in the locker room, he'd gone back to ignoring me. What did it say about me that I almost preferred him hating me over this feigned indifference? Probably that I wasn't quite as levelheaded as I had thought. Or that I wasn't as intelligent as I had imagined myself to be. Perhaps both.

I tried my hardest to avoid him during training and games,

subtly maneuvering myself away from his vicinity whenever possible as if he were the bane of my existence rather than the object of my increasingly vivid fantasies.

But no matter how I attempted to focus on drills and plays, my traitorous mind kept drifting back to him, painting highly detailed images of our heated exchanges and the crackling chemistry between us. The way his muscles rippled as he moved, the intensity in his brown eyes, the deep timbre of his voice...

I'd never felt this way about anyone, let alone a man, and the confusion it stirred within me was as thrilling as it was terrifying. The days blurred into one another like a Fado song, each day filled with soccer and school, as well as with longing and lamenting. The good news was that we were in the midst of the conference championships and were in an excellent position to proceed to the nationals.

The bad news was that no matter what I did, I could. Not. Stop. Thinking. About. Farron.

After the game against Butler, Coach decided Farron and I had mended fences and rescinded his threat of making us room together. I wasn't sure whether to be disappointed or relieved.

On a late afternoon training, I darted across the field, my cleats digging into the damp grass as I maneuvered around my teammates. My eyes flicked to Farron, standing tall and commanding at the center of our defensive line. I veered sharply left, putting more distance between us.

"Tore!" Jake called out, waving his arms.

I passed the ball to him, perhaps a bit harder than necessary. As Jake dribbled downfield, Coach's whistle sounded.

"Good hustle! Take five, then we'll run some more drills."

I bent over, hands on my knees, catching my breath. Sweat dripped down my face as I tried to calm my racing pulse. Once my lungs stopped protesting, I made my way to the sidelines, grabbing my water bottle and taking a long drink. My gaze drifted back to Farron, now chatting with some of the other defenders.

Our gazes collided, and the world around us melted away, the other players fading into the background. All I could see was him, and my need for him was an almost visceral pain inside me. Magnets irresistibly drawn to each other yet pushing each other away.

The only consolation was that he couldn't drag his eyes away either, his gaze so intense, I was surprised no one commented on it. But someone would. If I kept staring at him like this, others would notice, which was the last thing I wanted.

Through a fog, Coach's whistle signaled the end of our break. I forced myself to turn away from him, releasing a breath I'd been holding. With effort, I jogged back onto the field, deliberately positioning myself as far from Farron as possible.

My foot caught on an uprooted little patch of grass, and I stumbled, nearly face-planting on the grass. Farron stopped in his tracks, his chest heaving as he stared at me with an intensity that sent a shiver down my spine. It was as if he could see right through my carefully crafted facade, straight to the desires I'd been trying so hard to bury.

"Tore!" Coach Peterson called out. "Head in the game!"

If only he knew how much my head was anywhere but the game.

As practice dragged on, I found myself stealing more and more glances at Farron. Each time our eyes met, even briefly, it sent a jolt through my body.

"Tore! Look out!"

I turned just in time to see the soccer ball hurtling toward my face. With a yelp, I ducked, the ball whooshing past where my head had been moments before.

"Bloody hell!" I straightened to see my teammates staring at me with a mix of concern and amusement.

Farron jogged over, his brow furrowed. "You okay? Maybe you should sit the rest of practice out."

"No!" I said too forcefully. "I mean, no, thank you. I'm quite all right. Merely a momentary lapse in concentration."

Farron studied me for a long moment, his gaze so intense, my knees became weak. "If you say so. But be more careful, yeah? We need you in one piece for the game next week."

As he turned away, I couldn't help but wonder. Had he meant the team needed me? Or that he did?

Finally, the whistle blew, signaling the end of our grueling practice. I wiped the sweat from my brow, my muscles aching as I trudged toward the locker room with the rest of the team. As I was about to step off the field, I heard Farron's deep voice behind me. "Hey, Tore. Hold up a sec."

My heart leapt into my throat. I turned, trying to keep my face neutral. "Yes?"

Farron's eyes darted around, making sure the others were out of earshot. "I need to talk to you. Can you stick around for a bit?"

"Of course," I replied, hoping my voice didn't betray my nerves. "Where would you like to chat?"

He jerked his head toward the bleachers. "There."

He walked in front of me, his damp shirt clinging to his broad shoulders. I swallowed hard, forcing my eyes away. He held back until we walked side by side in silence, our cleats crunching against the gravel path that led away from the field. Neither of us seemed willing to fill the space between us with words. My throat felt dry, which was ludicrous after all the water I'd guzzled during practice.

"Under here should be good." Farron nodded toward the area

under the bleachers. His eyes scanned our surroundings, ensuring we were alone, and I followed him.

The space beneath the bleachers was cool and shadowy, a stark contrast to the bright, sunny field.

"Is this about me being distracted during training?" I asked. "I'll focus better next time."

Farron leaned against a metal support beam, the breadth of his shoulders more imposing in the semi-darkness. "It's not about soccer."

His voice was quieter now, stripped of its usual edge of authority.

"Then what—" The question died on my lips as something flickered in his eyes, an intensity that matched the quickening of my own pulse.

Farron ran a hand through his dark hair, a gesture I'd come to recognize as a sign of frustration. "Look, I'm not good at beating around the bush, so I'm gonna come out and say it."

My pulse quickened. What on earth was he about to say?

"I can't stop thinking about you. About our kisses. About touching you."

That was the last thing I had expected him to say, and I had no clue how to respond. "Farron..."

Farron's hands balled into fists at his sides, the veins on his forearms standing out like cords. "Every damn day... Every practice, every game, every dream, you're always there, taunting me. It's driving me fucking crazy."

The raw edge in his voice sliced through the quiet, and my heart pounded out a frantic rhythm. This admission, this frustration—it was about me. My thrill of elation was tempered by a flicker of fear. "Is it so terrible? To think of someone?"

He stopped his pacing and glared at me. "You don't get it, do you? It's not mere thinking. It's this constant distraction." His hand shot out, gripping my arm with a firmness that bordered on pain. "Why you? Why now? You're everything I can't stand, but there's something about you that's got me all messed up inside."

My breath caught in my throat. His touch sent a jolt up my arm, and I smiled despite everything else. This magnetic pull wasn't one-sided. "I don't know, but maybe it's because we're not as different as you think. And yes, I feel it too."

"Dammit!" Farron released me abruptly. "What are we supposed to do with this?"

I took a deep breath, gathering my courage. "What do you want to do? About us?"

Farron's brown eyes locked on mine, intense and conflicted. He was silent for a moment, and I could almost see the gears turning in his head. Finally, he let out a heavy sigh. "Maybe we should give in to it. Get it out of our systems."

My heart leapt into my throat. "You mean...?"

"Nothing serious could ever grow between us. We're too different, not to mention literally from different worlds. But we have this crazy chemistry, and I'm tired of fighting it."

"So you wanna stop fighting it and give in?" Was I understanding this correctly?

"It has to be purely physical, all right? No strings attached. And it stays between us. Nobody can know about this, especially not the team."

A mix of excitement and nervousness coursed through me. This was so far from anything I'd ever done, but I had never wanted anything or anyone more. "I agree to your terms. It shall be our secret."

At first, his face showed that same frustrated, angry look, but then a smile teased the corner of his lips. "Always so proper."

My cheeks heated. "So I've been told. But Farron, I... I want this. I want you."

The intensity in his eyes seemed to double at my words. "Fuck, Tore," he growled, taking a step closer to me. "You have no idea what you do to me."

I swallowed hard, my body thrumming with anticipation. "Perhaps you could show me?"

I barely had time to catch my breath before Farron's lips found mine. The force of it sent me stumbling back, my shoulders hitting the cool metal of the bleachers. His body pressed against mine, solid and warm, as his hands cupped my face.

Farron's tongue swept across my bottom lip, seeking entrance. I opened to him eagerly, moaning as our tongues met. He tasted intoxicating.

I gasped into his mouth, overwhelmed by the sensations. His stubble scratched against my skin and sent shivers down my spine, igniting a fire in my belly.

Our bodies pressed together in a desperate bid for connection, our hands exploring each other with fervent need. My hands found their way to his broad shoulders, feeling the muscles ripple beneath his shirt as he moved. The world outside our secluded spot ceased to exist. There was only Farron and the raw need that coursed through us.

"*Faen*," I breathed when we finally broke apart for air. My head was spinning, and I had trouble even remembering my own name.

Farron's eyes were dark with desire as he looked at me. "What does that mean?"

"It's Norwegian for... Well, it's not polite to say in English."

He chuckled, the sound sending vibrations through his chest and into mine. "Didn't know you had it in you. You're always so proper."

That was the second time he'd called me that. He wasn't

saying it in a negative way, yet it somehow grated me. "I'm not always proper."

"No?" He trailed his hand along my neck, and I instinctively tilted it sideways to give him access. "Are you saying you can be dirty?"

Before I could respond, his lips were on my neck, trailing hot kisses down to my collarbone. I had to fight to stifle the embarrassingly loud moan that threatened to escape.

"I can be anything you want," I panted, my hips instinctively bucking against his. The friction sent sparks of pleasure through my body, and I could feel how hard he was against me.

He groaned, pressing me harder against the bleachers. "Fuck, Tore. We need to stop."

I whined in protest, but he was right. We were still under the bleachers, where someone could stumble upon us at any moment.

"We can't." Farron pulled back enough to look me in the eyes. "Not here."

"Right." I nodded, struggling for composure.

"We need privacy. Colin's gone for training over the weekend, some special goalkeeper's thing in Pennsylvania. Meet me in my room?"

The prospect of being alone with him, truly alone without fear of discovery, was exhilarating. "What time?"

"I'll text you when he's gone."

"Okay."

"Good." He grinned, that rare expression that transformed his entire face.

I took a deep breath, running my fingers through my disheveled hair in an attempt to look presentable. "I should go first," I said, my voice still husky from our heated exchange. "We wouldn't want to arouse suspicion by leaving together."

Farron nodded, his dark eyes still smoldering with desire. "Good thinking."

"I'll see you at practice tomorrow, then?"

"Yeah," he replied, his expression softening for a moment. "I'll be the guy who can't take his eyes off you."

A thrill rushed through me. "And I'll be the one staring right back at you."

"Now, get out of here before I change my mind about letting you leave."

With one last lingering look, I slipped out from under the bleachers, my heart pounding as I scanned the area for any witnesses. Thankfully, the field was deserted. I straightened my shoulders and adopted what I hoped was a casual stride as I made my way to the locker room.

As I walked, my mind raced with thoughts of what had transpired. The feel of Farron's lips on mine, his strong hands gripping my hips, the intoxicating scent of his cologne mixed with sweat—it was all burned into my memory. I couldn't believe how quickly things had escalated between us. What on earth was I doing with him?

In two days, I would be alone with Farron in his room. The possibilities made my pulse quicken and my palms sweat. There was no going back now. I was in too deep.

And the scary thing was, I didn't want to find my way out.

15

FARRON

My heart pounded as I paced my small dorm room, glancing at my phone every few seconds. Where the hell was he? When I texted Tore that Colin had left, he said he'd be here in ten minutes. It had been fifteen.

I ran a hand through my hair, probably messing it up. Not that I cared about that preppy shit. But for some reason, I wanted to look good for him. Yet another item to add to the long list of things that had changed since meeting Tore. Some days, I barely recognized myself.

A soft knock at the door made me jump. I took a deep breath, willing my hands to stop shaking as I reached for the handle. Tore stood there, looking perfect as always in jeans and a crisp button-down. His blue eyes met mine and a jolt of electricity shot through me.

"Hello, Farron. My apologies for being tardy. I got a bit turned around in the corridors." He somehow managed to make that lame excuse sound hot.

I didn't bother responding but grabbed his shirt and yanked

him into the room, slamming the door shut behind us. Before he could say another word, I crushed my lips against his.

Tore made a small, surprised sound but quickly melted into the kiss. His lips were so soft, tasting faintly of mint. I ran my tongue along them, demanding entrance. He opened for me with a quiet moan that sent shivers down my spine.

My hands roamed over his lean body as our tongues battled for dominance. I'd been thinking about this for the last two days, fantasizing about what it would be like to touch and taste him again. The reality was so much better...

When we finally broke apart, gasping for air, Tore's cheeks were flushed and his hair disheveled. He looked dazed but eager. "That was quite the greeting."

I smirked, still gripping his hips. "What, they don't kiss like that in Norway?"

Tore laughed softly. "I must say, I rather enjoy the American way."

"Good." I growled. "'Cause I'm only getting started."

I pushed Tore against the wall, pressing my body flush against his. His breath hitched as I captured his lips again, my hands sliding under his shirt to explore the smooth skin beneath.

"Farron," he gasped between kisses, his fingers tangling in my hair. "This is... Oh, bloody hell."

I chuckled against his neck, nipping at the sensitive skin. "Can't form sentences? I must be doing something right."

Tore's hips jerked forward, seeking friction. "You're doing everything right. I've never felt quite like this before."

The admission sent a surge of desire through me. I ground against him, relishing the way he moaned. "Me neither," I admitted, surprising myself with the honesty. "But I can't seem to stop."

"Then can I strongly suggest you don't?"

I didn't need to be told twice. I claimed his mouth again, my hands roaming over his body as if I could memorize every plane and curve. Tore was equally eager, his fingers tracing the muscles of my back, then down to my ass.

We moved together, bodies rubbing and pressing, seeking more contact. The friction was maddening, not enough and too much all at once. He was so hard against my thigh, matching my own arousal.

"Fuck," I groaned, breaking the kiss to catch my breath. "Tore, I..."

He silenced me with another kiss, rolling his hips in a way that made me see stars. "Less talking," he moaned against my lips. "More of this, if you please."

I couldn't help but laugh. Even in the throes of passion, he was unfailingly polite. It was endearing as hell and only made me want him more.

Without breaking our heated kiss, I reached between us, fumbling with Tore's zipper. He gasped against my mouth, his hips jerking forward instinctively.

His moves were as clumsy as mine when he reached inside my sweatpants—unlike him, I'd dressed with the idea of taking my clothes off again as soon as possible—and found my leaking cock.

"Fuck yeah." I moved against his hand. "Touch me."

Tore didn't hesitate. His soft, manicured hands—so different from my own calloused ones—wrapped around me, and I nearly lost it right then and there. I bit back a moan, determined to make this last while I brought him to a climax as well.

Our movements were rough, urgent, and messy. There was nothing refined about the way we touched each other, stroking and pulling with desperate need. Tore's usual composure was gone, replaced by the same raw, animal desire that consumed me.

We couldn't find a rhythm and kept bumping into each other, but it didn't matter. Hands squeezed, pumped, stroked while our hips bucked, rolled, and jerked. I was lost in the sensations—the heat of Tore's skin, the sounds of our ragged breathing, the slick slide of flesh on flesh.

Tore whimpered. "I can't... Oh, bloody hell..."

His needy sounds sent me over the edge. My body tensed, waves of pleasure crashing over me as I came with a guttural groan, thick ropes flying from my cock, all over Tore's hand and our clothes. Tore followed seconds later, his body shuddering against mine as he coated my hand with his cum.

We collapsed against each other, breathing heavily. For a moment, all I heard was the pounding of my heart and Tore's labored breaths. Fuck, that had been intense.

"Well," Tore finally said, his voice shaky. "That was... Hell, I don't even know how to describe it."

I laughed, the sound muffled against his shoulder. "Let me know when you find the words, pretty boy. 'Cause I'm a little short on descriptions as well."

I took a deep breath, inhaling the scent of Tore's cologne mixed with sweat and sex. My body was still buzzing, every nerve ending on fire. I pulled back slightly, looking at Tore's flushed face. Then my eyes dropped lower, and I snorted. We looked like crazy fools, both our cocks still hanging out, our pants halfway down our hips, cum everywhere, and our hands sticky. "We should probably clean up."

He looked down, and a slow smile spread across his face. "Clean up would be good. You came all over my shirt. I may have to wash that."

"We have a whole weekend to take care of that."

He looked up and our eyes met. A whole weekend. We had a full forty-eight hours together. "Yes, we do," he said softly.

I stepped back, then grabbed some baby wipes from the drawer of my nightstand, handing a few to him. We cleaned ourselves up as best we could. I stole glances at Tore, noticing how his hands trembled slightly.

Our eyes met, and suddenly, the awkwardness melted away. I felt a surge of desire, different from before—less urgent but no less intense.

Without thinking, I reached out, my fingers tracing the line of Tore's jaw. He leaned into my touch, his eyes fluttering closed.

"Farron," he whispered. "I... I want..."

"Yeah," I breathed. "Me too."

Slowly, carefully, I began to unbutton Tore's shirt. My rough fingers fumbled with the delicate buttons, but Tore didn't seem to mind. He watched me with hooded eyes, his breath coming faster.

As I pushed the shirt off his shoulders, Tore's hands found the hem of my T-shirt. He tugged it upward, his soft hands skimming my abs. "You really do have that perfect six-pack."

I laughed softly. "You're not so bad yourself."

We took our time undressing each other, exploring newly exposed skin with gentle touches and soft kisses. It was so different from our frantic encounter earlier—tender, almost reverent.

What the hell was I doing? This wasn't me. I didn't do gentle or tender. But with Tore, it felt right. That alone should've scared the shit out of me, but somehow, it didn't. Or maybe I was still in denial. I didn't care at this point. All I wanted was him.

I pulled Tore closer, our lips meeting in a deep, languid kiss. Dressed in nothing but our underwear, we stumbled backward, never breaking apart, until the backs of my knees hit the edge of my bed. We tumbled onto the mattress, a tangle of limbs and heated breaths.

Tore's weight on top of me felt incredible, his soft skin velvety under my calloused hands as I ran them down his back. Our kisses grew more urgent, tongues exploring, teeth nipping. I was lost in the sensation, my mind hazy with desire.

Tore pulled back, his blue eyes meeting mine. There was a hint of nervousness in his gaze but also determination. "I've been doing some research."

I raised an eyebrow, curious. "Research?"

Tore's cheeks flushed pink, but he didn't look away. "Yes. About pleasuring another man. I want to try something if you'll let me."

My heart raced. "What did you have in mind?"

"I want to give you a blowjob."

I sucked in a sharp breath, arousal surging through me. That was a big step for a guy who, like me, had never been with another man. "Are you sure?"

He nodded eagerly. "I've never done it before, but I want to. For you."

The sincerity in his voice, the eagerness to please, it was almost too much. I cupped his face in my hands. "You don't have to do anything you're not comfortable with."

I surprised myself with how gentle my voice sounded.

Tore's lips curved into a smile. "I want to. Please, Farron. Let me try?"

As if I would say no when he said please. My body thrummed with need, and the thought of Tore's mouth on me was driving me wild. "I don't need convincing, pretty boy."

Tore's face lit up with excitement. He trailed kisses down my chest, his hands fumbling slightly as he pushed down my boxers. I lifted my hips to help, my breath catching as the cool air hit my heated skin.

"You're beautiful," he said simply, licking his lips as he stared at my cock, which was rapidly filling again—a testament to what he did to me as my usual refractory time was definitely longer than a few minutes.

"Thank y—"

My words cut off in a gasp as Tore wrapped his hand around me, giving an experimental stroke. His touch was hesitant, gentle, so different from my own rough handling.

"Is this all right?" he asked, looking up at me through his lashes.

"Fuck yeah," I breathed.

Tore nodded. He leaned down, his breath hot against my skin, and then... oh god... his tongue darted out, licking a stripe up my length.

I groaned, my hands fisting in the sheets. Tore's inexperience was evident in his tentative movements, but his enthusiasm more than made up for it. He explored with his tongue, mapping every inch of me before finally taking me into his mouth.

"Jesus Christ," I hissed, fighting the urge to buck my hips. The wet heat of his mouth was incredible, sending sparks of pleasure shooting through my body.

Tore hummed, the vibration sending another wave of sparks through me. He started to bob his head, finding a rhythm. It was sloppy and unpracticed, yet it meant somehow more than any blowjob I'd ever received before. He was so eager, so determined, and the sight of his pretty lips around my cock alone was almost enough to push me over the edge.

"Tore," I panted, reaching down to tangle my fingers in his hair. "Fuck, that feels amazing. You're doing so well."

He moaned around me, the sound sending tremors through my body. The pressure built inside me, my muscles tensing as I raced toward release again.

"I'm close," I warned him, tugging gently at his hair. "You don't have to—"

But Tore redoubled his efforts, taking me deeper. The feeling of his throat constricting around me was my undoing. With a strangled cry, I came, my body shuddering with the force of my orgasm.

Tore swallowed, choking slightly and pulling away for the rest, which hit his face. He looked utterly debauched with his red-rimmed eyes, his swollen lips, and my cum dripping off his chin.

"Was that... okay?" he asked, his voice rough.

For some reason, my usual gruffness had made way for a strange sappiness, a softness floating inside me I'd never felt before. "That was amazing."

He sat back on his heels, wiping his mouth with the back of his hand, a look of pride on his face. "Thank you."

"You did research?"

He nodded, his cheeks reddening again. "I read a number of articles. And then I called a gay friend and asked him for some extra tips. You have him to thank for the humming part."

Fuck, that was adorable.

He grabbed another wet wipe and cleaned his face. As soon as he was done, I pulled him close, our bodies intertwining as we lay on my narrow dorm bed. My heart was still pounding, and my mind raced with a confusing mix of desire and uncertainty.

Tore's breath was warm against my neck as he nuzzled closer. "I liked that more than I had expected."

"Yeah? Well, you're welcome to do it anytime." I swallowed. "I don't know if I can—"

"You don't have to. We'll do whatever you're comfortable with. It's a new journey for both of us."

It was a mindfuck, was what it was. And at this point, I wasn't even sure what the biggest issue was: the fact that I was into men —or at least, into Tore—or that I hated him yet still wanted him. "I never thought I'd end up here with you, of all people."

Tore chuckled softly. "Is that a good thing or a bad thing?"

I pretended to consider it for a moment. "Jury's still out on that one."

He rolled his eyes, but I could see the hint of a smile playing on his lips. "Oh, sod off. You're clearly enjoying yourself."

"Maybe a little," I admitted, pulling him closer. Our bodies were sticky with sweat and other fluids, but I couldn't bring myself to care.

Yeah, mindfuck was the right word. Maybe because, most of all, I wasn't sure if I still hated him.

16

TORE

Johan Cruyff, one of the most famous Dutch players and coaches, had a well-known saying: *every downside has its upside*. Luke's grandmother had passed away, which was super sad. He'd been crying when his mom had called him, and then, still sniffing, he'd packed his bag to go home for the weekend.

The upside, however, was that I had my dorm room all to myself, an opportunity I wanted to take full advantage of. In the two weeks since we'd agreed to work it out of our systems—whatever "it" was—Farron and I had managed two quick hook-ups, both hurried since we didn't have time or privacy. But now we could have both, so I sent him a message.

> Luke's gone for the weekend. Would you like to come over?

The response came almost instantly.

> Hell yeah. Be there at eight.

A thrill shot through me. He wanted this as much as I did.

I leapt into action, surveying my dorm room with fresh eyes. It wasn't exactly cozy, but I was determined to make it as inviting as possible. I hastily changed the sheets on my narrow bed, opting for the soft, Egyptian cotton set I'd brought from home. The familiar scent of lavender fabric softener filled the air as I smoothed out every wrinkle.

Next, I tackled the clutter, sweeping stray papers and books into drawers. I arranged a few scented candles on my desk, their soft glow lending the room a warm, intimate atmosphere. Or was that too much? Farron had made it clear that all he wanted was sex. But did that mean I couldn't make it a nice experience?

My cheeks flushed as I considered what might happen. Would Farron want to go further than we had before? The thought sent a shiver of anticipation through me. I'd thought about it a lot, and if he wanted to, I was ready for more.

With trembling hands, I reached into the back of my closet, retrieving the discreet, black bag I'd hidden there. After our conversation under the bleachers, I'd bought the contents on a whim, face burning as I'd placed my order online. Now, I took the contents into the bathroom and showered, taking extra care to ensure every inch of my body was clean, including the parts I hoped would see some action later.

Back in my room, I put a condom and a bottle of lube on the bedside table in case Farron wanted to explore beyond hand jobs and blowjobs. I wasn't getting my hopes up, but if the opportunity arose—pun intended—I wouldn't pass it up.

I changed my outfit three times before settling on a soft, blue sweater that brought out my eyes. I styled my hair, willing my hands to stop shaking. It was just Farron.

Except it was so much more than that, wasn't it? This was the boy who made my heart race, who filled my thoughts day and night, and whose arrival I was literally counting down to. This had disaster written all over it.

Despite expecting it, a knock at the door at eight sharp made me jump. I took a deep breath, straightened my sweater, and reached for the handle. There he stood, his broad frame filling the doorway, dark hair tousled from the autumn wind. Our eyes met and the world seemed to fall away. The intensity in his gaze sent a jolt through me, igniting every nerve ending.

"Hello," I managed, my voice barely above a whisper. "Won't you come in?"

Farron nodded, a hint of a smile tugging the corners of his mouth. "Hey, Tore."

As he brushed past me, his scent hit me, and I inhaled it deeply. I closed the door, my fingers lingering on the handle as I steadied myself.

When I turned, Farron was eyeing my meticulously cleaned room. "Damn, did you hire a maid or something?"

Heat crept up my neck. "I, ah, tidied up a bit. Wanted it to be nice for you."

Farron's eyes softened. "You didn't have to do that."

"I wanted to." I took a step closer to him.

Farron's gaze dropped to my lips, and I leaned in, drawn by an invisible force. Our lips met, softly at first, then with increasing urgency. I gasped as Farron's strong hands gripped my waist, pulling me flush against him.

My fingers tangled in his hair as our kisses deepened, tongues exploring, tasting. Farron nipped at my lower lip, eliciting a moan I couldn't hold back.

"Fuck, Tore," Farron breathed against my neck, his stubble scraping deliciously against my skin. "You drive me crazy, you know that?"

I arched into him, reveling in the feeling of his solid body against mine. "The feeling is quite mutual, I assure you."

Farron's hands slipped under my sweater, calloused fingers tracing patterns on my bare skin. Each touch sent sparks of pleasure coursing through me. I tugged at the hem of his shirt, desperate to feel more of him.

As we fumbled with clothing, I marveled at how right this felt. How perfectly we fit together. A part of me wanted to tell Farron how I felt, to lay my heart bare. But I held back, afraid words would ruin everything. Instead, I poured every ounce of my growing affection into our kisses, hoping Farron could feel what I couldn't yet say.

In between kisses, the last of our clothing came off, and we stood naked. Chest to chest, mouth to mouth, our hard cocks rubbing against each other. Nothing had ever felt more right.

I pulled back slightly, my heart racing. Farron's eyes were dark with desire, his chest heaving.

I swallowed hard, gathering my courage. "I want you to... I mean, if you're amenable... I'm willing to bottom for you."

Farron's eyes widened, his mouth falling open in shock. "You... what?"

I felt my cheeks flush but pressed on. "If you want to fuck me, I'd be okay with that."

For a moment, Farron just stared at me, his expression unreadable. "Have you ever...?"

"No, but I want you to be my first."

Farron exhaled sharply. "Fuck, Tore. That's... I didn't expect..."

"We don't have to," I said quickly, ignoring the pang of disappointment in my chest.

"I want to." Farron's eyes locked on mine with an intensity that made me shiver. "Fuck yes, I want to."

Relief and excitement flooded me. Farron cupped my face in

his hands, kissing me deeply. When he pulled back, a tenderness in his eyes made my heart skip. I'd never seen him look at me that way. "You sure about this?" he asked softly.

I nodded, unable to form words. Farron's thumb traced my lower lip, and I melted into his touch. "We'll take it slow, all right? I've never done this, so tell me if I'm doing anything wrong."

A little chuckle escaped me. "Neither have I, so I probably wouldn't know."

More of that softness that had my insides all aflutter. "We'll figure it out, but I don't want to hurt you."

Hurt. That was the one thing I was apprehensive about. My research had taught me that not everyone enjoyed anal and that, for some people, it hurt beyond what was pleasurable. What if I was one of them?

"Will you tell me if it's too much?" Farron asked.

I nodded again, desire and nervousness warring within me. Farron led me toward the bed, then gently pushed me onto the mattress. I lay back on the bed, my heart racing as Farron's eyes roved over my body. He joined me, his weight pressing me into the mattress as he captured my lips in a searing kiss. I moaned into his mouth, arching against him, craving more contact.

Farron's hands explored my body, leaving trails of fire in their wake. His dark eyes bore into mine as he reached for the lube. My cheeks flushed, but I didn't look away. I wanted him, craved him, needed him more than I'd ever desired anything.

Farron coated his fingers in the cool gel and then guided my legs apart. He knelt between my thighs, those deep, brown eyes never leaving mine. He leaned in, brushing a featherlight kiss against my inner thigh before trailing lower. I gasped, arching my hips involuntarily as his lips danced across my hole. It felt... good. So very good.

Then his finger was there, slick against me as it rubbed, softened, and teased. He sank it inside me, easier than I had expected, and I breathed out, closing my eyes. The intrusion was foreign but not unpleasant, and I had no trouble relaxing as he fucked me with his finger.

He added a second finger, which stung, but only for a moment. When he slid both fingers inside me as deep as he could, he brushed against a spot that lit up every nerve in my body. I moaned louder than I had intended, and he froze.

"Don't stop," I whispered. "That was... I've never felt anything like it."

A slow smile spread across his face. "Like this?"

He did it again, and it was like fireworks went off inside my ass. "Gods, yes. Right there."

Farron pumped his two fingers, ensuring he hit that spot on every single stroke, and his name spilled from my lips as he teased and tormented me. Every slide of his fingers left me arching my back and begging for more. I'd never imagined anything could feel this good, this right.

"Farron," I panted, "I want you inside me. Please."

He didn't make me wait. Instead, he sat back and reached for the condom. He rolled it on with ease, then, after a brief hesitation, added more lube. When he checked in with me, I nodded. I was so ready for him.

He palmed my thighs, spreading me wide as he positioned himself at my entrance. He looked into my eyes, his own darkened with lust and something else I couldn't quite place. "Breathe," he told me, and so I did.

When he pushed against my hole, I closed my eyes. I'd had sex before—though with girls, obviously—but somehow, that had never felt this intimate. I breathed out and bore down, as I had read, and my body gave way as he popped past that first resistance.

He was inside me. Farron was *inside* me.

I'd expected him to push deeper, but he waited, not moving until I'd opened my eyes.

"You good?"

I nodded. "Please, continue."

He snorted. "Please, continue? Like I'm giving a speech?"

My cheeks heated. "I meant..."

He leaned in and kissed me, such a casual, affectionate gesture that it took my breath away. "I knew what you meant. It was funny, is all."

The smile on my face transformed into a grimace as he sank deeper. For a moment, the stretching, burning sensation consumed me. I clenched my teeth, my nails digging into the mattress as I tried to adjust to the sensation of him filling me so completely.

"Tore?" Farron's voice held a hint of panic.

"One sec. I need one moment to..."

I willed my body to relax against the discomfort, and once I breathed out, that stinging ebbed away, making space for the most incredible sense of fullness. "Deeper. Go deeper."

He inched in farther until he was buried to the hilt. Some discomfort lingered, but strangely enough, it was intertwined with pleasure, as if the two were somehow inseparable. The promise of more coursed through my body, helping me relax. "You can move."

He was so much more careful than I had expected, his eyes never leaving mine as he moved slowly, filling me with precise, deep thrusts. Even the memories of the pain melted away, replaced by a euphoric high that radiated from my ass outward.

The room filled with the sounds of our gasps and moans, skin against skin. I'd never felt so vulnerable, so exposed yet so utterly safe in someone's arms. The way Farron looked at me, touched me, made me feel... It might be sex for him, but for me, it was a thousand times more. I was falling for him, hard and fast.

My hips bucked upward as I sought more of his delicious friction, and a litany of pleas spilled from my mouth. "Farron... Oh, so good... Mmm, yes, right there... Oh gods, harder!"

Farron grunted and moaned, his hands gripping my hips tighter as he moved faster and with more force, his hips rutting against mine in a primal rhythm that shook us both. "You feel amazing. So fucking tight and hot."

I'd never realized that bringing someone else pleasure could enhance my own, but it did, those simple words setting my whole body on fire. My orgasm built slowly in my belly, my balls, at the base of my cock, which lay untouched, caught between our bodies. It uncoiled, growing, spreading until every muscle was awake, alive, ablaze.

"Tore," Farron grunted. "I'm... I can't hang on much longer."

I wrapped my hand around myself and furiously pumped at the same tempo as Farron's thrusts, which became more staccato and less precise. His body jerked, and the moan he let out was positively sinful—also so positively loud, the whole dorm could probably hear it. He rutted a few times, then froze, throwing his head back as he came.

I couldn't take my eyes off him, his whole face pure ecstasy as he released. My own orgasm overtook me, flashing white-hot as it sent me flying high. I spurted out my load between us until I had nothing left to give. For a few seconds, we stayed like that, still connected, both panting.

He averted his eyes and held the base of his cock as he pulled out. "Gotta take care of this," he mumbled.

I winced, the sensation distinctly unpleasant. Farron tied the condom, scrambling to his knees on the bed.

"You can—" I started, but he was already getting up, sliding off the bed. With a well-aimed throw, he deposited the condom in the trash bin.

"That was amazing," he said, but he avoided looking at me. "Anytime you wanna do that again, I'm game."

I swallowed. "You can stay if you want. Luke won't be back until Sunday evening."

He got dressed at record speed. "I can't. Not tonight. But if you're up for another round later this weekend, let me know."

He was out the door before I could say another word. I sagged back on the bed, my body suddenly cold.

After wiping the remnants of my own cum off my stomach, I crawled under the covers, fighting against the tears.

This was on me. Farron had been crystal clear he wanted nothing more but sex. I was the one who'd fallen for him. I couldn't blame him for that.

But bloody hell, it hurt.

17

FARRON

I was a dick.

Walking out after sex had been an absolute dick move, and Tore would be right to never speak to me again after that. But sheer, utter panic had filled me, and I'd needed to get out of there fast. When he'd offered to bottom for me—and Jesus, that had been a shock—I'd thought it would be like any other hookup. Maybe even easier because women were much more likely to get a little clingy. Yeah, yeah, that was probably sexist, but I'd been there.

With Tore, sex should've been easy. Uncomplicated. Wham, bam, thank you... man. After all, we'd agreed this was nothing but sex.

But then we'd shared that experience, that absolutely mind-blowing experience, and I'd been shocked to my core. What should've been a quickie had turned into something so intimate and special that I'd been lost for words. It had been intense and raw, the sort of thing you couldn't unfeel. And Christ, did I feel it —an emotion that scared the hell out of me because it made believing my own lie that this was mere sex impossible.

My stomach twisted with regret. I'd panicked and pushed Tore away, but the truth was, I had wanted nothing more than to cuddle with him, to hold him. To stay. I'd never felt a connection like that before. It scared the shit out of me.

My mind kept replaying every moment with him, an endless memory of every touch, every moan, every gasp. The softness of his skin, his breathy whimpers, the way he'd looked at me with those gorgeous blue eyes, how he'd clung to me as I'd filled him, how he'd felt around my cock...

A beep from my phone interrupted my thoughts, and I subtly rearranged myself—boners in public were so embarrassing—as I checked the message. My heart sank like a stone in a still pond.

> Got the flu and can't do the interview. Hope you can find someone else.

With those few words, my carefully constructed schedule for the English assignment to interview a non-native English speaker crumbled to dust. Bogdan, my Bosnian roommate from last year, had been the perfect candidate, and now he'd canceled. The guy was sick, so I couldn't really blame him, but what a clusterfuck.

I needed to find a replacement, conduct the interview about the challenges of learning English, and write the entire damn paper. And it all needed to happen this weekend. Desperation clawed at my insides. Who would I be able to find at such short notice?

I scanned the library's main room, my gaze flitting over faces, familiar and unfamiliar, absorbed in their own worlds of study and leisure. No one I recognized fit the bill for my assignment. They'd either been born in the US or had lived here for part of their lives.

I needed someone with a story, someone new to the country who struggled with the nuances of the English language. And then, as if summoned by my frantic thoughts, Tore walked in and sat at a table, opening his laptop.

Could I...?

There had to be someone else. Anyone but him. But who would be available on such short notice?

Even if I asked him, he'd refuse. Not that I could blame him after how I had hightailed it out of his room the previous week. Like I said, it had been a dick move.

He was the epitome of what I didn't need right now—a reminder of privilege and ease—but he was also my last shot at salvaging this assignment. I couldn't afford an F, so I'd have to suck it up.

My jaw clenched as I approached him, my pride taking a back seat to necessity.

"Hey, Tore," I started, my voice surprisingly steady, given the turmoil I felt.

He looked shocked for a moment before he caught himself. "Hello, Farron."

"Look, I know I'm probably the last person you want to help, but I'm in a bind. My interviewee bailed on me for my English project. I need to talk to someone about the challenges they've faced learning English. Would you be willing to be interviewed?"

He turned those piercing blue eyes on me, his expression unreadable. There was a brief pause where the air between us seemed to hum with the history of my less-than-stellar behavior toward him. I braced myself for rejection, ready to turn and walk away.

"I would be delighted to help you with your assignment." The words rolled off his tongue with that distinctive accent that spoke of his impeccable upbringing.

Surprise must have painted my face because the corner of Tore's mouth lifted in the ghost of a smile. It was unsettling how easily he'd agreed to help, considering the chip on my shoulder I'd been carrying around since we met and how we'd parted ways last week, thanks to me.

"Really?" I asked, not able to mask my disbelief. "Even after...?"

"Yes." He closed his laptop with a soft click. "I can't promise my answers will be fascinating, but I'll share what I can."

"Thanks. I appreciate it, really. When do you have time?"

"I can do it now if that's convenient for you?"

"Now is perfect. Again, thanks."

He stood, gesturing for me to lead the way. "Shall we find a quiet place to talk?"

"Uh, yeah, sure." I shook off the shock and led him to one of the private study rooms reserved for group projects. The interview was back on track, but now it was with someone whose life couldn't be more different from mine. Someone who, despite everything, was willing to lend me a hand when I least expected it —or deserved it.

I observed him as he settled in. He wore a deceptively simple white tee and jeans, but on him, they seemed tailor-made, accentuating his physique. Even dressed down, he looked like he'd stepped out of a high-end fashion catalog—the kind I used to find crumpled up in the mailbox, immediately trashed because who cared about clothes that were pricier than my entire wardrobe? Everything about him seemed so damn effortless.

Before we started, I had to address the proverbial elephant in the room. "I'm sorry for running out the other day. After we had" —I made a gesture—"sex."

He cocked his head, his expression neutral. "Did I do something wrong?"

"No. Not at all. It was..." I sighed. "It's complicated, but it wasn't you. It was me."

"Well, that's reassuring in all its vagueness."

"I mean it. I was... a dick."

"I'm glad we agree."

Hearing him confirm it made me feel better, which was ridiculous but the truth, nonetheless.

"Anyway, you ready?" I asked.

"Absolutely. I'm curious to see what your assignment is about."

"The goal of the interview is to ask about your challenges in learning English as a foreign language. To verify, it is a foreign language for you, right?"

He chuckled. "Was it my charming accent that gave it away?"

I would never in a million years admit it, but his accent was charming. "When did you first learn English?"

He folded his hands. "In Norway, we start with learning English as a second language in the last two years of elementary school, but I started a little earlier than that. We had a British nanny, and she taught me the basics."

A nanny. Of course he'd had a nanny. Go figure. "How is English taught in schools in Norway?"

"There's a heavy focus on the grammar, especially initially, and it often comes at the expense of verbal fluency. Initially, my passive English far exceeded my verbal abilities."

How did he always manage to sound so smart? He was so comfortable using complex words and sentences, which was even more remarkable considering English was a second language for him. "Growing up in Norway, are you exposed to a lot of English?"

He nodded. "We are, as dubbing is not common, and we watch English movies and TV series in the original language but with Norwegian subtitles."

My eyes widened. "You can keep up with those? I struggle

watching foreign movies with subtitles. It's always too fast for me."

"It's a matter of experience, I think. We're so used to it that most of us have no issue with it. Kids learn it from a young age. And because we hear English and read the Norwegian, we automatically pick up a lot of the English language, though not always the correct or polite expressions."

"Like what?"

He chuckled. "My cousin and I watched the first three *Die Hard* movies together when we were ten or so. My English teacher did not appreciate us repeating the most famous catchphrase from those movies."

Oh my god. I couldn't hold back a laugh. "You said yippee-ki-yay in class?"

"Yes, but it was the word that followed that got us into trouble."

"I can't imagine why."

He leaned forward. "It's funny, but it does show a challenge. When you hear characters in a movie use certain language, like saying *shit* or *fuck* all the time, how are you to know you're not supposed to say that in polite society?"

He made a good point, actually, one I had never considered. "You're saying American media doesn't accurately represent American culture when it comes to language."

"Exactly, but that distinction is subtle and not easily understood, especially for teenagers. A friend of mine did an exchange program and went to an American high school for a year. He was also part of a church program there, and in the first week, he got in big trouble for using words like *shit*, *fuck*, and *damn* in youth group."

I winced. "I can't deny there's a certain double standard there."

"But generally speaking, idioms and expressions are the

biggest challenge, especially those connected to American phenomena."

"Like what?"

Thinking furrows marred his forehead, but then his face lit up. "Sports expressions. Like getting to first base or second base when you're referring to sexual activities. That made absolutely no sense to me until I understood it had to do with baseball."

"You don't have baseball in Norway?"

"We do, but it's not a big part of our culture, unlike here. And you have so many sports expressions. The other day, someone mentioned that the president needed to throw a Hail Mary to improve his approval rate, and I had no clue what that meant until Luke explained it was a football expression."

"I can see how those are a challenge." I jotted down some notes and then checked my list of prepared questions. "Can you think of any embarrassing situations where you got something completely wrong?"

"Well, my accent isn't always easy to understand. Last week, I asked for water at a restaurant. My accent must have been thick because the waiter brought me butter instead. He must've wondered what on earth I wanted butter for, as he hadn't brought out any food yet." He flashed a grin that had no business being as endearing as it was.

"How about pronunciation? What's been the biggest challenge there?"

His laugh was melodious. "You mean other than there being no rhyme or reason to it? Case in point is *Worcestershire*, where one only pronounces half the letters. Or *extraordinary*, which really should be pronounced extra-ordinary but instead becomes this glued-together jumble. Or the word *read*, which, depending on the meaning, can be pronounced in two different ways. Exact same word. I mean, really, the list goes on and on."

He was giving me some really good examples. "I can see why that's a struggle."

"Or plural forms. One mouse, two mice. But not one house, two hice. Or meese for two moose since it's also two geese."

I couldn't suppress a snicker. "Yeah, there's no logic there."

"None at all, which means you have to learn each one on their own. It's learning a lot of lists, like irregular verbs, irregular plural forms, and rules."

"What's been most useful for you in learning English?"

"Being immersed in English-speaking environments. I was fortunate to be able to travel a lot, and I've done immersive language courses in the UK, Australia, and New Zealand. Not being able to communicate in any other language than English is the best way to learn, even if it can be scary."

My grip on the pen tightened until my knuckles turned white. "Must've been nice to have those opportunities."

"Indeed, it was quite beneficial for my language development," he continued, apparently oblivious to the sharp edge in my voice. "The tutors were exceedingly helpful as well."

Tutors. Trips abroad. Nannies. His world was so far removed from mine that it wasn't even funny. My resentment swelled like a tide, threatening to spill over as I recalled the countless nights Mom worked double shifts and we still had to choose which bills to pay.

"Is something wrong?" Tore asked, concern creeping into his otherwise steady gaze.

"Nothing," I snapped, then forced myself to take a breath, reining in my emotions. "Let's focus on the interview."

As I asked more questions and Tore spoke of idyllic childhood experiences, my mind raced back to the cramped apartment where my siblings and I would huddle around a secondhand table, laughter often mingling with the stress lines on Mom's face.

She'd always tried to shield us from the worst of it, but you can't hide reality when it's banging on your door.

"Of course, having all those opportunities to perfect my English helped," Tore was saying, "but that doesn't mean I didn't have to work hard."

"Hard work..." I rolled my eyes. His version of "hard work" probably meant something entirely different from mine.

"You doubt I worked hard?" Tore's expression shifted from open and relaxed to something sharper, more defensive.

I shrugged. "Rich boy faces 'challenges' but has all the resources to overcome them. Must be tough."

The air between us crackled with tension, and this time, not the sexual kind. Tore's jaw clenched. "You think you know everything about me because I grew up with money?" His voice rose, a rare edge slicing through the usual calm. "You don't know the first thing about my challenges."

"Sure, but you never had to fight for anything. Not like some of us."

"Challenges aren't limited to money, Farron." His voice held a tremor, betraying a passion I hadn't witnessed before. "You think because I've had tutors and traveled that I haven't faced difficulties? That everything has been handed to me on a silver platter?"

"Hasn't it?"

"My struggles may not have been monetary, but that doesn't mean I haven't faced challenges." He stood abruptly, his chair scraping harshly against the floor. "Do you know what it's like to constantly be compared to those who came before you? To carry the weight of a future you didn't choose? To give up a dream that's within reach because of duty?"

His words hung heavy in the air, and my mind raced, struggling to reconcile this raw, emotional side of Tore with the poised figure he'd always shown me.

"So, yeah, I've had privileges," he continued, his voice dropping to a bitter tone. "But I've also been locked in a life that demands everything and allows for nothing personal. No choices, no freedom."

I swallowed. "I'm not sure I understand."

Tore gave me a long look, his anger fading to resignation as he sat down again. "No one ever does," he murmured, taking a deep breath as he composed himself. "Let's finish the interview."

As we resumed, my thoughts stuck on the glimpse he'd given me into his world—a world far more complex than I'd assumed.

I rushed through the remaining questions until I'd asked them all.

"Are we done?"

"Yeah, I have enough." I cleared my throat, setting aside the notebook. "Why did you agree to this? To the interview?"

"Because you asked," he said simply, and damn if that didn't make me feel like even more of an ass.

"Thanks," I said, and I meant it.

"You're welcome." His eyes held a hint of sadness I hadn't seen before. He walked out before I could say anything else.

Stunned, I sank deeper into my chair, my mind a whirlwind of confusion. The clarity with which I had always viewed Tore's life—privileged, pampered, perfect—was blurring. Had I failed to see his constraints, his lack of liberty in a gilded cage? He'd mentioned having to give up his dream of playing professional soccer, but maybe that hadn't been the only sacrifice he'd had to make? So maybe his life wasn't quite as perfect as I had imagined it to be.

But as much as this new understanding clawed at the walls I'd built around my heart, a bitter taste lingered on my tongue. Because no matter how gilded his cage might be, it was still a cage he could step out of. Unlike poverty, which clung to your skin, infused your bones, and defined your every waking moment.

The truth was, Tore's struggles might be real, but they didn't keep him awake at night, wondering if there would be enough food for his siblings or if the lights would stay on. They didn't force him to juggle school with a job or weigh on him with the constant pressure to succeed because failure meant more than personal disappointment; it meant letting down everyone who depended on you.

No, Tore might be a little more complex than I'd initially thought, but that didn't mean he and I were similar in any way... and we never would be.

18

TORE

The locker room buzzed with electric energy, a mix of nervous anticipation and fierce determination. I inhaled deeply, the sharp scent of sweat and deodorant filling my nostrils as I laced my cleats. Around me, my teammates were a flurry of motion: adjusting shin guards, pulling on jerseys, psyching themselves up for the battle ahead.

We were once again facing our archrivals, the Connor Condors, only this time, much more than honor was on the line. For the first time in decades, we stood a chance at winning the conference title.

"This is it, boys." Farron's gruff voice cut through the chatter. "Conference Championship. We can win this. I know we can."

"Damn straight," RJ chimed in, slapping Farron on the back. "Those Condors won't know what hit 'em."

A chorus of agreement rippled through the team. I nodded, trying to channel their confidence. "We shall give them a proper thrashing, yes?"

Farron snorted, the corner of his mouth twitching. "A 'proper thrashing'? Christ, Tore, you sound like you're inviting them to tea."

Heat crept up my neck. "I merely meant—"

"All right, Hawks!" Coach Gold's booming voice silenced us as he strode into the locker room. "Gather 'round."

We huddled close, the air thick with anticipation. Coach's eyes swept over us, pride evident in his weathered features. "Gentlemen, I want you to take a moment. Look around at your teammates. These are the men you've bled with, sweated with, fought alongside all season. The bond you've forged is unbreakable."

I met Farron's gaze again, a spark of something unnameable passing between us. My throat tightened. Even from across the room, the weight of his presence hit me. My heart raced, though whether from pre-game jitters or Farron's proximity, I couldn't say. We hadn't spoken since that interview for his English assignment a week ago, other than the necessary exchanges during practice and games.

Coach continued, his voice swelling with emotion. "I've watched you grow from a group of individuals into a cohesive unit. Your progress and your dedication are nothing short of remarkable. But our journey isn't over yet." He paused, letting the words sink in. "Out there, it's not about individual glory. It's about working as one. Supporting each other. Trusting each other. That's how we'll bring home that championship trophy. And that's how we'll head into nationals."

A ripple of determined nods swept through the team. I felt it, too, that sense of purpose, of belonging to something greater than myself.

"Now," Coach's eyes gleamed, "let's show those Condors what happens when you mess with a Hawk's nest."

We pressed in close, hands piling atop one another. The energy was palpable, crackling through our huddle like lightning.

"ONE TEAM!" Farron called out, and we all responded. "ONE DREAM!"

Our cry echoed off the locker-room walls, a battle cry that sent shivers down my spine. As we filed out toward the field, Farron caught my arm. "Are we good?"

How was I supposed to answer that? Considering his timing, I gave the only appropriate response. "Of course we are."

His answering grin was filled with relief. "Then let's go make history."

As I followed Farron out of the locker room, my heart raced. His touch lingered on my arm, a phantom warmth that sent tingles through my body. As if I needed another reminder of how aware I was of him.

But none of that mattered now. We took our positions, and with a whistle, the game started. It was time to play.

The roar of the crowd washed over me as the ball sailed through the air, a perfect arc that seemed to hang suspended for an eternity. I tracked its descent, my muscles coiled and ready. This was it. The Conference Championship. Everything we'd fought for all season came down to this moment.

I sprinted forward, my cleats digging into the freshly mowed grass. The scent of earth and sweat filled my nostrils as I jockeyed for position against a Condor midfielder. His elbow dug into my ribs, but I barely felt it. My focus was singular: the ball.

It bounced once, twice, and then I was there, my foot connecting with a satisfying thud. I sent it flying toward our striker, threading the needle between two defenders.

"Nice one, Tore!" Jake shouted as he streaked past me, chasing the play.

The game unfolded like a violent dance, both teams surging back and forth across the field. The Condors were good—damn good—but we were better. We had to be.

I glanced toward our goal, where Farron stood like a sentinel. His face was a mask of concentration, those broad shoulders tense as he barked orders at our defense. God, he was magnificent. A true captain in every sense of the word.

"Heads up!" someone yelled.

I snapped back to attention in time to see a Condor forward breaking through our midfield. Bloody hell. I sprinted to intercept, but he was too quick, too determined.

"Farron!" I shouted in warning, even as I raced to catch up.

But I needn't have worried. Farron was already moving, reading the play like it was second nature. He timed his tackle perfectly, sliding in with surgical precision to knock the ball away. The Condor went flying, landing in an ungraceful heap on the turf.

"That's how it's done, boys!" Coach bellowed from the sidelines. "Keep it clean, keep it tight!"

Farron was back on his feet in an instant, scanning the field. His eyes met mine for a split second, and I saw a flash of something there. Pride? Determination? Maybe even a hint of that connection we'd been building off the field? Whatever it was, it set my heart racing faster than any sprint could.

"Let's go!" Farron shouted, his voice carrying across the pitch. "We've got this!"

When the halftime whistle came, the score was still nil-nil. Not where we'd wanted it to be, but it could've been worse. The Condors had fumbled some real chances at scoring. On the other hand, we'd also had some good opportunities, but alas, their goalie had blocked every shot at goal.

But this was the championship title, so if we were still tied at the end of the ninety minutes of regular playing, we'd go into overtime. And then, penalty shootouts: the nightmare of every soccer player on the planet.

Coach had some encouraging words for us, as well as some instructions. "Tore, you're free to roam," he told me.

"Unleash the Tore!" the team yelled, and all I could do was grin.

In the second half, the crowd's cheers faded to a dull roar in my ears as I lost myself in the rhythm of the match, every fiber of my being focused on one goal: victory. The Condors had the same intention and attacked with relentless waves, keeping Farron busy.

Yet another Condors player broke through, but Farron intercepted his pass to their striker. Before he could send it up the field, however, the Condors player he'd bested tackle-slid into him. Everything slowed down as Farron cried out in pain, crumpling to the ground. My blood ran cold. The Condor player stumbled away from the scene, his face a mask of feigned innocence.

My heart pounded in my ears as I sprinted toward Farron, fury and concern battling for dominance in my chest.

"What the bloody hell was that?" I shouted. The referee blew his whistle, but I barely heard it over the roar of blood in my ears. I dropped to my knees beside Farron, my hands hovering uselessly over his body. "Are you all right?"

Farron's face was contorted in pain. "Fuck, that asshole came in cleats up."

The referee jogged over. Surely, he'd seen the foul play. But as he reached us, he merely waved for the medical team.

"No card?" My temper flared. "That was a blatant foul!"

The ref shook his head. "Free kick."

I opened my mouth to argue further, but Farron's hand on my arm stopped me. "Don't," he muttered through gritted teeth. "It's not worth it."

The medical team arrived, and Becca gently probed Farron's ankle. His cleat came off and then his socks, showing a clear imprint of a cleat. Farron had been right. That bastard had aimed for his ankle. Becca probed some more, then sprayed it and taped it. The sock came back on, then his cleat, but I had a bad feeling.

I watched, helpless and angry, as they carefully helped him to his feet. Farron tried to put weight on his injured foot but winced.

"Can you continue?" Coach asked, his voice gruff with concern.

Farron hesitated, the struggle evident in his eyes as his pride warred with the reality of his injury. Finally, he shook his head. "I don't think so, Coach."

Coach immediately gestured at Cooper, Farron's replacement, who had started warming up as soon as Farron went down.

As the medical team helped Farron off the field, a protective urge surged through me. I wanted to follow him, to make sure he was okay, to do something, anything, to ease his pain. But I couldn't. Not only would it lead to way too many questions I wasn't ready to answer, but more importantly, we had a match to win. And Farron would want me to focus on that.

But as I took my position again, I couldn't shake the image of Farron's face twisted in pain or the burning desire for justice that now fueled my every move.

A few minutes later, Cooper got a hold of the ball and sent it flying upfield. The ball sailed toward me, and I trapped it with my chest, letting it drop to my feet. Time seemed to slow as I surveyed the field, my senses heightened by a cocktail of adrenaline and rage. The Condors' defense spread before me like a fortress, but I saw the cracks, the weaknesses.

I feinted left, then cut right, my feet dancing over the grass. A defender lunged, but I was too quick, too determined. Everything else faded into the background as I focused solely on the goal ahead.

The Prince and the Player

"Tore!" Jake called out, indicating he was open, but I ignored him. This was personal now.

I dribbled past another defender, my heart pounding in my ears. The goalkeeper tensed, ready for my shot. In that split second, I remembered Farron's grimace of pain, his reluctant admission of defeat. It fueled me, propelling me forward.

With a final burst of speed, I struck the ball with everything I had. It curled through the air, centimeters beyond the keeper's outstretched fingers, and slammed into the back of the net.

The stadium erupted, but I barely heard it. I stood there, panting, a mix of emotions churning inside me. Pride, anger, worry for Farron—it all swirled together.

My teammates mobbed me, hugging me, jumping me, high-fiving me. "Thanks," I said again and again, my voice hoarse. "But we're not done yet."

As we reset for the kickoff, I caught sight of the Condor player who'd taken Farron out. He was smirking, looking far too pleased with himself. My jaw clenched, and a cold determination settled over me.

The whistle blew, and the game resumed. I bided my time, waiting for the right moment. It came sooner than I expected. The ball was knocked out of bounds near midfield, and as we jostled for position for the throw-in, I saw my chance. I body-checked the Condor player hard, shoving my full weight into him and sending him sprawling onto the turf.

The referee's whistle shrieked, and the expected yellow card came out. I didn't care. The satisfaction of wiping that smug look off his face was worth it.

"What the hell, man?" the player spat as he got to his feet.

I leaned in close, my voice low and controlled. "Next time, play the ball, not the man."

As I jogged back to my position, I caught Coach's eye. He

looked torn between approval and disappointment. I'd hear about it later, but in that moment, all was well.

After that, the game grew rough, but we held the line. Again and again, the Condors came at us, but we held them back until the final whistle blew.

For a moment, I stood frozen in disbelief. We'd done it. The Hawley Hawks had won the conference title. A roar erupted from our supporters, and suddenly, I was engulfed by my teammates. We jumped and hugged, shouting incoherently in our joy. Hands slapped my back and ruffled my hair, and the sensation of elation was beyond anything I'd ever felt.

"We fucking did it!" Luke bellowed, grabbing me in a bear hug that nearly knocked the wind out of me.

I laughed, caught up in the euphoria. "Indeed we did! Bloody brilliant, the lot of you!"

Coach approached, his usually stern face split by a wide grin. "Great job, boys! You've made Hawley proud today!"

I searched for Farron. He was there, only a few feet away from me, balancing on crutches, his face a mix of pain and pride. Our eyes met, and my stomach flipped. Then, someone else hugged me, drawing my attention away from Farron.

After the celebration died down and we'd showered, Farron stood waiting outside the locker room, still on crutches. I'd been the last one, needing some alone time to process. The corridor was empty, everyone else having left for the after-party.

"Hey," he said softly, his brown eyes warm. "That was one hell of a game."

I suddenly felt shy. "Thank you. I wish you could've been out there with us for the full game."

Farron's lips quirked up. "Me too. But thank you for what you did out there. Not just today but this whole season. You're..." He inhaled. "You're the reason we made it this far. We couldn't have done it without you."

Unsure of how to respond to that unexpected compliment, I opted for humor. "Maybe that tackle hit you harder than I thought. Did they check your brain?"

Instead of responding, he leaned in and kissed me. It was brief, gentle, but it sent electricity coursing through my body.

When he pulled back, I was breathless. "Farron, I..."

"I saw what you did," he murmured. "Standing up for me like that. It meant a lot."

My cheeks flushed. "I couldn't let him get away with hurting you."

Farron's eyes softened. "Like I said, thank you. I won't forget it."

Hope bloomed in my chest. Could this mean...? "Are you still interested in...?"

"Hooking up with you?" He cocked his head. "I am, but why would you be after that stunt I pulled last time?"

I shrugged. "No idea what you're talking about."

As we stood there, grinning at each other like fools, I felt a sense of possibility I'd never experienced before. Whatever this was between us hadn't run its course just yet.

19

TORE

I leaned against the brick wall of the dining hall, watching Luke devour his fourth slice of pizza. His appetite never ceased to amaze me.

"So," Luke said between bites, "what are your plans for Thanksgiving break?"

I shrugged, caught off guard by the question. "I hadn't really given it much thought, to be honest. We don't celebrate Thanksgiving in Norway, so it's not something I'm accustomed to planning for."

Luke's eyebrows shot up. "Wait, seriously? You don't have any plans at all?"

"Not as such, no," I replied, feeling a bit sheepish. "I suppose I'll stay on campus and catch up on some reading. Perhaps work on that political theory paper due after the break."

"Dude, that's not okay. I wish I could invite you, but we're at my grandpa's this year. After my grandma died, he needs us to be there for him. They were married for fifty years, you know."

"I'm so sorry, Luke. It must be hard for him."

He sighed. "It's part of life to lose people you love, but that doesn't make it easy."

"Is he your father's parent? The one who owned your farm before your father did?"

His eyes widened for a moment. "You remember the littlest details. It's impressive."

I could tell him I'd been trained in that, but that would only lead to questions. "I try to listen when people tell me something."

"Well, it's working. And yes, he is." He checked his watch. "We need to go. We have practice in a few minutes."

When I walked toward the trash can to throw out my half-eaten apple—it had been devoid of any taste and about the furthest thing from crispy one could imagine—I almost walked into Farron.

"Hey," I said, my cheeks immediately heating.

"You're staying here for Thanksgiving?" he asked, sounding almost angry.

I fronted. "How do you—"

"I overheard you talking to Luke."

"It doesn't make sense for me to go back home, especially since I already spent a few days there recently."

"You can't be here by yourself."

What was the problem? "I'll be fine, I assure you."

Farron crossed his arms, his brows furrowed. He seemed to be wrestling with something internally. I waited, curious about what was on his mind. After a moment, he cleared his throat. "Look, I... I know we're not boyfriends or anything, but no one should be alone on Thanksgiving. My mom would kill me if she found out. So, if you want, you can celebrate Thanksgiving with me."

I blinked, stunned by the unexpected invitation. My heart raced as I processed his words. "You're inviting me to spend Thanksgiving with your family?"

Farron rubbed the back of his neck. "Yeah, I mean, if you want to. It's not gonna be anything fancy, but you wouldn't be alone."

Warmth spread through my chest. The idea of spending a holiday with Farron, seeing where he came from, was thrilling. "Do you mean it? Or are you secretly hoping I'll say no?"

He jammed his hands into his pockets. "Have you ever known me to do something I don't want to?"

Not the most enthusiastic response, but I'd take it. "I would be honored, Farron. Truly. Thank you for the invitation."

"Yeah, whatever. I'll text you when I'm leaving."

"Okay."

"Don't tell anyone."

One more thing to add to my growing list of secrets. "Not a word."

But that turned out to be a promise I couldn't keep. We'd both forgotten about Luke, who had watched our exchange. He'd been too far away to overhear anything, but the fact that Farron and I were talking to begin with had shocked him. "What the fuck was that about?"

"What do you mean?"

He rolled his eyes. "You and Farron, obviously. You were talking."

"That's not allowed?"

"Don't treat me like an idiot. What the hell is going on?"

I didn't want to betray Farron's trust, but I also hated the idea of lying to Luke. If news of what Farron and I had been up to ever leaked, it would cost me my friendship with him. Could I count on Luke to keep our secret? He'd never given me any reason to doubt him.

"Not here," I said.

He held his tongue until we were outside, then looked around to ensure no one was close by. "What's going on?"

"You can't tell anyone. I mean it."

His eyes widened. "Oh my god, it's something big, isn't it?"

"Promise me."

He held up his hand. "I solemnly swear."

"Farron and I have been... seeing each other."

Luke came to an abrupt stop. "Get the fuck outta here."

"I'm serious."

"All that hate between you two was..."

I let out a deep sigh. "Foreplay. You could call it foreplay."

Luke resumed walking again, his face still showing his shock. "I'll be damned. That's about the last thing I expected."

"It's nothing serious. We have this crazy chemistry we're trying to get out of our system. It'll burn out soon, and then we'll go back to normal."

"Good luck with that 'cause I don't think it works that way. But I won't say a word."

I shrugged. "We'll see."

"But what were you guys talking about?"

I looked away, fearing that if Luke saw my face, he'd read too much from it. "He overheard me saying I'd be here alone for Thanksgiving, and he invited me to celebrate with his family."

Once again, Luke halted. "You're celebrating Thanksgiving with him?"

"Yeah, why?"

"Just sex, huh?" He patted my shoulder. "Keep dreaming."

We didn't speak of it again, instead hurrying to soccer practice.

All during practice, my mind raced with thoughts about the upcoming holiday. I'd never experienced an American Thanksgiving, and the prospect of sharing it with Farron and his family filled me with excitement and a touch of anxiety.

What would his family be like? Would they accept me? I hoped they wouldn't find me too foreign or out of place. The significance of this invitation wasn't lost on me, despite me downplaying it to Luke. Had he truly only done it out of some cultural sense of obligation?

Farron was letting me into a personal part of his life, something he didn't do lightly. This Thanksgiving would be more than a meal; it was a chance to understand Farron better, to see the world that had shaped him.

* * *

I was ready to go when he texted me the next morning. Luke had already left and our building seemed mostly empty as I hurried down the steps and slid into the passenger seat of Farron's beat-up Chevy, throwing my weekend bag in the back seat.

The landscape rolled by as we rumbled down the highway. Ohio was vast—endless fields of golden corn stubble stretched to the horizon, interrupted only by the occasional red barn or silo. It was a far cry from the fjords and mountains of Norway, but it held its own simple beauty.

At first, our conversation was stilted, but then I started discussing the latest matches in the Premier League with him, and time flew by. He was a Manchester United fan, while I cheered for Manchester City—I had to, considering Erling Haaland, their star striker, was Norwegian and played for our national team—which gave us yet another point of contention.

"I find it interesting he's playing for Norway," Farron said. "He has dual citizenship, right?"

"He does, and he could choose to play for England."

"So why doesn't he? The English national team is far better than the Norwegian—no offense."

"It is, which is why that choice means so much. He could've

led England to a victory in the World Cup, but instead, he chose to represent the country he feels most connected to. He's always played for Norway, even as a youth."

Farron slowly nodded. "It speaks to his integrity and character, I think."

"Agreed."

We turned off the main road onto a narrower one, where the houses stood close together, and the lawns were tiny.

"Almost there," Farron said, a hint of tension in his voice.

We pulled up to a modest, two-story house with peeling, white paint and a slightly sagging porch. Before I could fully take it in, the front door burst open and two younger versions of Farron came bounding out.

"Far! You're home!" the youngest girl—that had to be Calista—squealed, launching herself at Farron as soon as he stepped out of the car. I took a deep breath and got out as well, plastering on my most charming smile.

Farron hugged the girl tightly. "Hey, ladybug. So happy to see you."

Rowan was a little more reserved, but he also embraced Farron. Then a woman who could only be Farron's mother emerged from the house, wiping her hands on a dish towel. She looked tired, but her smile was genuine.

"You must be Tore," she said warmly, extending her hand. "I'm Linda. Welcome to our home."

I shook her hand, noting the calluses and strength in her grip. "Thank you so much for having me, Mrs. Carey. I truly appreciate your hospitality."

She waved off my formality with a laugh. "Oh, honey, call me Linda. And we're happy to have you. We're excited to meet one of Farron's friends."

Caspian, a lanky teenager trying very hard to seem unimpressed, came outside as well, and Farron affectionately gave him a noogie. "Good to see you, dude."

As we made our way inside, I couldn't help but notice the worn furniture, the faded curtains, the many stains on the walls, and the slight draft from the windows. But there was also warmth here—countless family photos crowding the walls, the smell of bacon, the sound of laughter.

I caught Farron watching me, a guarded look in his eyes. I smiled at him, hoping to convey without words that I was honored and grateful to be here.

We'd arrived in time for lunch, which consisted of club sandwiches, served with a big pickle and a little bag of potato chips on a collection of mismatched plates. Linda was still making the last few ones in the tiny but spotlessly clean kitchen.

"Can I help with anything, Mrs... I mean, Linda?" I asked, feeling oddly out of place.

Linda smiled warmly. "That's sweet of you, Tore. Could you two set the table?"

I nodded eagerly, glad for something to do. As Farron guided me to the drawer with the silverware, his shoulders were tense, his movements stiff.

"Your family seems lovely," I said softly, trying to ease the tension.

Farron grunted, not meeting my eyes. "Yeah, they're all right. Look, it's not much compared to what you're used to, but—"

I cut him off gently. "It's perfect, Farron. Truly."

He finally looked at me, a mix of defiance and vulnerability in his eyes. My heart ached at the conflict I saw there. Finally, he nodded, relaxing a little.

As we all sat down to eat, I was struck by the simple homeyness of it all. I might be used to more formal meals, but this had so much more atmosphere. "This looks absolutely delicious," I said sincerely.

Linda beamed. "We're glad you could join us, honey. Now, dig in."

As we ate, I made an effort to engage with Farron's siblings, complimenting Rowan on a drawing I'd noticed in the living room that had his name on it and asking Caspian about his interests—soccer, what a shock. Farron was watching me, his posture gradually relaxing as the meal progressed.

"So, Tore," Linda said between bites, "Farron tells me you're on the soccer team with him. How are you liking Hawley so far?"

I swallowed a mouthful. "Oh, I'm loving it. It's quite different from home but in the best way. Everyone's been so welcoming, especially Farron."

I caught Farron's eye as I said this, and a small smile tugged at his lips. For a moment, I forgot about the worn tablecloth and the cramped kitchen. All I could see was the warmth in Farron's eyes, the way his family laughed together, the love that filled this home.

As I helped clear the dishes later, I realized that this simple meal had given me something I'd rarely experienced in all the grand state dinners and royal banquets of my childhood: a sense of belonging.

After lunch, Calista tugged at my sleeve. "Tore, do you want to play a game with us?"

I glanced at Farron, who nodded encouragingly. "I'd be delighted," I said, following the younger siblings into the living room.

Rowan was already setting up a board game on the coffee table. "We're playing Monopoly," he announced, his eyes gleaming with excitement.

"Ah, a classic." I settled on the worn carpet. "I must warn you, though, I'm rather rubbish at this game."

Caspian snorted. "Yeah, right. You're probably some kind of Monopoly shark."

I laughed, shaking my head. "I assure you, I'm not. My sisters always beat me soundly."

Farron joined us, sitting close enough that our shoulders brushed. The warmth of his body next to mine was distracting in the most delightful way. The game started and, as was common with Monopoly, quickly became heated, but in a playful way.

"Ha! Pay up, Tore," Calista crowed as I landed on her New York Avenue. "That'll be two thousand dollars."

I handed over the colorful bills, chuckling. "You drive a hard bargain, my lady."

As the game wound down, with Calista emerging as the victor, Caspian stood up. "Soccer time."

Farron nodded. "Soccer time."

Five minutes later, everyone had changed into soccer uniforms and cleats, including Calista, and we walked across the street to a playground with a small grass field next to it. On either side stood two small vertical wooden poles, which would be our goals.

"Farron and me against you three," Caspian decided.

Farron and I grinned at each other. Of course we would be on rival teams. It made sense, considering.

Caspian was good. Really, really good. We wouldn't have stood a chance if not for the fact that I was faster and Rowan and Calista were also great players, especially considering their age. In all fairness, Farron went easy on them in the tackles—as he should.

But our main weapon was my speed and the fact that I was in such great shape, having done so much conditioning training. Farron didn't stand a chance at keeping up with me at full speed, and even Caspian had to admit I left him in the dust.

We played for an hour, and the game ended in a tie, with

Farron and I conspiring to make that score happen. Caspian knew it was rigged, but he went along with it, and Rowan and Calista were delighted we hadn't lost.

"You're really fast, Tore," Calista said. "It was fun playing with you."

"Thank you. I had fun too."

Farron leaned in, his breath tickling my ear. "You're good with them," he murmured.

His words sent a shiver down my spine. "They're wonderful," I whispered back. "Just like their brother."

Our eyes met, and for a moment, the rest of the world faded away. The intensity in Farron's gaze made my heart race.

"You guys coming?" Caspian asked, breaking the spell.

"Yeah," Farron said, his voice hoarse.

Dinner consisted of meatloaf, mashed potatoes, and green beans, and we gobbled it all up, hungry after the game. Everyone had chores, I discovered, with Calista and Rowan in charge of the dishes while Caspian took out the trash and wiped down the table.

Farron and I found ourselves alone in the living room.

"Want to go for a walk?" Farron asked, his voice low.

I nodded, my mouth suddenly dry. We slipped out into the cool, night air, walking side by side down the quiet street. Our hands brushed, and without thinking, I laced my fingers through his.

Farron stopped, turning to face me. In the soft glow of a streetlight, his eyes were dark and intense. "Tore," he breathed, and then his lips were on mine.

The kiss was electric. Farron's mouth was hot and demanding, his stubble rough against my skin. I melted into him, my free hand coming up to tangle in his hair. His tongue swept across my lower lip, and I opened for him with a soft moan.

When we finally broke apart, both of us breathing heavily, I rested my forehead against his. His arms tightened around me. "Fuck, Tore," he muttered. "What are you doing to me?"

I didn't have an answer, but as we stood in the darkness, holding each other close, I knew that whatever was happening between us was far more powerful than I'd ever anticipated.

20

FARRON

I woke to the gentle rhythm of Tore's breathing, his chest rising and falling against my back. Warmth radiated from his body, seeping into my skin. For a moment, I let myself sink into the comfort of his embrace, savoring the feel of his arm draped over my waist.

Then reality hit like a bucket of ice water. What the fuck was I doing?

My heart raced as memories of last night flooded back—the heated kisses, roaming hands, clothes hastily discarded. I'd dragged an extra mattress into my room for him to sleep on, but he'd never made it into his own bed. After making each other come, we'd cleaned up and fallen asleep.

I squeezed my eyes shut, trying to block out the images. This wasn't me.

I didn't cuddle. I didn't do relationships. And I sure as hell didn't do it with spoiled, rich boys.

But as Tore shifted in his sleep, pulling me closer, a traitorous part of me wanted to stay right here in his arms. I wanted to memorize the feel of his body against mine, the scent of his skin.

Jesus, I had to get out of here before he woke up. Before I did something stupid like kiss him good morning.

Carefully, I began to extricate myself from Tore's embrace. His arm tightened reflexively, and I froze, holding my breath. After a moment, his grip relaxed, and I slowly slid out from under the covers.

My feet hit the cold floor, and I winced, searching for my clothes in the dim, morning light. I found my boxers and jeans crumpled by the bed, pulling them on as quietly as possible. Where the hell was my shirt?

As I hunted for the rest of my clothes, I glanced back at Tore. He looked so peaceful, his face relaxed in sleep, golden hair tousled against the pillow. Something tugged in my chest and I quickly looked away.

This was exactly why I needed to get out of here. These... feelings, or whatever the fuck they were, were dangerous. This was sex, nothing more. I couldn't afford it to be. Tore and I were as different as fire and ice.

I finally spotted my T-shirt hanging off the back of a chair and grabbed it, along with my shoes. The floorboards creaked as I tiptoed to the door, and I cringed, glancing back. Tore stirred slightly but didn't wake.

My hand was on the doorknob when his sleep-roughened voice stopped me in my tracks. "Farron? Where are you going?"

Shit. I turned slowly, meeting Tore's confused blue eyes. "I didn't wanna wake you this early."

Tore frowned, propping himself up on one elbow. The sheet slipped down, revealing his bare chest, and I forced my eyes away. "It's almost nine. It's not early at all."

Double shit. "I thought you might want to sleep in." I fumbled for the doorknob behind my back. "Go back to sleep. I'll see you later."

Before he could respond, I slipped out the door and shut it quietly behind me. I leaned against it for a moment, my heart pounding. What the hell was wrong with me?

As I hurried down the hall, pulling on my shirt, I tried to shake off the lingering warmth of Tore's touch. This was sex. Nothing more. We'd hook up a few more times, and then this crazy attraction to him, this obsession, would fade. It had to.

But even as I told myself that, I knew it was a lie. The memory of Tore's lips on mine, the way he'd thrown himself into that blowjob, the incredible sensation of being inside him, his radiant smile, that charming accent, even the way he'd looked at me last night like I was something precious—was all burned into my brain.

I needed to get my head on straight. I had responsibilities, goals, a plan for the future. What I didn't need was some Prince Charming distracting me.

No matter how much I wanted him to.

Of course, when Tore showed up downstairs a few minutes later, looking all fresh and cute, my resolution went right out the window. Everyone else was still asleep, apparently, so it was just us.

"I thought you were gonna sleep in?" I asked gruffly.

He chuckled. "I never sleep in. Nine is about as late as I've ever gotten up."

Oh. We had that in common, then. "Want some breakfast?"

The second I asked it, I regretted it. We usually didn't have many breakfast options beyond cereals.

"I'm starving."

I made a split-second decision. "Let's go to Mabel's Diner. My best friend, Wesley, his parents own it, and it's the best food you've ever had. Best milkshakes in the state of Ohio too. They'll be open for breakfast only and then close for the rest of today and tomorrow."

Tore studied me for a moment, his eyes narrowing, then nodded. "I'd love to if you'll allow me to treat you as a thank you for inviting me."

Oh, he was smart, wasn't he? The way he'd framed that made it all but impossible for me to refuse. "If you insist."

"I do."

It wasn't like he couldn't afford it, so whatever. I could swallow my pride in this case. "You can't hold my hand," I said softly. "Not in the daylight. I don't want people to think that..."

"I know."

"Okay. I could give you a tour of the town after if you want."

"I do want," Tore said, his smile warm and genuine. "I'd like to see where you grew up and learn more about you."

Something in my chest tightened at his words. Why did he have to be so nice? It would be so much easier if he was just another entitled rich kid.

"All right, let's go."

Mabel's Diner hadn't changed a bit since I'd graduated from high school. It was still a slightly rusty, retro-style building with a large neon sign. The bell above the door jingled when we walked in, and Auntie Mabel—Wesley's mom, who I'd started calling Auntie when I became friends with Wesley—looked up from behind the large counter.

"Well, I'll be... Look what the cat dragged in."

I grinned. "Hi, Auntie Mabel."

She came from behind the counter, wearing her standard, red-checkered apron. "Gimme a hug, boy."

She gave the best hugs, my body pressed against her soft curves. Somehow, her hugs made everything better, just like my mom's. "It's so good to see you," I mumbled.

"You too, honey. Who's your friend?"

I stepped back. "Tore, meet Mrs. Mabel Williams. Auntie, this is Tore. He's an international student from Norway, and he's on my soccer team."

She wiped her hand on her apron, then shook Tore's. "It's a pleasure to meet you, ma'am," he said, unfailingly polite as ever.

"Right back atcha, and don't you have the prettiest accent?"

He blushed. "Thank you, ma'am."

"And so polite too." She sent me a pointed look. "Some people could do with some of those manners."

"Hey," I protested. "I'm always polite to you."

She huffed. "Like when you and Wesley ate the last of my banana cream pie and denied up and down you had?"

If she was gonna bring up all my childhood sins, I was in trouble, so instead, I leaned in and kissed her cheeks. "I apologize, Auntie. Now, can we get a table? We're starving."

Appeased, she nodded, pointing. "Table fifteen. Two daily Mabel specials?"

"Yes, pretty please and thank you." I turned to Tore. "Vanilla, banana, or strawberry?"

"Excuse me?"

"Milkshake flavors."

"We're doing... Oh, okay. Vanilla, please."

"Two specials and two vanilla shakes coming up," Auntie Mabel said, and I led Tore to the table.

"I thought I heard your soft baritone," a voice said, and I spun around.

Wesley sauntered toward us, a knowing grin plastered on his face.

"Wes!"

We exchanged a hug. "Mom told me you'd walked in," Wesley said.

"You were helping in the kitchen?"

He nodded. "Like old times." Then he turned to Tore and extended his hand. "Hi, I'm Wesley."

"You're Farron's best friend," Tore said, immediately rising to his feet and shaking Wesley's hand. "Tore Haakon, a pleasure to meet you."

"Tore, huh?" Wesley shot me a look that said I had some explaining to do later. "You wouldn't be that student from Norway Farron's mentioned a few times, would you? The one from his soccer team?"

"That's me." Tore beamed.

"Farron's told me so much about you."

I shot Wesley a warning glare, but he ignored me.

"Has he now?" Tore asked, glancing at me with a soft smile that made my stomach flip. "All good things, I hope."

"He's celebrating Thanksgiving with us," I said, trying to keep my voice casual. "Just wanted to show him the town."

Wesley's eyes sparkled with mischief as he looked between us. "Oh, I bet you did. By the way, this explains a lot."

My heart pounded as I struggled to decipher Wesley's cryptic remark. What the hell was he implying? I wanted to grab him and demand an explanation, but I couldn't bring myself to do it. Not with Tore standing right there, looking at me with those piercing blue eyes. "I don't have a clue what you mean."

"You'll figure it out." Wesley slapped my shoulder. "I should get going. Pops asked me to pick up some milk before the store closes. It was a pleasure meeting you, Tore. Truly enlightening."

I'd never been happier to see my best friend disappear. His timing was excellent, as his mom brought us our food, which we wolfed down in no time.

"You weren't exaggerating," Tore said, rubbing his belly after slurping the last bit of his milkshake. "This food is amazing, and that was, by far, the best milkshake I've ever had."

"Told you."

He grabbed the check Auntie Mabel had dropped and took a quick look at the amount. Instead of paying with a card, like I'd expected him to do, he took cash from his pocket and put it inside the leather fold.

"Let's go," he said.

I checked how much he'd put in there. Wait, a hundred bucks? That was way too much. "You don't need change?"

He avoided my eyes. "No, it's fine."

The bill couldn't have been more than thirty bucks. Was he truly giving her a seventy-dollar tip? "Tore..."

"I said it's fine." Before I could say anything else, he got up and walked toward the door.

"Was the food to your liking, Tore?" Auntie Mabel called out.

He spun around, flashing her one of his radiant smiles. "Best breakfast I've ever had, and that milkshake was divine."

"Aw, that's so kind of you. Come back now, you hear?"

After a last quick hug, I followed Tore outside. "Let's give you the tour."

Tore's eyes were wide as he took in the small-town charm of my hometown. We continued down the street, passing the old movie theater where I'd had my first kiss, the park where I'd learned to ride a bike, and with each landmark, I shared stories, surprised by how easily they flowed out.

As we walked back home, I snuck glances at Tore. He looked so out of place here. Even his relatively simple outfit screamed elegance and money, yet he seemed genuinely interested in everything I showed him. No judgment, no condescension. Just curiosity.

Maybe I'd been too quick to judge him. Maybe there was more

to Tore than his wealth and background. The thought both excited and terrified me.

"Thank you for showing me around," Tore said as we approached my home. "I feel like I understand you better now."

I swallowed hard, caught in the intensity of his gaze. "Yeah, well, thanks for listening, I guess."

Jesus, I needed a distraction, something that would prevent me from looking at him all day.

As soon as we walked into the living room, I tossed him a controller. "Let's see if you can handle some real competition. We're playing FIFA."

Tore caught the controller with surprising grace, a determined glint in his eye. "I may surprise you. I've been known to have quite the deft touch with my fingers."

I felt my cheeks heat at his words, but before I could respond, Caspian and Rowan burst into the room, shoving each other playfully.

"Dibs on playing the winner!" Caspian shouted, flopping onto the couch next to me.

As we started playing FIFA, I kept stealing glances at Tore. He sat cross-legged on the floor, his tongue poking out slightly as he concentrated on the screen. It was cute. Fuck, I needed to get a grip.

"Oh, come on!" Tore exclaimed as I scored a goal. "That was clearly offside!"

I laughed, feeling some of the tension ease from my shoulders. "Welcome to the real world, pretty boy. Sometimes the ref makes bad calls."

We played for hours, the room filled with laughter, trash talk, and the occasional victory dance. To my surprise, Tore held his own, even managing to beat Caspian in a nail-biting match.

The smell of roasting turkey and sage drifting from the

kitchen eventually lured us away from the game. As we gathered around our small dining table, I felt a twinge of embarrassment. Our mismatched chairs and chipped plates were a far cry from the fancy dinners Tore must be used to.

But Tore didn't seem to notice or care. He complimented my mom's cooking enthusiastically, talked to Calista about how much fun Legos were over playing with dolls, asked Rowan about his art projects, and engaged in a heated debate with Caspian about soccer strategies.

"This stuffing is absolutely delightful, Linda," Tore said, helping himself to seconds. "I don't suppose you'd be willing to share the recipe?"

My mom beamed, her cheeks flushed with pleasure. "Of course. It's a simple family recipe, nothing fancy."

I watched as Tore leaned in, genuinely interested, as my mom explained the secret to her perfect stuffing. There wasn't a hint of him being patronizing, only warmth and appreciation.

As the meal went on, something shifted inside me. The chip on my shoulder, the one I'd been carrying for so long, began to feel a little lighter. I had been too quick to judge Tore based on his background. He'd shown nothing but kindness.

"Hey," I said softly, nudging Tore as we helped clear the table. "Thanks for being so cool with my family. I know it's probably not what you're used to."

Tore's hand brushed against mine as he reached for a plate, sending a jolt of electricity through my body. "This has been an amazing experience. Your family is wonderful."

As we finished cleaning up, our eyes met across the table. The air between us crackled with tension once again. Would that ever change? Would we ever be able to burn through it somehow? I wanted to close the distance between us, to feel those soft lips against mine.

"Who wants pumpkin pie?" my mom called from the kitchen, snapping me out of my thoughts.

I shook my head, trying to clear it. What the hell was happening to me? This was Tore, for fuck's sake. But as I watched him laugh at one of Caspian's terrible jokes, his whole face lighting up, warmth spread through my chest.

As we settled onto the couch for some post-dinner TV, I was hyperaware of every movement, every laugh, every accidental brush of his arm against mine.

"You all right there, Captain?" Tore asked, his blue eyes twinkling. "You seem a bit distracted."

I cleared my throat, trying to focus. "Yeah, food coma, I guess."

But it wasn't the turkey making my heart race. It was the realization that I'd been so wrong about Tore. All my preconceived notions about rich, entitled assholes were crumbling in the face of his genuine kindness and warmth.

As the night wore on and my family drifted off to bed, Tore and I found ourselves alone in the living room. The TV droned on in the background, but I couldn't focus on anything but the way the soft light caught his profile.

"Farron," Tore said softly, turning to face me. "I wanted to thank you for inviting me. This has been lovely."

I snorted, trying to deflect the sudden intensity of the moment. "Lovely? Who the fuck says lovely?"

Tore grinned, leaning in closer. "I do, you uncultured swine."

Before I could stop myself, I closed the distance between us, pressing my lips to his. For a moment, everything froze. Then Tore's hand was in my hair, pulling me closer, and I was lost.

The kiss deepened, passionate and hungry. I traced the curve of his jaw with my fingers, marveling at the softness of his skin. Tore moaned softly into my mouth, the sound sending shivers down my spine.

"Fuck," I breathed as we broke apart, both panting. "Not here..."

"Your room," Tore whispered. "Let's go to your room."

We slid up the stairs, careful not to wake anyone, then tiptoed into my room, where we fell back on my bed, a tangle of limbs and heated kisses. Eventually, our kisses slowed, becoming softer, more languid.

"We should probably get some sleep," I said reluctantly, not wanting the moment to end.

Tore nodded, stifling a yawn. "Please don't tell me to go to my own bed."

He should. He really should.

Instead, I pulled him closer. As we drifted off to sleep, limbs intertwined in my full-size bed, I made a last, desperate attempt to convince myself.

Sex. This was nothing more than sex.

If I said it often enough, maybe I'd believe it.

21

FARRON

Tore was on my mind all the freaking time. It was as annoying as it was fascinating, considering how I had hated his guts mere weeks ago. Thanksgiving had changed something for me. Seeing him in my home, with my siblings, witnessing his genuine interest firsthand had made me see him in a different light.

And now I couldn't stop thinking about him. I thought it had been bad before, but since Thanksgiving, it had gotten even worse. We hadn't had an opportunity to hook up again. Privacy was ridiculously hard to find when we both had roommates, teammates, and friends in general cockblocking us every step of the way. But if we won this game, we only had two more games to play after this—if we made it all the way—and the season would be over. Surely, after that, we'd find a way to get together.

I'd recovered from the hit I'd taken in the game against the Condors, though Coach had benched me for one more game to be safe. I couldn't blame him. As much as we both wanted to win, it couldn't come at the expense of my health and safety.

I couldn't believe we'd made it to nationals. This had been my dream since my freshman year, and here we were, making it a reality. Two rounds in, and we were still standing. Granted, some luck had been involved, including a dubious offside call in our favor in our last game, but that was all part of it. College soccer didn't have VAR—video assistant referee—like the big pro tournaments had.

No matter how much Tore was on my mind, as soon as the whistle blew, everything else faded away. There was only the game, the ball, my teammates. I'd worked too hard for this to allow myself to be distracted, and luckily, Tore showed the same focus, as did the rest of the team. By now, we moved as one unit, anticipating each other's moves.

With ten more minutes to play in this game against St. Andrew's College from somewhere in California, we were tied one to one. Our opponents had clued in to the danger Tore formed, and he constantly had man-on-man coverage. But that didn't mean they could keep up with him. All he needed was one moment, one opportunity to get away from his defender.

In the final minute of regular time, Tore finally got a breakaway. I held my breath as he approached the goal, his lean body a blur of motion. With a powerful kick, he sent the ball sailing past the keeper.

The stadium erupted. We'd won, bringing us one step closer to becoming the national champions. My teammates swarmed Tore, lifting him onto their shoulders. Pride and joy swelled in my chest. He was so damn good.

The celebration on the soccer field was electric, the night air charged with the euphoria of victory. I stood in the middle of the sea of blue and yellow, my teammates chanting and whooping, their joy infectious. In that moment, we were brothers-in-arms, victorious warriors after a hard-fought battle.

"Let's carry this momentum to finals, Hawks!" Coach bellowed over the din, rallying the team. We answered with a resounding cheer, our voices rising to the stars above Hawley College, our shared dream of glory binding us tighter.

We paraded into the locker room, whooping and hollering. The excitement was infectious as the guys clapped each other on the back, reliving the best moments of the game. RJ dumped a cooler of water over Coach's head as we all laughed. Coach took it in his stride, grinning broadly.

"Party at the Phi Delta house!" Jake yelled.

RJ high-fived him. "Hell yeah, we earned it!"

As the noise died, Coach—still dripping wet—gathered us for a final huddle. "Great work out there, boys. You should be proud. Now go celebrate. Responsibly."

We all put our hands in. "Hawks on three! One, two, three, HAWKS!"

I led the cheer, yet at the same time, I was detached from it, as if I was watching myself from afar. We'd worked so hard to get here, but now that we were so close I could taste it, it came with a startling realization.

I wasn't good enough.

Standing under the hot spray of the shower, I let it sink in. All my life, I'd dreamed of going pro, of playing for a club—and now I knew it would never happen. I wasn't good enough. Throughout my four years of college, I'd kept the hope that scouts would see me, would recognize my potential, and would offer me a deal.

But they hadn't.

And now I realized why. I wasn't good enough. I'd expected that truth to sting, but it didn't. It left me feeling... melancholy, for lack of a better word, but not bitter or angry. I loved soccer. Always had and always would, but now that my college career was coming to an end, it was somehow enough.

Even if we didn't win nationals, I could look back at what we had achieved with so much pride. My freshman year, we hadn't even made the playoffs. My sophomore and junior years, we'd come close to winning the conference, coming in second both times. This time, we'd won, and now we were playing at nationals.

It was enough.

Soccer would always be a part of my life in one way or another, but it wouldn't be my day job. At least, not as a player. And I was okay with that. Strangely okay, in fact.

"Farron..."

I looked up to find Tore looking at me. He was fully dressed, and the locker room was silent. Somehow, I'd missed everyone else leaving while lost in my thoughts.

"Are you okay?" Tore asked.

I took a deep breath as I turned off the shower. "Have you ever had a true epiphany?"

He frowned as he leaned against the wall. "Not that I recall. Why?"

"I just had one."

"Would you like to share?"

Always so goddamn polite. I toweled off, not in the least bothered by him watching me. "I realized I'll never become a pro player."

His soft gasp made me look up. "What? You can't give up hope. Maybe—"

I stopped him with a hand signal. "I'm okay with it. That's the epiphany part, that somehow, I'm okay with giving up on that dream. I don't know how or why, but it's okay."

He pushed off the wall and stepped closer. "I know from experience how hard it is to let a dream like that go."

I wrapped the towel around my waist and secured it, more out of habit than out of an issue with Tore seeing me naked. "It must've been even harder for you because you had the talent to make it. I'm not good enough. No, don't protest. I'm good, and I've excelled at the collegiate level, but I'm not good enough for the pros... and that's okay. I've made my peace with it without even realizing it."

Before I knew what was happening, he was hugging me, wet towel be damned. I resisted for one moment, then gave in and leaned into his embrace.

"It's still hard," he whispered. "Letting go of a dream is never easy."

Funny how I felt so seen with those simple words. "Thank you."

He hugged me a little longer, then let go.

"Did everyone else leave?" I asked, making my way back to the locker room itself.

Tore nodded. "They were quite eager to attend that party."

"Are you going?"

"I doubt it. It's not my scene."

We fell into silence, the air thick with unspoken words. I got dressed, hyperaware of Tore's presence a few feet away. The locker room felt smaller suddenly, more intimate. It was like the air itself was shimmering with the heat between us, waiting for a spark to ignite.

"Farron," Tore said softly, and I turned to find him much closer than I expected. My breath caught in my throat.

"Yeah?" I managed, my heart racing.

Tore's blue eyes searched mine, filled with an intensity that made my skin tingle. "I can't stop thinking about Thanksgiving."

I swallowed hard, heat rising to my face. "Me neither," I admitted, the words tumbling out before I could stop them.

"Something changed."

"Yeah."

Without warning, Tore's hand was on my arm, his touch

sending electricity through me. "I know you're confused," he murmured, "but I felt something real. Didn't you?"

My mind screamed at me to pull away, to deny it. But my body had other ideas. I found myself leaning into Tore's touch, drawn to him like a magnet. "I... Yeah. I did."

The next thing I knew, Tore's lips were on mine, soft yet insistent. A groan escaped me as I kissed him back, my hands finding their way to his waist. The taste of him, the feel of his body against mine—it was intoxicating.

I'd missed him. In the ten days since I'd last kissed him, held him, touched him, I had missed him. How insane yet how true.

My hand found the nape of his neck, pulling him closer toward me. Our tongues tangled, and the dam inside me broke. The kiss was hungry, urgent, as if we were trying to consume each other whole. Tore's mouth was insistent against mine, his tongue tracing my lips before delving inside, tangling with mine in a dance that stole my breath away.

I pushed Tore against the lockers, our kisses growing more heated. My hands roamed his body, relishing the firm muscles beneath his damp jersey. He tangled his fingers in my hair, pulling me closer. My skin burned where his fingers dug in, and I reveled in the pain, the pleasure, the overwhelming reality of Tore in my arms.

"Farron," he gasped between kisses. "I want—"

The locker room door suddenly burst open with a loud bang. We sprang apart, but it was too late.

"Holy shit!"

My blood ran cold. RJ stood frozen in the doorway, his eyes wide with shock.

"RJ," I choked out, panic rising in my chest. "I can explain—"

"Explain what?" RJ's gaze darted between Tore and me, taking in our disheveled appearance and flushed faces. "That you were sucking face with the guy you supposedly hate?"

I cleared my throat. "I don't hate him."

RJ snorted. "No kidding, considering you guys were making out. And aren't you both straight?"

How the hell was I going to explain this? I barely understood it myself. "It's not... I mean, we're not..."

"We're figuring things out," Tore interjected calmly, placing a reassuring hand on my arm. The simple gesture steadied me, and I leaned into his touch.

RJ's eyebrows shot up. "Figuring things out? So this isn't a one-time thing?"

I took a deep breath, forcing myself to meet my co-captain's gaze. "No," I admitted, surprised by how certain I felt. "It's not."

I took Tore's hand and squeezed it.

"Does Coach know?" RJ asked.

"No, but we'll..." I checked with Tore, who nodded. "We'll tell him. And the others."

"Jesus..." RJ looked from me to Tore and back. "I'll be goddamned." Then he grinned. "I'll text the team to come back. Hell if I'm gonna keep this quiet until tomorrow."

True to his word, he messaged everyone, and within a few minutes, the whole team was back in the locker rooms. There were some grumbles about having to leave the party, but mostly, the guys were curious, sensing there had to be a reason RJ had asked them to come back.

"Cap, you have the floor," RJ announced when everyone was present.

Oh fuck. Tore gave me a small nod, his blue eyes filled with encouragement. Emboldened, I held out my hand, and he took it, stepping close to me. A hushed silence fell over the room. "Yeah, so... Tore and I are... together. As in, dating." The words felt foreign but right, tasting of freedom and fear all at once.

"Like holding hands and making daisy chains together?" Ethan quipped, breaking the silence. A ripple of laughter followed, easing the tightness in my chest.

"Very funny." I rolled my eyes. "More like 'skip practice to make out in the locker room' together."

"Ooh," came the drawn-out chorus, followed by a round of playful jeers and wolf whistles.

"Guess that means you'll be playing defense in more ways than one, huh?" Colin called out, and even I couldn't suppress a grin.

"All right, knock it off," I said, though I didn't mind the teasing. It was better than I'd expected—no anger, no disgust. Just the guys being guys. A wave of relief washed over me, though I was a bit confused too. This wasn't how I'd expected things to go at all.

Then Ethan asked the question I'd been fearing. "But I thought you hated him?"

I looked at Tore, my cheeks heating. "Yeah, it turns out I didn't hate him so much after all."

After that, the teasing was endless until the guys streamed out of the locker room again, eager to attend the party. Once again, Tore and I were alone.

"You okay?" he asked, and his concern touched me.

"Better than I had expected, considering I came out in more ways than one."

"You're not upset with me?"

I cupped his cheek. "This wasn't your fault. We both knew this was the risk we were taking."

Plus, I was relieved everything was now out in the open, but I didn't have the right words to express that feeling. My head was still a mess, with relief and fear and excitement and worry all battling with each other.

I wasn't upset that we were now officially dating or whatever it was. This wasn't some fling or an experiment gone too far. There was something between us that went deeper than lust, more profound than physical need.

No, it wasn't the idea of being with Tore that scared me; it was the intensity of what I felt for him... and the fear of what would happen to me if it ended.

When it ended.

Because this was no fairy tale, and in the real world, guys like him didn't end up with the likes of me.

22
TORE

I couldn't take my eyes off Farron as he lounged on his dorm room bed, his muscular frame relaxed against the headboard. My heart raced, still not quite believing this gorgeous man was now officially my boyfriend. We had been forced to say something after RJ caught us, but Farron had still chosen to call what we had a relationship. He could've said it was a fling, a one-time thing, but he'd stated we were dating. So, boyfriends we were.

"You're staring again," Farron said with a smirk.

My cheeks flushed. "Can you blame me? You're pretty nice to look at."

"True." He winked at me.

"Plus, I still have to pinch myself sometimes to make sure this is real."

Farron's expression softened. He reached out and pulled me onto the bed beside him, wrapping his strong arms around me as we turned on our sides, lying face to face. I melted into his embrace, relishing the warmth of his body against mine.

"I'm still coming to terms with it myself," Farron murmured, his lips brushing my ear. "It's been intense and confusing."

"I'm glad you gave me a chance," I said softly. "I know I'm not your normal type."

He let out a short laugh. "No kidding. You have certain body parts that are new to me, plus..."

"Plus I'm rich."

"Yeah. No offense."

I stiffened slightly at his words, guilt twisting in my stomach. If only he knew the full extent of my wealth and status. But I pushed those thoughts aside, focusing instead on the man beside me. "None taken. I understand."

Farron was quiet for a moment, his fingers tracing idle patterns on my arm. When he spoke again, his voice was hesitant. "When you were with me for Thanksgiving, you saw where I'm from. And that's not even the small apartment we grew up in. My mom only bought that house a few years ago, when I was able to work and contribute."

"It's an amazing thing you've done for your family, stepping up like that."

He was quiet for a long time. "I shouldn't have had to. If my father's family had done what they should have..."

"What do you mean?"

"I told you about my dad, right?"

"He died in a car crash, yes. Drunk driver. And you were in the car with him."

"Exactly. Well, my father came from money." Farron's voice turned tight. "Old money. But after he died, his family turned their backs on us. On my mom, my siblings, and me. Left us with nothing."

I felt a surge of anger on Farron's behalf. "That's horrible. How could they do that?"

Farron's laugh was bitter. "Because they're rich assholes who only care about themselves. They didn't want anything to do with my mom. She grew up in a trailer park, so they considered her trailer trash. They never thought she was good enough for their precious son. So after he died, they cut her loose and broke off all ties with her and with us, their grandkids."

His words stung, hitting too close to home. He wasn't talking about me specifically, but I still felt defensive. Not all wealthy people were like that. But I bit my tongue, knowing this wasn't the time to argue. "What happened after that?"

Farron's eyes grew distant. "It was rough. Mom worked multiple jobs, but we still struggled. I started working as soon as I could, trying to help out. We relied on food stamps, the food bank, and a local church that helped us. I hated it. Hated feeling helpless, hated seeing my mom work herself to exhaustion, hated seeing my siblings go hungry at times. Especially because our lives had been fine before that. We hadn't been rich, but my dad had held a good job as an accountant, and we'd never had issues paying the bills. We lived in a nice home, had two cars, and my mom only worked part-time at the hospital."

My chest tightened as I imagined a young Farron shouldering so much responsibility. It was a world so far removed from my privileged upbringing that I could scarcely comprehend it. "I'm so sorry you had to go through that. You've overcome so much."

Farron's fingers tightened around mine. "Soccer was my way out. My ticket to a better life. That's why it means so much to me."

And now he'd had to come to terms with not playing for a pro team like he'd dreamed of for so long. My dream had been shattered when my father put his foot down, but it had never been about money for me or about survival. Soccer had been my passion, but not a way to a better life. "Is that why you pushed yourself so hard? Why you expect so much from the team?"

"I couldn't afford to fail. This scholarship, this opportunity, it was everything to me. To my family. And it's a little different now that I've accepted my future isn't in soccer. At least, not as a player. But for many years, it was the only way I could see myself and my family rise out of poverty."

The weight of his words settled over us. I felt humbled by his strength, his determination. But a nagging voice in the back of my mind whispered I was deceiving him. That I didn't deserve his trust. "What your father's family did was reprehensible. But not all rich people are like that. Many wealthy individuals use their resources for good."

Farron's eyebrows knitted together, his posture stiffening slightly. I pressed on, determined to make my point. "Take Bill Gates, for instance. He's donated billions to charitable causes. Or Warren Buffett, who's pledged to give away most of his fortune. Bono has always stood up for causes he believes in. Even celebrities like Angelina Jolie use their wealth and influence to make a difference."

I watched Farron's face, searching for any sign that my words were getting through. His jaw was set, but I could see a flicker of uncertainty in his eyes. "I'm not saying all rich people are saints, and I know that there are bad apples among them," I continued, my voice soft. "But wealth itself isn't inherently evil. It's how people choose to use their money and power that matters."

Farron was quiet for a long moment. "I get what you're saying, Tore. And I know you're different. You've shown me that. The way you treat everyone on the team, how hard you work, how generous you are..."

My heart swelled at his words, even as guilt gnawed at my insides.

"But it's not that simple," Farron continued. "I can't flip a switch and change how I feel. This bitterness... It's been a part of me for so long."

I nodded, understanding the complexity of his emotions. "I

don't expect you to change overnight. I just wanted to offer my view, show you a different side."

Farron's lips quirked in a small smile. "You're always trying to see the best in people, aren't you?"

I shrugged, feeling a blush creep up my neck. "I suppose it's how I was raised. To look for the good, even when it's not immediately apparent."

"It's one of the things I lo—" Farron caught himself, clearing his throat. "One of the things I admire about you."

My heart raced at his near-confession. I wanted to hear those words, to say them back. But the weight of my secret held me back. Instead, I leaned in and kissed him softly, hoping to convey everything I couldn't say aloud.

As our lips parted, a charged silence fell over the room. I gazed into Farron's deep, brown eyes, searching for any hint of suspicion or doubt. But all I saw was warmth and affection, which only intensified my guilt. Here was Farron, opening up about his past, his fears, his prejudices, and I was holding back the most fundamental truth about myself. The weight of my royal lineage pressed down on me, threatening to crush this fragile connection we'd forged.

Farron's calloused hand cupped my cheek, his thumb tracing my jawline. "You okay? You seem... I don't know, distant all of a sudden."

I forced a smile, hoping it didn't look as strained as it felt. "I'm fine. Just thinking about everything you've shared. It's a lot to process."

"Yeah, I did dump quite a bit on you. Sorry about that."

"No, no," I said quickly. "I'm glad you told me. I want to know you, Farron. All of you."

The irony of my words wasn't lost on me. Here I was, encouraging honesty while hiding behind a facade of half-truths.

Farron leaned in, pressing his forehead against mine. "I want that too, Tore. With you."

My heart ached at the sincerity in his voice. I wanted to blurt out the truth right then and there, consequences be damned. But fear held my tongue.

Instead, I kissed him again, desperately, as if I could somehow make up for my dishonesty through physical affection. Farron responded eagerly, his strong arms wrapping around me, pulling me closer.

When we finally broke apart, breathless, I knew I had to leave before I completely lost my resolve. "I should go." I reluctantly disentangled myself from his embrace. "Early practice tomorrow."

Farron nodded. "Yeah, of course. I'll see you on the field, yeah?"

"Absolutely." At the door, I turned back for one last look. Farron sat on his bed, hair mussed, lips swollen from our kisses. The sight of him, so open and trusting, nearly broke me.

I hurried back to my dorm room, each step heavier than the last. By the time I reached my door, I was practically running, desperate to escape the suffocating weight of my guilt. Once inside, I leaned against the closed door, sliding to the floor. The silence of my empty room pressed in on me, amplifying the turmoil in my mind.

I needed to talk to someone who would understand and be honest with me, but who could I turn to? My eyes fell on my phone, and suddenly, I knew. Floris. I could always count on him to be direct with me. Others sometimes perceived it as rude, but I didn't. He simply spoke the truth, and sometimes, people took offense.

With trembling fingers, I pressed Call. Each ring felt like an eternity until, finally, I heard his familiar voice.

"Tore? Is everything all right?" Floris asked, concern evident in his tone.

"I've royally mucked things up, Flo," I blurted out, wincing at my unintentional pun. "I need your advice."

I heard rustling on the other end, then Floris's voice again, clearer this time. "I'm listening. What's going on?"

Taking a deep breath, I launched into my tale. He already knew about Farron since he'd been the one I asked about blowjobs, so I shared the new developments and my growing guilt over hiding my true identity. "He hates rich people," I said, my voice cracking. "He's had such a rough life, and I'm lying to him every day. I don't know what to do."

There was a moment of silence on the other end. Then Floris spoke, his words measured and careful. "Tore, you need to tell him the truth."

"But what if he hates me?" I asked, voicing my deepest fear.

"He might," Floris admitted. "But if you don't tell him, and he finds out some other way, it'll be much worse. Trust me on this."

I collapsed onto my bed, staring at the ceiling. "You're right. I know you're right. But how do I even begin that conversation?"

"There's no easy way," Floris said gently. "But the longer you wait, the harder it'll be. You need to come clean before this goes any further."

He was right, but bloody hell, the thought of telling Farron filled me with dread. How would he react? "Thanks," I said softly. "I knew I could count on you to tell me the truth."

Floris chuckled. "It's the only way I know. Now go get some sleep. You've got a big conversation ahead of you."

After we hung up, I lay in bed, my mind racing. How would Farron react? Would this be the end of us before we'd truly begun? The uncertainty was agonizing, but I knew Floris was right. I had to tell Farron the truth, no matter the consequences.

All I had to do was figure out how.

23

FARRON

I rested my ass on the edge of my bed, my notebook forgotten on the floor as I powered up my laptop. This was officially one of the weirdest things I'd ever done, but desperate times called for desperate measures. Tore would be spending the night—Colin had a girlfriend now and would be meeting her parents over the weekend—and I needed to be ready.

So far, Tore had initiated most of our sexual encounters. Sure, I had kissed him first, but after that, he'd been the one to step into the shower with me, he'd offered me a blowjob, and he'd suggested anal. In other words, he'd been way ahead of me the whole time, and while this wasn't a competition, it still didn't sit well with me that he'd bested me. Yeah, not the right term, but whatever.

I needed to offer him something in return, and hell if I was gonna suck at giving oral, no pun intended. You'd think I'd know how to give a blowjob, considering girls had done it to me, plus Tore, of course. But giving was very different from receiving. The last thing I wanted was to choke, literally or figuratively, so I needed some guidance. Tore deserved my best effort. And he'd admitted he'd done research too, so I had to do the same.

Gnawing on my lower lip, I typed *how to give a blowjob* into the search bar. The first result was a video titled *Beginner's Guide to Mind-Blowing Blowjobs*. I took a deep breath, reminding myself this was for Tore, and pressed play.

A woman with more cleavage than I thought humanly possible was on her knees in front of some dude who was straining against his pants. I turned the audio down to one bar to avoid giving my neighbors a show, focusing on her every move as she unzipped his fly, her hand brushing against what looked like a very sizable package.

The guy moaned, and I swallowed hard, my mouth suddenly as dry as the Sahara. Jesus. This was weird. I'd watched porn a gazillion times before and it had never bothered me, but somehow, it now felt wrong. As if I was cheating on Tore, which was ridiculous. This was for research purposes only.

The woman had her mouth on his cock now, and damn, she was working it. I took mental notes: one hand at the base, the other on his shaft, and don't forget the balls. Hmm, her tongue technique was interesting too. She licked him like a lollipop in between sucking him, and every now and then, she also suckled on the tip only. Maybe to give her jaw a break? 'Cause that dude was packing and she was shoving that thing down until his pubes hit her nose.

She looked up at the camera, her eyes half-lidded in supposed pleasure, though it felt too over the top for me. And hell to the no was I making those moany sounds as I sucked Tore off. I'd leave the audio part to him since he was always so much more vocal than me—which I loved, especially those high-pitched little whimpers he made.

All right, enough with the fake pleasure. I clicked close on the video, then hit the next link on the search results, which was an article. Ah, that was so much better. It only offered drawn illustrations, which worked fine for me. I made some more mental notes, then closed the search page and called it a day. I'd wing the rest.

Colin was due back any moment, and I wasn't gonna let him catch me. He was on my ass enough about Tore, though not in a mean way. None of the guys were, but they sure knew every gay joke and double entendre on the planet.

As soon as Colin left that night, I did a quick swipe of my room to make it presentable, even changing the sheets. Mine weren't as fancy as Tore's, but they were clean and smelled fresh. That was about as good as it was going to get. Then, all I could do was wait for Tore to show.

When Tore arrived, his shoulders were tense and his brow was furrowed.

"Hey," I said, frowning at the stress that radiated off him. "Everything okay?"

Tore sighed, dropping his bag by the door. "I had a rather taxing day, I'm afraid."

I stood, studying him. The usual sparkle was missing from his blue eyes, replaced by a weariness that made my chest ache. All thoughts of my own nerves evaporated. Right now, all that mattered was making Tore feel good. I could offer to talk about it, but I sucked at comforting people, so maybe I could use a different way of helping him de-stress?

I closed the distance between us, cupping his face in my hands. "How about I make you feel better?"

I captured Tore's lips with mine, pouring all my desire and determination into the kiss. His body tensed for a moment, then melted against me as he responded with equal fervor. My hands slid down to his waist, pulling him flush against me.

"Farron," he gasped when we broke apart. "I must say, I very much approve of your method of de-stressing."

I grinned, trailing kisses along his jawline. "I figured you might. Just let me take care of you tonight."

My fingers found the hem of his shirt, slowly inching it upward. Tore raised his arms, allowing me to pull the garment over his head. I tossed it aside, my breath catching as I took in the sight of his lean, toned torso.

"Fuck," I whispered, running my hands over his smooth skin. "You're so gorgeous."

A light blush colored Tore's cheeks. "I'm not convinced that's an accurate assessment, but I appreciate the sentiment nonetheless."

I chuckled, shaking my head. "Trust me, it's accurate."

My hands moved to his belt, fumbling slightly as I worked to undo it. Nerves fluttered in my stomach, but I pushed them aside. This wasn't about me. It was about making Tore feel good.

I slowly slid his belt free, then popped the button on his jeans. As I lowered the zipper, my heart pounded so hard, I was sure Tore could hear it. But when I looked up, his eyes were closed, his head tilted back slightly.

Taking a deep breath, I hooked my thumbs in the waistband of his jeans and boxers, easing them down his long legs. Tore stepped out of them, now completely naked before me.

"Christ," I breathed, drinking in the sight of him. Lean muscles, smooth skin, and not an ounce of body fat. He looked like he'd been carved from marble by some Renaissance master.

My hands roamed over Tore's body, exploring every inch of him. I traced the lines of his abs, marveling at how defined they were. As my fingers skimmed lower, Tore's breath hitched. My hands continued their journey, caressing his thighs, then moving back up to tease his nipples.

Tore gasped, arching into my touch. "You're driving me mad."

"That's the idea." I pressed a kiss to his collarbone, then gently pushed him backward until he sat on the bed, frowning slightly.

My heart was racing as I slowly sank to my knees between his legs. This was it. Pushing aside my nerves, I looked up at Tore. His blue eyes were dark with desire, his chest rising and falling rapidly. Keeping my eyes locked on his, I leaned forward and licked his crown.

Tore let out a strangled moan, his hands flying to my hair. "Oh, bloody hell."

"This okay?"

"Very okay. Very, very okay."

With a smile, I wrapped my hand around his base, then moved in again. Funny, but the faint smell of his sweat wasn't deterring me at all. If anything, it spurred me on. I licked around his entire length, using my tongue to trace patterns and alternating with butterfly kisses. They might not give him the most pleasure, but they satisfied my need to show him how much I wanted him and wanted to do this for him.

Taking a deep breath, I suckled the tip of his cock—a little drop of precum pearling—into my mouth. The taste was different than I'd expected, not unpleasant but definitely unique.

Encouraged by Tore's sounds and him gripping my head, I relaxed my throat and took in a little more. I hollowed my cheeks, sucking gently, and was rewarded with another moan from Tore. All my doubts and hesitations seemed to melt away in the face of Tore's pleasure. If he was enjoying it, that meant I was doing it right.

His hips began to move in a slow, sensual rhythm, and I gladly followed his lead. I applied more pressure, bending my neck to take him deeper into my mouth. The feeling of him in my mouth, the knowledge that I was the one causing these sounds of pleasure, was intoxicating.

Giving oral was also hard work. After a minute or two, my jaw began to tense and my tongue got tired. Who knew this would be a workout? But luckily, Tore's grip on my hair tightened, his moans becoming more ragged. "Close. Really close."

That was all the encouragement I needed. I picked up the pace, desperate to bring him over the edge. Tore's moans crescendoed, his hips bucking. I pulled back just in time when, with a final, shuddering gasp, he came. He sprayed his load all over my face, and instinctively, I caught some on my tongue. Again, not off-putting, but I was glad I hadn't tried to swallow.

As Tore came down from his high, I rose and grabbed some wet wipes to clean myself up, then him. Maybe I should've cuddled first or waited a bit longer, but the sensation of drying cum on my face was not one I particularly cared for.

"Well," Tore said after a moment, his voice still breathless, "that was unexpected. Thank you."

"I did research," I said, then wanted to facepalm because why had I felt the need to mention that? "Wanted to make it good for you."

"You more than succeeded."

I sat next to him. "Sorry I didn't swallow. That was still a bridge too far."

He half-turned and cupped my cheek. "It was perfect."

He kissed me, and what started out soft and tender quickly grew frantic again. We spent a long, drawn-out moment lost in each other's mouths, the heat between us igniting into a raging inferno.

I moaned into his eager mouth as he pushed me down. With him still naked and me fully dressed, it was a bit weird, but apparently Tore felt the same way because he yanked on my T-shirt. I raised my arms and awkwardly pushed myself up so he could drag it over my head.

My pants came next, and before I knew it, I was naked too. So much better. My cock, which had grown hard as steel when blowing him, was still erect. Did Tore's actions mean he was interested in more?

As if he could read my mind, he rolled on top of me, our eyes meeting. "Will you fuck me again?"

"You sure?"

He nodded. "I loved it, and we haven't done it since."

"Well, we've been a little busy with other things like soccer and coming out."

He flashed me one of his sunny smiles. "I've been really eager to do it again."

I cupped his cheek in my hand, my thumb brushing his cheekbone lightly. "So have I."

I kissed my way down his jawline, along the column of his neck, and down to his chest. His breath hitched in anticipation as I took a nipple between my teeth, teasing it with the lightest of bites. Tore arched against me, moaning my name as I trailed kisses down his abs, every muscle of his lean, athletic body taut with desire.

His cock was making a valiant attempt at recovery, but it would have to wait. Instead, I reached for the lube on my nightstand. Preparing him was easier than last time, both of us knowing what to do now, and I had him ready for me in no time. I rolled on a condom, slicked myself up some more, then checked in with Tore. "You good?"

He nodded, turning on his stomach and pushing himself to his hands and knees. "I want to try this. It's supposed to feel really good because you can go deeper."

"An experiment I am happy to participate in."

He chuckled, relaxing, which had been my intention. I positioned myself at his entrance, my cock hard and aching, and with one deep breath, I began to push inside. His tight heat enveloped me, hot and wet and clenching around me like a glove. The sensation was indescribable, and I had to grit my teeth to keep from coming right then and there.

Tore moaned, his body trembling beneath mine as I inched in and out of him, sinking a little deeper each time. He'd been right. This position was easier. The angle was better, and because I was on my knees and didn't have to push myself up, I could focus all my strength on fucking him.

"Oh fuck, this feels so good," Tore moaned.

The man was cursing. The guy who, other than the occasional "bloody hell," never uttered a swear word, was cursing. If nothing else, that showed me how much he wanted this, how much he loved this.

His words fueled the fire inside me, and I picked up the pace, withdrawing almost all the way before slamming back in harder this time. Tore fisted the sheets, holding on for purchase, but he had a hard time bracing against my onslaught.

I stopped for a moment and gently pushed between his shoulder blades. "Lie down on your stomach."

With a little sigh, he did as I told him, spreading his legs. The angle was a little different now, but I quickly got the hang of it and resumed my pace. Fuck, this was perfect. I could go much harder like this, our bodies colliding as I fucked him into the mattress with a hunger I never knew I possessed.

As we moved together, bodies slick with sweat and the sounds of our passion filling the room, a deep peace filled me. This was it. This was what it felt like to be complete. It was as if every piece of my life up until this moment had been leading me here, to this moment, to be with this man...

Now, all I had to do was hold on to him.

24

TORE

I stood in front of my locker, fingers trembling as I closed the metal door with a clank. The chatter of my teammates faded to the background as if coming to me through headphones. This was it, the finals of the nationals. Everything we'd worked for all season came down to the next ninety minutes as we played Elkin College, a highly ranked college near Boston. Our host was some university in Pennsylvania—neutral ground for both teams.

So many emotions were coursing through me that I didn't even know where to start. I was incredibly grateful and proud that we'd made it this far. Being in the finals was an honor, no matter the outcome.

But I was also relieved that the season would be over. We were all exhausted from playing multiple games every week since the beginning of the school year. I had struggled to keep up with homework, and I wasn't the only one.

Plus, Farron and I had barely managed to spend time together in between practice and games. After Christmas break, we would only do conditioning training, and once spring started, some friendly matches, so we'd finally have time to hang out.

Speaking of Christmas, would Farron and I be able to celebrate Christmas together? He'd probably want to go home, and I wouldn't mind joining him, but it would be so much better to have him come home with me. Norway was stunning in the winter, and I'd love to show him the beauty of my country.

Of course, that meant coming clean about who I was first. After my call with Floris, I'd been determined to tell Farron the truth, but then I'd realized the potential consequences. If Farron took the news badly, it could affect the team and our season. I couldn't let that happen, so I'd decided to wait until after the season was over. Surely, those few days extra wouldn't matter.

Coach's voice cut through the noise. "All right, Hawks, circle up!"

As we gathered, I caught Farron's eye across the huddle. He gave me a slight nod, his jaw set with determination. My heart fluttered.

"You've all worked your butts off to get here, and I couldn't be prouder of you," Coach said. "You all know what to do because you've been doing it all season. Get out there and get it done."

A cheer went up. I tried to join in, but my voice caught in my throat.

We did our team huddle, and then we streamed out of the locker room. Farron grabbed my shoulder as we filed out. "You've got this. Go shine."

I managed a weak smile. Bloody hell, I'd never been this nervous about a match before. "I'll do my very best to make you and the team proud."

As we jogged onto the pitch, the roar of the crowd hit me like a wall. My legs felt like jelly. I took deep breaths, trying to center myself.

"Nervous?" Farron asked, still beside me.

"Me? I'm as cool as a cucumber."

He chuckled. "Yeah right. You look like you're about to puke."

"I prefer to think of it as pre-match jitters."

Our eyes met.

"Good luck," I whispered.

"You too."

We took our positions for kickoff. The ref blew his whistle. Game on.

As we battled back and forth across the pitch, my nerves settled. This was what I loved: the thrill of competition, pushing my body to its limits. Elkin played hard but fair, attacking at every opportunity, which kept Farron and the rest of our defense busy.

We were well-matched, ball possession going back and forth. These kinds of games where both teams preferred an offensive rather than defensive style were my favorite.

I sprinted forward, positioning myself for a potential cross from Farron. The crowd's roar swelled as he dribbled past one defender, then another. My heart raced, hope surging through me. This could be our chance.

Farron sent the ball arcing toward me, the perfect height for a header. I leapt, my forehead connecting with the ball solidly, and turned my head to give it a spin in the right direction. Time seemed to slow as I watched it sail toward the goal. The keeper dove, fingers outstretched...

And tipped it over the crossbar.

"Bloody hell," I groaned, landing hard on the pitch. The disappointment was a heavy weight in my chest as I pushed myself up.

Farron jogged over, offering a hand. "That was close, man. We'll get the next one."

I accepted his help, trying to muster a smile. "Right. Next one."

But as the match wore on, that elusive goal seemed to slip further and further away. Every shot was blocked, every pass intercepted, every attack countered. The frustration was palpable among our team, shoulders tense and faces grim.

As halftime approached, I was near our own goal, helping defend against yet another Elkin assault. Their striker, a hulking bloke with surprising agility, managed to slip past our centerback.

I raced to intercept, but I was a fraction too slow. The Elkin player's foot connected with the ball as I arrived, sending it sailing past Colin's outstretched hands and into the net. The crowd erupted, but it wasn't the joyous sound I'd been hoping for all match. Elkin's fans were celebrating while our own supporters fell into a stunned silence.

I stood there, hands on my knees, trying to catch my breath and process what had happened. We were down one to nil, with only moments left before halftime. Psychologically, that was bad timing, but at least we still had forty-five minutes to play.

Coach gave a rousing speech at halftime, which most of us spent guzzling down energy drinks and eating whatever we could stomach. Farron, who never sat down because he said it made his muscles lock up, kept checking in with me non-verbally. Underneath that grumpy exterior really beat a soft, caring heart.

The second half began. I took a deep breath, steeling myself for the battle ahead. We had forty-five minutes to turn this around, and I was determined to give it my all.

Elkin came out strong, their offensive line pressing hard against our defense. I sprinted down the field, trying to create space for a pass, but their midfielders were relentless.

Jake launched the ball in my direction. I trapped it with my chest, my heart pounding as two Elkin players converged on me. I dribbled left, then quickly cut right, barely managing to squeeze between them. The crowd roared as I broke free, charging toward the goal.

I hesitated for a split second. Should I take the shot or pass? In that moment of indecision, an Elkin defender slid in, knocking the ball over the line. We had the throw-in, but our momentum had been stopped, and we immediately lost the ball again, thanks to Cooper's sloppy aim.

We charged onto the field with renewed vigor, but Elkin's defense was impenetrable. Every time we pushed forward, they seemed to anticipate our moves. I sprinted down the wing, calling for the ball, but our passes were constantly intercepted.

As the minutes ticked away, a sense of desperation began to creep in. We were running out of time, and the realization that we might actually lose this match started to sink in. Elkin was outplaying us at every turn. Their defense was a fortress, and our attacks felt increasingly desperate.

In the final minutes of the match, I found myself with the ball at my feet, facing a wall of Elkin defenders. I tried to channel all my years of training, all the skills I'd honed, into this one moment. I feinted left, then right, searching for an opening. But there was none. An Elkin player slid in, cleanly taking the ball from me and ending our last real chance at equalizing.

As the final whistle blew, I stood rooted to the spot, my chest heaving. We had lost. We were in second place. The disappointment was crushing, a physical ache in my chest.

"Good game, mate," an Elkin player said, offering his hand.

I shook it mechanically, barely registering the gesture. My mind was a whirlwind of emotions: disappointment, frustration, and an overwhelming sense of letting everyone down.

As we walked off the field, I caught sight of Farron, who stood talking to the Elkin's captain. His devastated expression nearly broke me. I'd wanted so badly to win this for him, for my team, for Hawley.

"You played your heart out," Luke said, throwing an arm

around my shoulders. "We all did. Sometimes, it's just not enough."

I nodded, unable to form words. The reality of our second-place finish was sinking in, and with it came a flood of questions about my future, about my relationship with Farron, about everything I'd been avoiding thinking about. This loss wasn't just about soccer. It was the end of a chapter and the beginning of something new, and it terrified me that I didn't know if it would be a good or a bad thing.

The locker room was a somber place as we filed in, the air heavy with the weight of our defeat. The usual post-game chatter was absent, replaced by the sound of shuffling feet and muted sighs. I slumped onto the bench, my muscles aching from the exertion of the match.

Coach cleared his throat, drawing our attention. His weathered face bore the lines of disappointment, but there was a glimmer of pride in his eyes as he surveyed our team. "Gentlemen, I know this isn't the outcome we hoped for. But I want you to look around this room. Each one of you has poured your heart and soul into this season. You've pushed yourselves beyond what you thought possible, and you've done it together."

I glanced around at my teammates, noting the mix of emotions on their faces. Some nodded along with Coach's words, while others stared at the floor, lost in thought.

"Second place in the nationals isn't a failure," Coach continued. "It's a testament to your hard work, dedication, and spirit. You've made Hawley proud. You've made me proud."

His words resonated with something inside me, and I felt a small spark of warmth cutting through the disappointment. We had come far, hadn't we?

"You've come farther than any Hawley team has in two decades, and that's an amazing accomplishment. So tonight, we celebrate," Coach said, a smile breaking through. "We celebrate how far we've come, and we look forward to where we're going next."

There was a murmur of agreement, and I found myself nodding along. Coach was right, of course. We should be proud. And yet...

As the team began to stir, talking in low voices about plans for the evening, I remained seated, a knot of uncertainty forming in my stomach. Coach's words about looking forward struck a chord. What was next for me? My future at Hawley was unclear, shrouded in a fog of doubt. I wanted to stay at Hawley for another year at least, even knowing Farron wouldn't be there, but would my father let me? Our agreement had been for one year only.

"You all right, Tore?" RJ asked, pausing by my locker.

I mustered a smile. "Just processing."

"You played your heart out all season." He clapped me on the shoulder. "We'll get 'em next time, yeah?"

I nodded, not trusting myself to speak. *Next time*. Would there be a next time for me at Hawley? The thought sent a pang through my chest, sharper than the ache of our loss.

As I slowly began to change out of my kit, my mind wandered to Farron, to the truth I needed to tell him. The end of the soccer season meant I could no longer hide behind the excuse of not wanting to disrupt the team. It was time to be honest, to reveal who I really was.

The thought filled me with a mixture of dread and anticipation. How would he react? Would this be the end of something beautiful before it had truly begun? One thing was certain: whatever came next, nothing would be the same.

Then Farron stood before me, gesturing for me to stand, which I did. "What's—"

He cupped my face in his calloused hands and pressed his lips to mine. The world around us faded. His kiss was fierce, passionate, and utterly public. My heart raced, and for a moment, I forgot how to breathe. When we finally broke apart, I blinked at him in astonishment. A beat of silence, and then the locker room erupted in cheers and whistles.

"We would've never made it this far without you, so thank you," he whispered.

I blinked. The team knew about us, of course, as did Coach, but Farron had never publicly kissed me. "Thank you."

Farron grinned at me, his thumbs gently caressing my cheeks. "I'm done hiding, Tore."

My chest swelled with emotion, even as guilt gnawed at me. I managed a smile, trying to push down the anxiety bubbling inside me. "You can kiss me any time."

As our teammates offered good-natured ribbing, I couldn't shake the weight settling on my shoulders. Farron had bared his heart to me, to everyone. And here I was, still keeping secrets.

I couldn't put it off any longer.

Tomorrow. I would tell him everything tomorrow.

25

FARRON

My body was funny. Six days a week, I woke up at five-thirty on the dot for soccer practice, but somehow, on Sunday, I was able to sleep in. Well, that was a relative term, as I'd still wake up around nine, but for me, that was sleeping in and a luxury I appreciated. Waking up slowly, without having to immediately jump into action, was a treat, and so I took my time slumbering before finally forcing myself out of bed.

Colin was spending the weekend with his girlfriend, so I had the room to myself. Tore and I had both been exhausted after yesterday's match, so we'd decided sleeping in our own beds would be smart. But we'd see each other today.

I did my morning routine, made my bed—a habit my mom had instilled in me as a kid—then checked my phone to see if anything earth-shattering had happened while I was asleep.

Tore had texted.

> Family emergency. Had to go home. Will text you later.

I frowned, checking the time stamp. He'd texted at five in the morning. Family emergency? What could be so urgent that he'd have to leave at that time? Worry settled in my gut.

I texted back.

> Everything okay? Let me know what's going on when you have a chance.

Impatience clawed at me as I waited for his answer. What could be wrong that he'd have to drop everything and fly home? I didn't know much about his family other than that he was the oldest and had two younger siblings. But it had to be something bad, right?

To distract myself from the gnawing worry, I made myself coffee and started scrolling through my phone, thumb flicking over the screen without much interest, until a trending video caught my eye:

Norwegian King Collapses at Public Event: LIVE UPDATES.

Norway. Tore's connection to Norway wasn't something we talked about much, but it was his home. It was where his roots ran deep.

Could his sudden departure have anything to do with this? Nah, that was crazy. It wasn't like I'd fly home if our president died or something. But something niggled in the back of my mind, and I hit play on the video as I sipped my coffee.

The king—who was much younger than I had expected for some reason—had been giving a speech to commemorate the opening of a new hospital, the commentator explained. Dressed in a nice suit, he'd been mid-speech when he'd suddenly keeled over, people around him lunging forward in a futile attempt to catch him.

"Jesus," I muttered under my breath, tapping on the link with a sense of foreboding I couldn't explain. The page loaded, and I was met with the somber faces of news anchors, their expressions grave as they relayed the unfolding tragedy.

"King Ragnar of Norway has passed away after collapsing during a public function earlier today, a spokesperson for the Norwegian royal family has confirmed," the anchor said in a somber tone. "Despite immediate life-saving measures at the scene and in the hospital, doctors were unable to revive him. The nation of Norway is in mourning as they come to terms with the sudden loss of their beloved monarch, who was only fifty-six."

I leaned forward, elbows digging into my knees, as I watched clips of the king's life flash across the screen: images of him waving from balconies, shaking hands with world leaders, smiling kindly at children. I didn't know the man, but fifty-six was way too young to die, especially that publicly.

"Details regarding the cause of death have yet to be released, but Gustav von Glücksburg, the crown prince, will be crowned king sometime in the future. The line of succession is clear, with Gustav's son, the young Prince Harald von Glücksburg, being next in line, followed by his two-year-old brother, Prince Olav," she continued as the screen showed pictures of all these people.

Then an image popped up beside the anchor: a familiar face, a smile I knew too well, blue eyes I could never forget. Tore. "With the death of King Ragnar, Prince Tore von Glücksburg, the nephew of the king, is now third in line to the throne," the anchor said, her words slamming into me with the force of a soccer ball to the gut.

I blinked, certain I'd misheard. But there he was, the man who had so unexpectedly conquered my heart, splashed across the screen with a regal bearing and an undeniable air of nobility. The picture shifted to one of him in a suit, standing beside individuals who must've been his royal relatives.

The room suddenly spun around me. This had to be some sort of twisted joke, a deepfake or something, right? But the undeniable truth stared back at me from the screen, and my mind struggled to make sense of it all. Tore? A prince?

My mind raced, piecing together fragments of conversations I'd had with Tore about his family. The offhand remarks he'd made about his obligations back home that I'd never thought to question in depth. He'd mentioned an uncle once, but he'd always glossed over the details with that self-deprecating humor of his, making it sound unimportant.

It suddenly felt like I'd been missing a massive piece of a puzzle I hadn't even realized I was a part of. I snatched my laptop from my desk, the metal cool under my fingers as I flipped it open with more force than necessary. My breaths came out in ragged huffs, and the cursor blinked at me impatiently as I typed Tore's name into the search bar. Tore Haakon von Glücksburg stared back at me from dozens of search results, each a punch to the gut, confirming the unbearable truth.

The Football Prince one headline read, the words blurring as I scrolled through article after article. Photos of Tore as a teen, clad in various soccer uniforms. Articles about him turning down an offer from Ajax. He'd told me about that, but he'd left out the part where the family obligation he'd mentioned was being part of the Norwegian royal family.

More official pictures of him, standing tall and regal beside his parents and with the Norwegian King and Queen—who were his uncle and aunt, I now understood. He looked different somehow—more poised, every inch the prince he never told me he was.

My heart hammered against my ribs like it wanted to break free, but I couldn't tear my eyes away from the screen. It was all there: the heritage, the lineage, the duties that came with being born into a royal family—a life so far removed from my own, it might as well have been fiction.

"Son of a bitch," I muttered to no one, anger simmering beneath the surface of my skin. Why? Why would Tore hide this? What game was he playing by pretending to be just another student, another teammate? He'd never denied being rich and privileged, but being of royal blood was a whole 'nother level he should've been honest about.

The room felt suddenly claustrophobic, the walls closing in around me. My hands clenched around my coffee mug, still half-full, though the coffee had to be cold by now.

"Damn you, Tore," I whispered, betrayal tightening its grip around my throat. He had seen me, known everything about my distrust for the wealthy, my disdain for privilege, yet he'd never told me this.

It wasn't the lie itself that clawed at me. It was the trust I'd placed in him, the belief we had something real. The memories of our time together flooded in—every glance, every accidental brush of skin, every shared laugh. They were tainted now, poisoned by the truth of his identity. I had let down my guard and allowed myself to believe in our connection. All those late-night conversations, the confidences we'd shared, the complete trust I'd had in him. They twisted inside me now, each memory more painful than the previous.

Tore and I had shared secrets under the cover of darkness, our bodies entwined, whispering about dreams and fears. I had opened myself up to him, let him see parts of me no one else had ever glimpsed. And all the while, he'd been hiding behind a mask, playing a role that now made every touch feel like a deception.

"Should have known," I muttered, a laugh devoid of humor bubbling from my chest. "A guy like that, mixing with the likes of me?" It was a farce, a cruel joke—and I'd fallen for it hook, line, and sinker.

And beneath the anger, beneath the sense of betrayal, was an ache so profound, it threatened to swallow me whole, a sense of heartbreak so intense, it left me breathless.

I wanted to throw something, punch a wall, yell out loud, anything to release the pressure building inside me. My grip on reality—and my mug—faltered.

"Shit!" I cursed as the ceramic slipped from my grasp, crashing onto the floor. It shattered into a million pieces... just like my heart.

26

TORE

I had been asleep, in the middle of a really nice dream about Farron and me, when my phone rang. The familiar melody of *"Ja, vi elsker dette landet"*—Norway's national anthem—filled my dorm room. I'd set that ringtone for my father.

I checked the time. A quarter to five. Wait, what? My father knew the time difference. My stomach dropped. "Pappa? *Hva er galt?*"

"It's your Uncle Ragnar. He died," my father said in Norwegian, his voice grave.

The world tilted on its axis. My throat constricted as I gripped the phone tighter. "What? No, that can't be right."

"He collapsed a few hours ago. Medical personnel did everything possible to save him but were unable. We need you to come home immediately."

I stared blankly at the wall adorned with a Norwegian flag. Uncle Ragnar's smiling face flashed through my mind: teaching me to fish, making bad dad jokes, taking me on his snowmobile. He'd been the king, yes, but to me, he'd also been my uncle, and now he was gone. Just like that.

"I'll start packing right away," I managed, my voice cracking.

"A car will pick you up in fifteen minutes."

"Okay. Pappa, *jeg beklager*."

"I'm sorry too, Tore. He will be deeply missed."

The next hours passed in a blur. I vaguely recalled packing a suitcase, informing a sleepy Luke I had to go home for a family emergency, and firing off a text to Farron. Before I knew it, I was stepping off the private jet onto Norwegian soil.

Even years later, I could barely remember anything about that week as we mourned as a family and nation. There were meetings to be held, a country to be reassured, and family to console. I functioned on autopilot, doing what needed to be done.

The funeral, held a week later, was a grand affair, as befitting a king. I stood stoically beside my parents and sisters, painfully aware of the eyes of the nation upon us.

"*Herregud*," I muttered under my breath as the casket was carried past. "This can't be real."

My sister Astrid squeezed my hand.

I swallowed hard, straightening my back. A prince didn't cry in public. But oh, how I wanted to.

The service dragged on, a mix of pomp and circumstance that Uncle Ragnar would have found amusing. I could almost hear his dry chuckle in my ear. *All this fuss over little old me?*

As we followed the casket out of the cathedral, the reality of the situation hit me like a punch to the gut. This wasn't about losing a beloved uncle. The entire power structure of our family—of our country—had shifted. My cousin, Gustav, was now king at only twenty-eight years old, with his oldest son next in line. And I was one step closer to a throne I'd never wanted.

"You all right?" Andor, my best friend since childhood, murmured as we walked.

I gave a slight shake of my head. "*Nei*. But I have to be, don't I?"

He nodded solemnly. "That's the curse of royalty, my friend. The show must go on."

And go on it did. I stood tall as we processed through the streets of Oslo, waving stoically to the mourning crowds. Inside, I was screaming. I wanted to run back to Hawley, to lose myself in the simplicity of college life. To be just Tore again, not His Royal Highness Prince Tore von Glücksburg.

But as I caught sight of my father's grief-stricken face, I knew that wasn't an option. My family needed me. My country needed me. But Farron was never far from my thoughts, a beacon of hope in the stormy sea of my new reality. In between, I fired off texts at him... but he never replied. I had no idea why and deep inside me, despair took root that something was horribly wrong, but I had no time to let it surface.

The day after the funeral, I stood in my father's study, the weight of tradition pressing down on me as heavily as the ornate oil paintings of our ancestors lining the walls. My father's eyes, rimmed with red from days of mourning, bore into mine with an intensity that made me want to look away. But I didn't. I couldn't.

"Tore, you must understand. With Ragnar gone, our family's duties have multiplied tenfold. We need you here, son."

I took a deep breath, steeling myself for the argument I knew was coming. "Pappa, I understand the gravity of the situation, but I can't abandon my studies. I've made commitments—"

"Commitments?" My father's eyebrow arched. "Your commitment is to this family, to Norway."

"And I have always honored that commitment." My hands clenched at my sides. "But finishing my education at Hawley is part of that. It's preparing me to serve our country better."

Father sighed, pinching the bridge of his nose. "Tore, this isn't some gap year adventure. The stakes have changed."

"I know that," I said, softer now. "But I also know that Uncle

Ragnar would have wanted me to finish what I started. He always emphasized the importance of a well-rounded education, remember?"

A flicker of grief passed over my father's face at the mention of his brother. For a moment, I thought I'd gone too far. But then his shoulders sagged slightly. "One semester," he conceded. "You may finish this semester at Hawley. But after that, we reevaluate. Agreed?"

Relief washed over me. "Agreed. Thank you, Pappa."

As I turned to leave, my thoughts immediately drifted to Farron. God, how I missed him. His strong, calloused hands. The way his eyes crinkled when he laughed. Even that infuriating stubbornness of his.

I pulled out my phone, desperate to reach out, to hear his voice. But then I hesitated. What could I even say? *Sorry I disappeared. Oh, by the way, I'm a prince?*

I needed to tell him the truth, but not over the phone. It could wait until I got back. Between meetings with advisors and comforting my grieving family, I sent more messages.

> I'm sorry for disappearing. I promise I'll explain when I get back.
>
> I miss you.
>
> Farron, please let me know you're okay.
>
> I'm coming back to Hawley in a few days.

Each unanswered text felt like a punch to the gut. Was he ignoring me? Had something happened to him? The possibilities swirled in my mind, each worse than the last.

But I couldn't go back to Hawley just yet. Christmas had arrived, and with it, a new round of grief at celebrating the holidays without Uncle Ragnar. We went through the motions but our heart wasn't in it.

Then again, I'd left my heart in Ohio.

By the time my plane touched down in Ohio in early January, I was a man possessed. I barely registered the drive from the airport to campus, my heart pounding a frantic rhythm in my chest. The familiar sights of Hawley College blurred past my window, but I only had eyes for one destination: Farron's dorm.

I practically sprinted across the quad, my sneakers slipping on the damp grass. Students turned to stare, but I couldn't bring myself to care about maintaining my usual composure. All that mattered was finding Farron.

I burst into his dorm building, taking the stairs two at a time. My hand shook as I raised it to knock on his door, hesitating for a moment. What if he didn't want to see me? What if I'd ruined everything by disappearing without explanation?

But I had to know. I had to see him, to explain, to make things right. I took a deep breath and knocked, my heart in my throat as I waited for an answer.

The door swung open, and there he was. Farron's broad frame filled the doorway, his dark eyes widening in surprise as they met mine. For a moment, we stared at each other, the air thick with tension.

"Tore," he said, his voice low and guarded. "I'm sorry about your uncle."

My heart clenched at his words, a mix of grief and gratitude washing over me. "Thank you," I managed, my voice hoarse. But then it hit. My uncle. I'd only mentioned a family emergency.

"Farron, I—"

But he cut me off, his expression hardening. "Yes, I know who you really are... Your Highness."

The title hit me like a slap. The blood drained from my face as

I realized the full extent of what he was saying. He knew. Somehow, he'd discovered my true identity.

"Farron, please," I pleaded, reaching out instinctively. He flinched away from my touch, and I let my hand fall uselessly to my side. "Let me explain. I never meant to—"

"To what?" His voice was sharp with hurt and anger. "To lie? To pretend to be someone you're not?" His eyes blazed with a mix of emotions: betrayal, anger, and so much pain that my own heart broke in response.

"No, that's not... I didn't want to lie to you. I wanted to be normal, to be just Tore. I wanted you to know me, not my title."

Farron laughed bitterly. "Know you? How could I know you when everything about you was a lie?"

"Not everything," I insisted, desperation creeping into my voice. "My feelings for you, they're real. They've always been real." I stepped closer, willing him to see the truth in my eyes. "I'm so sorry, Farron. I never meant to hurt you. Please, let me explain."

I could see the conflict in his eyes, the way he wavered between anger and something softer. For a moment, I dared to hope that he might listen, that I might have a chance to make things right.

But then his jaw clenched, and the walls came up behind his eyes. "You've explained enough, Your Highness," he said, his voice cold and formal. "Now, if you'll excuse me..."

As he began to close the door, panic surged through me. I couldn't let it end like this. I couldn't lose him. "Farron, wait!" I cried. "Please, I lo—"

But the door shut in my face, cutting off my desperate declaration. I stood there, staring at the closed door, my heart shattering into a million pieces. What had I done?

I pressed my forehead against the cold wood of Farron's door, my breath coming in ragged gasps. The finality of that slamming door echoed through my body, leaving me feeling hollow and lost.

"Farron, please," I pleaded, my voice barely above a whisper. "I know I messed up. I know I hurt you. But please, give me a chance to explain."

There was no response from the other side of the door. I couldn't even hear movement. Was he standing there, as frozen as I was? Or had he walked away, leaving me talking to an empty room?

I swallowed hard, trying to push down the lump in my throat. "I never meant to lie to you. I just... I wanted you to see me. The real me. Not the prince, not the title. Just Tore."

"Fuck off, Prince Tore." Farron's voice finally came through the door, thick with emotion. "I don't want to hear your excuses."

His words were like a knife to my gut, but at least he was talking. I latched onto that tiny glimmer of hope. "They're not excuses. I know I was wrong. I should've told you the truth from the beginning. But I was scared, Farron. Scared of losing you before I even had a chance."

I heard a thud from inside the room like something being thrown against a wall. "You don't get it, do you?" Farron's voice was closer now, angrier. "You had me. You fucking *had* me, Tore. And you threw it away with your lies. We're done. Go back to your castle. This commoner's made his decision."

His words hit me like a physical blow. I had to brace myself against the doorframe to keep from stumbling. "I'm sorry," I whispered, knowing it wasn't enough but not knowing what else to say. "Please, Farron."

But there was only silence from the other side of the door.

My legs gave out, and I slid down the wall, landing hard on the floor. Tears burned in my eyes as the reality of the situation hit me. I'd lost him. I'd lost Farron. The one person who'd made me feel alive, who'd shown me a world beyond my royal duties and expectations. And it was all my fault.

I buried my face in my hands, my shoulders shaking with silent sobs. How could I have been so stupid? So selfish? I'd thought I could have it all: my royal life and Farron. But in trying to keep both, I'd lost the one thing that truly mattered.

I didn't know how long I stayed there, lost in my grief and regret. But eventually, I forced myself to stand. My legs were shaky, and my chest ached with each breath.

I'd lost the person I loved, and I had no one to blame but myself.

27

FARRON

I missed soccer.

If it had still been soccer season, maybe I wouldn't have spent so much time thinking about Tore. Hell, I wouldn't have had the time for all those useless, stupid what-ifs that now played through my brain.

Christmas had been awful, New Year's even worse, and now that school had started again and Tore was back, every day was agony. I was angry every day, all day, all the time. Hurting and pissed off and just so fucking lost that I didn't know what to do with myself.

I slammed my locker shut, the metallic clang echoing through the almost empty locker room. My jaw clenched as I grabbed my gym bag, the fabric rough against my calloused hands. To stay fit, we did sessions in the gym three times a week: a combination of strength, conditioning, and flexibility training. As usual, I'd arrived early so I wouldn't have to face Tore in the locker room.

"Dude, what's got your panties in a twist?" Colin's voice grated on my last nerve as he sauntered up, that stupid grin plastered on his face.

I shot him a glare that could melt steel. "None of your goddamn business."

"Whoa, easy tiger. Just asking." He held up his hands in mock surrender. "You've been a real ray of sunshine lately."

"Yeah, well, maybe I don't feel like dealing with your shit today." I shouldered past him, my footsteps heavy on the worn linoleum.

Colin jogged to catch up. "Come on, man. I'm trying to help."

I stopped abruptly, turning to face him. "You want to help? Then back the fuck off." The words came out harsher than I intended, but I was too wound up to care.

His eyes widened slightly, hurt flashing across his face before he masked it with indifference. "Whatever, dude."

As he walked away, guilt gnawed at my insides. I was being an asshole, but I couldn't seem to stop myself. Every time I thought about Tore, about his lies, about how easily he'd played me, rage bubbled inside me like molten lava.

Should I tell the team about Tore's true identity? So far, I seemed to be the only one who knew, though I wasn't sure if Tore had told Luke. Those two had become close friends, but other than sending me dark looks every now and then, Luke hadn't said a word to me about it.

It would be so easy to expose Tore, to watch his carefully constructed facade crumble. But every time I considered it, something held me back. Despite everything, despite the anger and the hurt, I still cared about him. And that realization pissed me off more than anything else.

As if on cue, Tore stepped into the gym, looking all kinds of perfect in his running shorts and tank, though his face was pale and he had bags under his eyes. My heart did a traitorous flip, desire warring with anger. I hated how easily he affected me, how even now, after everything, I still wanted him.

My stomach dropped as Tore's eyes met mine across the gym. For a moment, I saw a flicker of something—Regret? Longing?—before he looked away and headed to the rowing machine.

I tried to focus on the burn in my muscles as I pushed myself harder and harder on the stair climber. But my gaze kept drifting to Tore, to the graceful way he moved, to the determined set of his jaw.

Memories of our time together flooded my mind: the heat of his skin against mine, the soft sighs he'd make when I kissed that spot behind his ear, the way he'd look at me like I was his whole world. I gritted my teeth, forcing the thoughts away. It had all been a lie, hadn't it?

As practice wore on, the tension between us grew thicker. Every time we came near each other, electricity crackled in the air. I could feel his eyes on me, burning into my back, but I refused to give him the satisfaction of looking. I was a mess of conflicting emotions. Anger, desire, hurt, and longing all tangled together in my chest, threatening to suffocate me.

Finally, Tore headed toward the locker room, his shoulders slumped. Part of me wanted to follow him, to confront him, to demand answers. But another part, the part that was still raw and bleeding from his betrayal, held me back. I wasn't ready to face him, to hear his excuses or explanations.

So, instead, I stayed behind in the gym, punishing myself with another round of burpees, feeling more alone than I ever had in my life.

When I was done, I showered and dressed, then headed outside. A thin blanket of snow covered the ground with more lazily drifting down, and my boots left big footprints. Then, I came to a full stop. Tore was sitting on a bench, head in his hands, looking utterly defeated as he ignored the falling snow. The sight sent a pang through my chest.

The Prince and the Player

I hesitated, warring with myself. Part of me wanted to go to him, to comfort him, but the anger still simmering beneath the surface held me back. As I stood there, frozen in indecision, Tore looked up and our eyes met.

For a moment, time seemed to stand still. His blue eyes, usually so bright and full of life, were dull with sorrow and guilt. It was like looking into a mirror of my own pain.

He got up, stepping in my way. "Farron, I—"

"Don't." I cut him off, my tone harsher than intended. "Just... don't."

I pushed past him, my shoulder brushing against his. Even that brief contact sent a jolt through my body, and I cursed internally at my traitorous reactions.

Back in my dorm, I couldn't shake the image of Tore's sad eyes from my mind. Why did it matter to me that he was hurting too? He was the one who had lied, who had betrayed my trust.

***

Spring break arrived, but I'd opted to stay. With everyone gone, I'd be able to get a lot of uninterrupted studying in, and I'd requested extra shifts at Walmart. My mom must've seen through my feeble excuses as to why I wasn't coming home as usual, but she hadn't pushed.

"You sure you don't wanna come to Florida with us?" Colin asked, tossing clothes into his suitcase.

I shook my head, not looking up from my textbook. "Nah, man. Gotta work."

"All work and no play makes Farron a dull boy," he sing-songed, dodging the pillow I chucked at his head.

"Fuck off," I growled, but there was no real heat behind it.

The truth was, I needed the distraction, needed something to keep my mind off Tore and the ache that had taken up permanent residence in my chest.

As the campus emptied out, I threw myself into work and studying. Stocking shelves, running the register, memorizing psychology terms—anything to keep my thoughts from wandering to a certain blond midfielder with sad blue eyes. Tore was going home with Luke, I heard through the grapevine, so at least I wouldn't run into him.

But no matter how hard I tried, I couldn't escape him completely. He haunted my dreams, leaving me restless and frustrated. More than once, I woke up achingly hard, the ghost of his touch still lingering on my skin. The thought of Tore's smile, the way his eyes would light up when he talked about something he loved, sent a pang through my chest. God, I missed him.

On the last day of spring break, I was walking across campus on my way back from a study session in the library when I saw Luke. Out of habit, I always checked out Tore's building when I walked past, and I caught Luke walking in, a weekend bag slung over his shoulder. Did that mean Tore was back too?

Before I knew it, I found myself standing outside Tore's dorm room, my hand poised to knock. I don't know what compelled me to come here. Closure? A masochistic need to torture myself further?

I rapped my knuckles against the wood before I could talk myself out of it. My heart pounded as I waited, equal parts hoping and dreading that he'd answer. What would I even say if he did? *I miss you even though I hate you? I can't stop thinking about you even though you betrayed me?*

Luke opened the door, his face lighting up in surprise when he saw me. "Farron? Everything okay?"

I jammed my hands into my pockets. "Is Tore here?"

Luke's expression softened, and something in his eyes made

my stomach clench. "No, he's not. Farron, there's something you should know..."

My chest tightened as Luke gestured for me to come in, his eyes full of sympathy. "What is it?" I asked, trying to keep my voice steady.

Luke sighed. "Tore's gone, man. He left for good."

The words hit me like a punch to the gut. "What do you mean, gone? He can't just... leave."

"He did," Luke said softly. "Packed up most of his stuff and took off. Said he wasn't coming back after spring break."

I stumbled backward, my legs hitting Tore's bed. I sank down onto it, my mind reeling. "But why?"

Luke shrugged, leaning against the desk. "He didn't say much, but..." He hesitated, watching me carefully. "He's heartbroken over your breakup. I don't know what happened between you two, but he's hurting. I think he went home to get away from it. From you."

I swallowed hard, memories of our last encounter flashing through my mind. The hurt in Tore's eyes, the tremor in his voice. Fuck.

"And he's not coming back next semester?"

Luke shook his head. "Nah, man. He's done here."

I nodded numbly, my eyes burning. The reality of it all was slowly sinking in. Tore was gone. Really gone. And I'd never even gotten the chance to...

To what? Apologize? Make things right? The thought of never seeing him again, never hearing his stupid British expressions or watching him light up when talking about books... It felt like someone had ripped a hole in my chest.

It made no sense because we'd already been broken up, but somehow, the finality of it made it a thousand times worse. As long as he'd been here, I'd had the option of seeing him, talking to him. Now that possibility was gone, and I was left with nothing but memories... and regret.

"You okay, dude?" Luke's voice broke through my spiraling thoughts.

I looked up, realizing my cheeks were wet. Hastily, I wiped at my face. "Yeah. It's nothing."

Luke didn't look convinced, but he didn't push it. "Listen, if you want to talk or anything..."

"Thanks." I rose abruptly. "I should go. Thanks for... you know."

I bolted from the room, ignoring Luke's concerned call after me. I needed to get out of there, away from Tore's lingering presence and the crushing weight of what I'd lost.

I stumbled out of the dorm building, the cool spring air hitting my face like a slap. My feet carried me aimlessly across campus, past the soccer field where Tore and I had spent countless hours training together. The memory of his lithe form darting across the grass, his blond hair catching the sunlight, and the brilliance of his smile every time he scored made my chest ache.

"Fuck," I muttered, kicking at a pebble on the path. "Fuck, fuck, fuck. What have I done?"

The realization hit me like a freight train. I'd pushed away the one person who'd seen past my tough exterior, who'd challenged me and made me laugh and made me feel things I'd never felt before.

"I'm in love with him," I said aloud, the words tasting foreign on my tongue. "I'm in fucking love with Tore."

The admission brought no relief, only a deep, gnawing ache. I'd fallen for a guy—a prince, no less—and I'd been too stubborn, too afraid to admit it. Now he was gone, thinking I hated him.

"I'm such a goddamn idiot." I sat down on a bench and groaned, burying my face in my hands.

I sat there for what felt like hours, replaying every moment with Tore in my head. The way he'd look at me when he thought I wasn't paying attention. The electricity I'd felt every time we touched. How had I been so blind?

As the sun began to set, casting long shadows across the campus, I made a decision. I couldn't let it end like this. I had to find Tore and tell him how I felt, even if it was too late.

I pushed myself off the bench, my muscles stiff from sitting for so long and my body like an icicle since it really wasn't that warm yet. The campus was quiet as I made my way back to my dorm. A lot of students were still gone for spring break. Each step felt heavy, weighed down by regret and the enormity of what I had to do.

As I entered my room, I caught sight of myself in the mirror. My hair was a mess, I had dark circles under my eyes, and I was pale as a ghost. I looked like shit, but that was the least of my concerns.

I grabbed my phone, hesitating for a moment before pulling up Tore's contact. My thumb hovered over the call button, but I couldn't bring myself to press it. What would I even say? *Hey, sorry I was a complete asshole. By the way, I think I'm in love with you.*

Nope, that wouldn't work. I tossed the phone onto my bed. I needed a plan for how to fix this mess I'd created. And I'd better come up with something spectacular too, if I wanted him to forgive me.

I froze, an idea forming. The phone wouldn't do. I needed to see him in person. I had to travel to Norway.

Fuck, this was crazy. I had no idea where in Norway Tore lived —a palace?—no money for a plane ticket, and no guarantee he'd even want to see me. But for the first time in weeks, I felt a spark of hope.

28

TORE

I stared out the floor-to-ceiling windows of my bedroom, watching raindrops race down the glass panes. The lush gardens of the royal estate stretched before me, a sea of green dotted with colorful spring blooms, appearing early this year due to an unseasonably warm spring. Inside, luxurious furnishings surrounded me: antique mahogany furniture, silk drapes, priceless artwork. But none of it brought me comfort.

My fingers traced the cool surface of my phone screen, hovering over Farron's name in my contacts. I ached to hear his voice, to see his crooked grin. But the memory of our last conversation, of the hurt and anger in his eyes, made my chest tighten painfully.

A soft knock at the door roused me from my brooding. "Come in," I called, my voice hoarse from disuse.

My mother glided into the room, elegant as always in a pale-blue dress. Her eyes softened with concern as she took in my disheveled appearance. "*Oh, min kjære,*" she murmured, sitting beside me on the window seat. "You look terrible."

I attempted a smile, but it felt more like a grimace. "*Takk*, Mamma. Just the boost my ego needed."

She smoothed my messy hair, her touch gentle. "Talk to me, Tore. What's troubling you?"

For a moment, I considered brushing her off with a vague excuse. But the weight of my secrets felt unbearable. "I've made a proper mess of things," I admitted, my voice barely above a whisper.

"How so?" she prompted, her hand rubbing soothing circles on my back.

I took a shaky breath. "There's... someone. At Hawley. Someone I care about very much."

Understanding dawned in her eyes. "Ah, I see."

"It's a boy, Mamma. And I'm in love with him. Really in love."

She quirked one well-groomed eyebrow. "A boy? Farron Carey, perhaps?"

I gasped. "How did you know?"

"You're not exactly subtle, Tore. You've been talking about him nonstop since you got back, and every time you do, your eyes light up... only to turn sad again. I told your father to expect your coming out. You know him. He doesn't handle unexpected news very well, and what with him still grieving Ragnar, I figured now wasn't a good time for another shock."

"I'm sorry, Mamma."

"Sorry for what? For being yourself? For falling in love?"

I made a vague gesture. "I know it would've been easier if I'd fallen for a girl."

"Easier for whom?"

"For you and Dad. For the country."

She put a strong hand on my shoulder. "You can't choose who you love, *min sønn*. But tell me what happened."

"He didn't know who I was until he saw the news about Uncle

Ragnar and my picture popped up. He's furious that I lied to him. And he's right. I kept it from him, from everyone. And now..." My voice cracked. "Now I've lost him."

"Oh, child." She pulled me into a warm embrace, and I allowed myself to sink into her comfort. "Love is never easy, especially for those in our position. But if this boy is truly important to you, you must fight for him."

I pulled back, wiping my eyes. "But how? He won't even speak to me now. And I feel so guilty for lying to everyone. I loved playing for the Hawley Hawks, Mamma, being part of a team again."

"Then why did you come home?"

"It was too much, seeing him every time. It hurt too much. Plus, Pappa told me to."

Her eyes narrowed. "Your father said you needed to come home?"

"Yes. He said the family needed me, that the country needed me."

She took a deep breath, then cupped my face in her hands, her gaze earnest. "Your father is wrong, Tore. I know it's harder for him to see since he's known nothing but a life of duty, but the times have changed. Your happiness matters more than anything else. You don't have to sacrifice yourself to be a prince."

"No?"

"No. Also, Ingrid is pregnant, so soon, you'll be fourth in line again. It's not been officially announced yet because we're waiting for her to pass the fourteen-week mark, but once we do, that's one more step away for you."

Ingrid was my cousin Gustav's wife, now the queen of Norway. "That's wonderful news."

My mother smiled. "She's only twenty-six, Tore. I expect her to have at least two more kids, and every single one will mean more freedom for you."

I breathed a sigh of relief. "That makes me feel so much better."

"As for your boy..."

"Any advice?"

"Be yourself. Allow him and your friends there to see the real you. Open your heart to him. And if he's worth it, he'll understand. If he can't accept all of you, then he's not the one for you."

I nodded, feeling a small spark of hope ignite in my chest. "Thank you, Mamma. I... I'll try."

She pressed a kiss to my forehead. "That's my boy. No worries, I will talk to your father and sort things out with him." She clicked her tongue. "That man worries too much. Now, come downstairs for dinner in an hour and eat with us, okay? You're far too thin."

I managed a genuine chuckle this time. "*Ja*, Mamma."

As she left, a resolve washed over me. My mother was right. I needed to be honest, not just with Farron, but with everyone. The Hawley Hawks deserved to know the truth about who I really was.

I grabbed my phone, my fingers trembling slightly as I opened our team group chat. For a moment, I hesitated, the cursor blinking accusingly at me. What if they hated me for lying? What if they thought I was some entitled, rich kid playing at being normal like Farron did? But even then, I owed them the truth.

I opened the group chat and took a deep breath, then started a video recording.

"Hey, everyone. Maybe you've heard by now that I have left Hawley College and I'm back home in Norway. My time with you has been one of the best times of my life, and I owe you all so much for making me feel part of your team.

"Because of that, I need to tell you something. My real name is

Tore Haakon Anders von Glücksburg... and I'm a prince. My cousin Gustav has just become the king of Norway after my uncle passed away unexpectedly. I kept this from you all because I wanted to be treated like a normal student, a normal teammate. I was afraid that if you knew, you'd see me differently. That you wouldn't want me on the team or that you'd only befriend me because of my title.

"I realize now that wasn't fair to any of you. You've all become such important parts of my life, and you deserve to know the real me. I'm still the same Tore who loves literature, struggles with American idioms, and occasionally scores a decent goal. I just... have a slightly more complicated family tree.

"I understand if you're angry or feel betrayed. I'm truly sorry for not being upfront from the beginning. I hope you can forgive me and that this doesn't change things between us. You guys mean the world to me, and I'd hate to lose your friendship over this. If you have any questions, I'm here to answer them honestly. No more secrets."

I pressed send before I could second-guess myself, and a mix of relief and anxiety washed over me. The truth was out there now, for better or worse. All I could do was wait and hope my teammates—my friends—would understand. And maybe Farron would see it and change his mind?

I flopped back onto my plush bed, staring up at the ornate ceiling of my bedroom. The weight of the secret I'd carried for so long had been lifted, but in its place settled a gnawing ache in my chest. Farron's face flashed in my mind, his dark eyes and cocky grin making my heart clench.

My phone buzzed, and I scrambled to check it, hoping against hope it might be Farron. Instead, I saw a string of notifications from the team. My stomach churned as I opened the group chat.

> Holy shit, dude!
>
> A prince? For real?
>
> This explains so much...

The messages kept coming, a mix of shock, confusion, and... acceptance? A small smile tugged at my lips, but it faded quickly. There was one person whose reaction I cared about most, and his name was conspicuously absent from the chat.

Desperate for a distraction, I called Andor. We talked for a while, Andor trying his best to cheer me up with his wild college stories and bad jokes, but even his usually infectious optimism couldn't penetrate the cloud of melancholy that had settled over me. I appreciated his efforts, but nothing could fill the Farron-shaped hole in my heart.

Dinner was a quiet affair with my mom, Astrid, and me. Anna, my other sister, was at a friend's, and my dad had a meeting with Gustav. My mom didn't mention anything we had discussed, which I was grateful for, and dinner was a good distraction. No phones were allowed at the dinner table, so I'd left mine in my room.

After dinner, Astrid persuaded me to watch a couple of episodes of *Ted Lasso* with her, so by the time I went back to my room, it was almost ten. My phone was blowing up with notifications from the team chat, and I smiled as I scrolled. Then I froze.

A Snapchat notification glowed on the screen, and I nearly dropped the device when I saw the name: *Farron*.

With trembling fingers, I opened the app. His message was simple, yet it sent my mind reeling:

> Can we talk? Call me when you can.

I stared at the words, reading them over and over. My pulse raced, hope and fear warring within me. Did he want to reconcile, or was this a final goodbye?

Out of habit, I checked his location. He'd never turned that off, so I could still see where he was, which was usually one of three locations: his dorm, the gym, or Walmart. I should probably feel guilty about this since it could be seen as invasive, but if he hadn't wanted me to see, he should've turned it off, right?

The map loaded, and I searched for Farron's Bitmoji. My eyes widened in disbelief as the map zoomed in on a familiar city: Oslo. Farron's Bitmoji stood proudly in the center of the Norwegian capital, right next to a hotel icon.

He was here. In Oslo.

I blinked hard, certain I must be hallucinating. But when I looked again, there he was, his little cartoon avatar grinning at me from the screen. My mind raced with questions. *How? Why?*

My heart hammered against my ribs, a mix of excitement and anxiety coursing through my veins. Farron was here, in my city, mere kilometers away. The realization hit me like a tidal wave, leaving me breathless and dizzy. Surely, he hadn't traveled all this way to end things once and for all. If he was here, if he wanted to talk, that meant there was still hope.

I paced my room, my fingers hovering over the call button. Should I ring him now? It was late, but he had asked me to call. What if he was jet-lagged and already asleep? Or worse, what if he answered and I made a complete fool of myself?

Bloody hell, I was overthinking this. But the weight of the situation bore down on me. This wasn't a casual call to a teammate or a friend. This was Farron, the man who had turned my world upside down, who had made me question everything I thought I knew about myself. And now he was here, in Oslo, presumably for me.

I needed to see him. In person.

29

FARRON

I stared at my phone for what felt like the hundredth time, willing a message from Tore to appear. The screen remained stubbornly blank, however. It had been two hours since I'd messaged him from the Oslo Gardermoen airport, a name I hadn't even attempted to pronounce.

With a frustrated groan, I tossed the device onto the hotel nightstand and flopped back onto the plush king-size bed. My eyes were gritty from lack of sleep, and my body ached from being crammed into tiny airplane seats for way too many hours. I'd left Hawley yesterday afternoon, changing planes in Charlotte before the long haul on a red-eye to London Heathrow. Then, yet another layover, and now here I was in Oslo, chasing after a guy I'd pushed away.

It had been the craziest day of my life. What the hell was I thinking? I'd blown well over a thousand dollars of my savings on a last-minute ticket to Norway, not even thinking about the fact that I might need a visa until I'd landed in Oslo. Luckily, US citizens didn't need one. Phew.

But once I was here, I hadn't known what to do. It wasn't like I could knock on the front door of the mansion he lived in—I'd seen pictures online, and it was every bit as massive as I had imagined—and ask to see him. He might not have Secret Service-level protection, but I highly doubted they let just anyone walk in from the streets.

I rubbed my eyes, trying to fight off the exhaustion. The rational part of my brain knew I should shower and try to adjust to the time difference, but I couldn't bring myself to move. Not until I heard from Tore. Despite my best efforts, I felt myself drifting off. The last coherent thought I had was of Tore's blue eyes and gentle smile...

A loud knocking jolted me awake. I sat up with a start, my heart pounding as I tried to get my bearings. Where the hell was I? The unfamiliar room swam into focus as memories of my impulsive trip flooded back. I'd fallen asleep on the bed, still fully dressed.

"Shit," I croaked, my voice rough with sleep. "Coming!"

I stumbled out of bed, nearly face-planting as my foot caught on a rug. The knocking came again, more insistent this time. I blinked rapidly, trying to clear the fog from my brain as I hurried toward the door. My bare feet sank into the plush carpet with each step.

Who the hell could it be at this hour? And what time was it anyway? I had no idea how long I'd been out.

I reached for the doorknob, stifling a yawn, then swung the door open. My jaw dropped. Standing in the hallway, looking as perfect and put-together as ever, was Tore. For a split second, we stared at each other. Then something inside me snapped. Without thinking, I grabbed his arm and yanked him into the room, slamming the door behind us.

"Farron, what—"

I cut him off, pushing him against the wall and fusing my lips to his. The kiss was desperate, hungry. All the longing and frustration I'd been bottling up poured out as I pressed my body against his. Tore tensed for a moment, then melted into me with a soft moan that sent shivers down my spine.

His lips were even softer than I'd remembered, and he tasted faintly of mint. I deepened the kiss, one hand tangling in his silky blond hair while the other gripped his hip. Tore's arms wrapped around me, pulling me even closer.

"Fuck," I breathed when we finally broke apart for air. My heart was racing, and I could feel Tore's rapid pulse beneath my fingertips, where they rested on his neck.

"I... I must say, I wasn't expecting quite such a warm welcome," Tore said, his voice breathy and accent thicker than usual. His cheeks were flushed, blue eyes dark with desire.

I couldn't help but laugh, resting my forehead against his. "Yeah, well, I wasn't exactly planning on jumping you the second I saw you. But damn, Tore. I've missed you."

I stepped back, suddenly aware of how much I'd jumped the gun here. My body ached at the loss of contact, but I needed to catch my breath and process what was happening. Tore stood there, looking disheveled and confused, his usually immaculate hair mussed from my fingers. "Not that I'm complaining, Farron, but what on earth are you doing in Oslo?"

"I, uh..." I ran a hand through my hair, suddenly feeling foolish. "I came to find you. To talk to you. Shit, I don't even know what I was thinking."

Tore's eyes widened. "You really flew all the way to Norway for me?"

I nodded, feeling heat creep up my neck. "Yeah. Look, I... I'm sorry, okay? I've been a stubborn asshole. I shouldn't have shut you out like that."

"Farron, I—"

"No, let me finish." I needed to get this off my chest before I lost the courage. "I missed you, Tore. I missed you so much. I tried to convince myself I didn't, but... Fuck, I couldn't stop thinking about you. But somehow, I thought there would be time, until Luke told me you'd left for good. And I realized I should've given you a chance to explain. I freaked out and pushed you away."

Tore's expression softened, and he took a step toward me. "I missed you too, Farron. More than I thought possible."

His admission made my heart race. I reached out, taking his hand in mine. "And I'm sorry I judged you based on your wealth without really knowing you. That wasn't fair."

Tore's eyes softened, his hand reaching up to cup my cheek. "Farron, you don't need to—"

"No, I do," I insisted, leaning into his touch. "I've always had this chip on my shoulder about rich people, and I was judging you based on your background from the moment we met."

"And you didn't even know all of it..."

I chuckled, shaking my head. "Be glad because I probably never would've even given you a chance, and I would've missed out on so much. Your background doesn't define you, and I was wrong to think it did. You're disciplined, hardworking, you give your all for the team, and you're generous. The thing is, I've realized it's not about the money. It's about who you are as a person. And you, Tore Haakon von whatever-the-hell-your-last-name-is, are pretty damn amazing."

Tore's eyes widened slightly, a faint blush coloring his cheeks. "Glücksburg," he murmured.

"What?"

"My last name. It's von Glücksburg."

I rolled my eyes. "As if I even stand a chance at pronouncing that correctly. Anyway, the point is, I'm sorry for being such an ass."

"Thank you. That means the world to me."

"Can we start over?"

Tore's expression shifted, guilt and remorse evident in his blue eyes. He squeezed my hand, his touch sending a familiar jolt through my body. "I'm the one who should be apologizing. I lied to you about who I was, and that was inexcusable. I'm truly sorry."

I swallowed hard, feeling the weight of his words. "Why did you do it?"

Tore sighed. "I so desperately wanted to be normal for once. To not be treated differently because of my royal background. I had to beg my parents and uncle to let me go undercover for a year and attend Hawley. It was my one chance to just be me. Not Prince Tore, not part of the royal family. Just Tore."

His vulnerability struck me. I'd never considered how isolating his position might be. "I get that, but—"

"No, you're right to be upset," Tore interrupted, his eyes locked on mine. "I should've been honest with you, especially after..." He made a vague gesture.

"Especially after what?" I teased him.

"After we became more than teammates."

"You mean after we had sex."

He looked away. "Was that all it was, sex?"

I tugged on his hand until he met my eyes again. "If it had been about sex, do you really think I would've flown halfway across the world for you?"

Relief washed over Tore's face, and before I knew it, we were kissing again. This time it was slower, more deliberate. I poured all my forgiveness into that kiss, my hands cupping his face as I drew him closer. Tore's arms wrapped around my waist, holding me tight as if afraid I might disappear.

When we finally broke apart, both breathless, I couldn't help but grin. "So, Your Highness, huh?"

Tore groaned, burying his face in my neck. "Please, don't start with that nonsense."

I laughed, the tension from the past weeks finally dissipating. "Hey, at least I didn't bow."

"Thank goodness for small favors."

I caressed his cheek. "I'm glad you disclosed the truth to the team. They took it pretty well."

He nodded. "I owed them that much, and yes, they did. Much better than I had expected."

"Yeah, I was the only asshole. I know."

"That's not what I—"

"But I was. Probably because..." Hell, how did I even put into words what I felt for him?

He tilted his head. "Why'd you fly here? You could've simply messaged me."

I winced. "I wasn't sure if that would be enough. Figured you'd need a bigger effort on my part to convince you I meant it."

"You mean your apology? I assure you that a message would've been enough. I would've accepted that."

"No, not that. Well, yeah, to start with, but mostly because..." I took a deep breath, suddenly feeling vulnerable. "I wanted to tell you in person that your wealth, your title... They don't matter. Not when it comes to how I feel about you."

Tore let out a soft gasp. "And how do you feel about me?"

I was standing on the edge of a cliff, teetering between fear and exhilaration. And then, without really thinking about it, I took the plunge. "I'm in love with you. It makes no sense, and at the same time, it's the most natural thing ever. You make me happy. Being with you makes me happy. You make me want to be a better man, you know? I smile more, I laugh more, I'm..." I threw up my hands in a helpless gesture. "I'm happy. Somehow, you get me. You see me like no one else does, and you awaken parts of me no one else can. Those weeks without you were horrible, and all I could think about was you. There's probably some romantic, poetic way to tell you all this, but I've been up for well over twenty-four hours and I'm exhausted yet so happy to see you, to be with you. That's all I want, is to be with you. I love you."

After that acute verbal diarrhea, I closed my mouth again, my cheeks heating.

Tore's blue eyes bored into mine, filled with an intensity that took my breath away. "I love you too, Farron," he whispered, his voice thick with emotion. "God help me, but I do."

Without another word, Tore took my mouth again in a deep kiss, reigniting the passion that had been simmering between us. I kissed him back with equal fervor, my hands sliding under his shirt to feel the warmth of his skin. Our tongues danced as we pressed our bodies closer, desperate to eliminate any space between us.

As we continued to kiss, an overwhelming wave of exhaustion washed over me. The adrenaline that had kept me going was wearing off, and my eyes felt increasingly heavy.

"Tore," I mumbled against his lips, fighting to keep my eyes open. "I'm sorry, but I'm so damn tired."

Tore pulled back, concern etched on his face. "Oh, Farron. I completely forgot about your long journey. You must be knackered."

I tried to protest, not wanting to ruin the moment, but a massive yawn escaped me instead.

Tore chuckled softly. "Let's get you to bed."

He helped me undress until I was left in my boxer shorts, my limbs feeling like lead. I crashed onto the bed and somehow managed to crawl under the blankets. As soon as I put my head on the pillow, my eyes drifted shut.

"Sleep, *min kjære*," he whispered, pressing a gentle kiss to my forehead. "I'll be here when you wake up."

Tore's arms wrapped around me, pulling me close. I nestled into his warmth, breathing in his familiar scent. My last coherent thought before succumbing to sleep was how right this felt: being here, in Tore's arms, our bodies intertwined.

It felt like coming home.

30

TORE

Watching someone else sleep was perhaps a tad creepy, but I couldn't help myself. He'd still been asleep when I woke up, not even stirring when I got up to relieve myself, then snuck back into bed. He must've been exhausted.

And now I lay in bed on my side, staring at him. I'd missed him so much that I had to take my fill of him. I suspected this deep incredulity that he was here and that we were together for real now would last a while. I still couldn't believe this incredible man was mine, that he'd chosen me despite our differences.

He loved me.

Farron loved me.

And gods, I was in love with him. Seeing him again had only confirmed that. I was watching him sleep, for goodness' sake. That was about as infatuated as a person could get, no?

I couldn't resist tracing my fingers along the defined muscles of his chest, marveling at how perfectly he fit against me. His eyes fluttered open, a slow smile spreading across his face.

"Good morning," I murmured, leaning in to capture his lips in a tender kiss—morning breath be damned.

Farron's strong arms wrapped around me, pulling me closer as he deepened the kiss. His tongue teased mine, igniting a familiar heat in my core. I tangled my fingers in his dark hair, relishing the silky strands against my skin.

"Mmm, now that's a wake-up call." Farron chuckled, his voice still husky with sleep. His calloused hands roamed my back, leaving trails of fire in their wake.

I peppered kisses along his jaw, savoring the slight scratch of stubble. "I've missed this," I breathed against his neck. "Missed you."

Farron tilted my chin, his brown eyes intense as they met mine. "Me too, Tore. These past few weeks apart were torture."

My heart swelled at his words. "Same."

As much as I wanted to stay cooped up with Farron all day, we were on a bit of a schedule, unfortunately. With a reluctant sigh, I pulled back slightly. "As much as I'd love to keep you in this bed forever, there's somewhere I'd like to take you today."

Farron quirked an eyebrow. "Oh? And where might that be?"

I took a deep breath, suddenly feeling nervous. "Well, I was hoping you might like to meet my parents. They're eager to meet the man who's stolen my heart."

I had texted them yesterday after Farron had fallen asleep, letting them know where I was. Not that they wouldn't know otherwise, as my phone had a tracker on it, but still. Common courtesy and all that.

They'd invited us over for breakfast, which meant we'd need to leave in less than half an hour. Not ideal, but since both had obligations throughout the rest of the day, it was the only opportunity we'd get.

Farron's eyes widened, a flicker of uncertainty crossing his face. "Your parents?"

I cupped his cheek, wanting to soothe his apprehension. "I promise they'll adore you as much as I do."

Farron bit his lip, a habit I found utterly endearing. "Are you sure? I mean, I'm not exactly..." He gestured vaguely at himself.

"You're exactly who I want," I assured him firmly. "My parents will see that. They just want me to be happy, and you make me happier than I've ever been."

A slow smile spread across Farron's face, chasing away the last traces of doubt. "Well, when you put it like that... I guess I better make myself presentable to meet royalty, huh?"

I laughed, pulling him in for another kiss. "You're perfect as you are. Though perhaps we should both shower first."

Farron's eyes gleamed mischievously. "Care to join me? Conserve water and all that."

As if I could resist such a tempting offer. I let Farron lead me to the bathroom, my heart light with anticipation for the day ahead.

***

By the time we approached the grand oak doors of my family's Oslo residence, Farron's nerves had returned in full force. I took his hand and threaded our fingers together in a quiet show of support.

"Ready?" I asked, glancing at Farron. His face was a mix of awe and trepidation as he took in the imposing facade.

"As I'll ever be."

I gave his hand a reassuring squeeze before pushing open the door.

The foyer was awash in morning light, the crystal chandelier casting rainbow reflections across the marble floor. Farron did a sharp intake of breath, and I felt a twinge of self-consciousness. It was easy to forget how overwhelming this could all seem.

"Mamma? Pappa?" I called out, my voice echoing slightly. "We're here!"

The sound of footsteps from the direction of the dining room sent my heart racing. I glanced at Farron, noting how his free hand trembled slightly at his side. I wanted nothing more than to wrap him in my arms to shield him from any discomfort, but this was a moment we had to face head-on.

My parents appeared in the doorway, followed closely by my sisters. The moment seemed to stretch, filled with an electric anticipation that made the air feel thick.

"Mamma, Pappa," I began, my voice steadier than I felt, "this is Farron. Farron, these are my parents, Per and Sonja, and my sisters, Anna and Astrid."

Farron stepped forward, his hand outstretched. I could see the slight tremor in his fingers as he introduced himself. "It's an honor to meet you, Your Royal Highnesses."

I hadn't expected him to know how to address them, and if I'd had more time to prepare him, I certainly would've discussed protocol with him, but he must've looked it up. Bonus points for him, and my parents appreciated it, too, judging by the quick look they shared.

My father clasped Farron's hand. "It's a pleasure to meet you, Farron," he replied warmly. "We've heard so much about you from Tore."

The tension in Farron's shoulders eased slightly, and relief filled me. As my mother stepped forward to greet him, I caught Anna's eye. She gave me a subtle thumbs-up, and I had to bite back a grin.

"Shall we move to the dining room?" my mother suggested. "Breakfast is ready, and I'm sure you boys are hungry."

As we followed my family into the dining room, I leaned close to Farron. "See? Nothing to worry about," I whispered.

He shot me a look that was equal parts relief and lingering nervousness. "Easy for you to say, Your Highness," he muttered back, but there was a hint of a smile playing at the corners of his mouth.

Conversation flowed easily as we enjoyed delicious croissants and pastries—which I was certain my mom had made in Farron's honor, as we didn't usually eat those—and, of course, our standard bread and *brunost*.

Farron frowned as he took a bite, looking pensive as if he was trying to figure out what he was eating. "It's caramel," I told him. "That flavor in the cheese you can't figure out? It's from milk sugars caramelized during the production process."

"Caramel cheese..." His face filled with wonder. "It's delicious."

"It's something Norway is known for, as well as for our salmon."

"I've never had salmon," Farron said. The simultaneous gasp of both my sisters had him looking up, his cheeks coloring.

"Salmon is expensive in America," I said, coming to his aid. I wasn't gonna spill details about his background to my sisters, but I did want them to understand where he was coming from. "Especially in landlocked states like Ohio, where it all has to be flown in from Alaska or Scotland or from salmon farms across the world. Most of what you see is pre-frozen, and what they sell as fresh salmon is, in fact, a few days old by then. Fish, in general, is not a staple of the American diet."

"That's interesting," my mother said, though I was certain I wasn't telling her anything new. "I suppose we're spoiled with having such easy access to fresh, high-quality salmon."

"I want to learn about Norway," Farron said, a slight tremor in his voice. "I know me being a foreigner isn't ideal, especially an American who knows next to nothing about the world outside the US. I haven't traveled much and the only reason I had a passport is because I wanted to be ready to travel in case I had an opportunity to play soccer somewhere. So I'm well aware I know nothing about your country other than what Tore has told me, but I want to learn. I'll do whatever is necessary to be worthy of him."

My eyes grew moist as my heart filled to capacity with love for him.

"We truly appreciate that," my mom said. "We know this is far from an easy world to step into. Our Tore comes with a lot of baggage. Baggage we value, but baggage, nonetheless. And please know that we will do whatever we can to help you adjust. We want you to feel welcome, both in our family and in our country."

Leave it to my mom to say the perfect thing at the perfect time. I'd never appreciated her genuine kindness and warmth more.

Farron's shoulders relaxed, the last of his tension melting away. "Thank you," he said, his voice thick with emotion. "I can't tell you how much that means to me. And how much Tore means to me."

Anna piped up, her eyes twinkling. "Does this mean we get to embarrass Tore with childhood stories now?"

I groaned but couldn't keep the smile off my face. "Please, have mercy."

As laughter filled the room, a warmth spread through my chest. This was more than I could have hoped for, my family accepting and welcoming Farron with open arms.

As the laughter died, I noticed my parents exchange a meaningful glance. My father cleared his throat, his expression growing more serious. "As thrilled as we are for you both—and we truly are—we do think it's best if you keep your relationship private for now. At least until we can develop a proper press strategy."

I blinked, processing his words. It made sense, of course. The media would have a field day with this news. But still, the idea of hiding our love didn't sit well with me.

"We're not ashamed of you," my father added quickly, reading the expression on my face. "It's more that the public reaction can be unpredictable. Not so much the Norwegian press but the international tabloids. We want to protect you both and ensure you're ready for that."

Farron's thumb rubbed small circles on my hand, a gesture of comfort. I glanced at him, and he wasn't upset, which was a relief. "I would appreciate some advice and training in how to handle all that, as I have zero experience with it," he said. "The last thing I want is to embarrass Tore or you or cause some kind of incident."

My mother nodded, relief evident in her features. "Exactly. We need time to prepare you both and help you figure out a strategy. That way, we can also control the narrative."

I took a deep breath, feeling torn. Part of me wanted to shout our love from the rooftops, consequences be damned. But I knew the weight of my position, the responsibilities that came with it. "We understand. We'll do our best to keep things under wraps for now."

Farron squeezed my hand. "We can do this, Tore," he murmured, his eyes never leaving mine. "It's not forever, right?"

I nodded, feeling a surge of love and gratitude for this man willing to navigate the complexities of royal life for me. "Just until we're ready."

"I'm glad we're on the same page," my father said. "I will reach out to Hans, our press secretary, today and ask him to sit down with you and start working on a strategy."

"So," I said, trying to lighten the mood, "about those embarrassing childhood stories..."

After breakfast, my father had to head out for an appointment with the prime minister, and my mom was taking Anna and Astrid for a dress fitting for a wedding they were attending, so Farron and I were on our own. Instead of giving him a tour of the house, which would only drive home the differences between us, I suggested we head into town to do some sightseeing. Farron was immediately game, even when I stressed we couldn't hold hands or show affection in case someone recognized me despite me disguising myself somewhat.

I adjusted the oversized sunglasses on my face, tugging the brim of my baseball cap lower. "Ready for your grand tour of Oslo?"

Farron's eyes sparkled with excitement. "Lead the way."

I had our driver drop us off outside the city center so no one would notice, and then we walked to Karl Johans gate, the main street of Oslo. The spring air buzzed with energy, tourists and locals alike bustling about. A thrill coursed through me at the thought of exploring my city with the man I loved, even if I couldn't show it.

"This street's named after King Carl III Johan," I explained, gesturing at the wide pedestrian thoroughfare. "He was actually born Jean Baptiste Bernadotte in France. Quite the character, as he started as a soldier and ended up King of Sweden and Norway."

Farron whistled. "Talk about a career change. That offers hope for me, a lowly commoner, as I'm now dating a prince."

I laughed, the sound bubbling from deep in my chest. "Oh, you have no idea. The stories I could tell you about royal history..."

We strolled down the street, my heart swelling as I pointed out landmarks. The Storting, the grand building that housed our parliament, stood proud and imposing. "That's where all the political action happens. Though sometimes I think the real decisions are made over *aquavit* and *tørrfisk*."

"Over what now?" Farron's nose wrinkled adorably.

"*Aquavit* is vodka infused with certain herbs, like dill. It's not my favorite, but it pairs well with fish, including *tørrfisk*. It's a traditional way of drying cod, which is then used for other dishes, like *lutefisk*, dried cod treated with lye. It's... an acquired taste."

Farron's expression was priceless. "You're shitting me, right? Fish soaked in poison?"

"Language, darling," I chided playfully. "And it's perfectly safe. Mostly."

Farron opened his mouth, then closed it again. "I'll try it at least once. For you."

I patted his shoulder. "Perfect answer. Very diplomatic."

We continued our walk, passing by the National Theatre. I recounted tales of Henrik Ibsen and other Norwegian playwrights, delighting in Farron's genuine interest. His questions were thoughtful, his observations keen. I found myself falling even deeper in love with him, if that was possible.

As we approached the Royal Palace, I felt a mix of pride and nervousness. "And this," I said, gesturing to the impressive building, "is the home of my cousin Gustav and his wife, Ingrid, now King and Queen of Norway. Well, one of their homes, anyway."

Farron's eyes widened. "It's huge."

"It's not all living space, you know. There are offices, reception rooms... Oh! And a lovely park behind it. We should explore that later."

As we walked away from the palace, happiness filled me. Sharing my world with Farron made everything I loved about Oslo feel new and exciting again.

"You know," I said, leading him down a narrow cobblestone

street, "there's this little café I adore. They make the most divine *kanelboller*—cinnamon rolls."

Farron grinned, his eyes crinkling at the corners. "I'm always down for some sugar."

I playfully nudged his shoulder. "I thought I was all the sweetness you needed."

"Smooth talker," he chuckled, then lowered his voice. "But you're not wrong."

As we entered the café, the rich aroma of cinnamon and coffee enveloped us. I ordered in Norwegian, conscious of Farron watching me intently. We found a quiet place in a corner, with no one paying us any attention.

"I love hearing you speak Norwegian. It's sexy."

"Well, perhaps I should teach you a few phrases then."

"Yeah?" Farron leaned in, his brown eyes sparkling with interest. "Teach me something."

"All right then," I said, clearing my throat. "*Jeg elsker deg.*"

Farron's brow furrowed as he attempted to repeat the phrase. His pronunciation was endearingly awful, but I found it utterly charming. "What does it mean?" he asked.

I hesitated for a moment, suddenly feeling vulnerable. "It means I love you."

Farron's expression softened. "In that case, *jeg elsker deg* too, Tore."

EPILOGUE
TORE

Three years later

"Tore Haakon!"

I walked onto the stage in my gown and cap, proudly sporting the summa cum laude stole, as thunderous applause broke out. The loudest of all was Farron, sitting in the first row, right next to my parents and sisters and, of course, his mom and siblings. They'd all shown up for my graduation ceremony.

"Tore is graduating summa cum laude. He'll be pursuing his master's degree in International Relations and Diplomacy at the University of Oslo. He also holds the honor of being the all-time top scorer for the Hawley Hawks, leading them to their third national title in as many years in his second year as team captain," the dean announced, his last words drowned out by a standing ovation.

I proudly accepted my diploma as I shook the dean's hand, posing for the photographer. As soon as I was off the stage, Farron was there to congratulate me, kissing me in front of everyone. That picture would make the news in Norway and perhaps the

US, but neither of us cared. In the almost three years we'd officially been together, we'd learned to navigate the press.

"I'm so proud of you," Farron said once the ceremony was over and I'd shaken a thousand hands. Well, it might not've been quite that many, but it sure felt like it.

"Thank you." I kissed him quickly. "Are you ready for our next adventure?"

"*Ja, jeg er klar.*"

I grinned. "Your Norwegian is coming along nicely."

He rolled his eyes. "My pronunciation is horrible, and you know it, but I'll keep trying."

"*Jeg elsker deg.*"

His expression softened. "I love you too."

It was the first sentence I'd taught him, and one he said often. As reluctant as he'd been about us initially, he now expressed his love for me every chance he got.

Farron had changed. He'd shed some of his gruffness and the chip on his shoulder was gone. He'd never become a sunshine like me, but that was fine. He'd found peace, and that was all that mattered.

After Farron and I made up and decided to be boyfriends officially, I'd decided to go back to Hawley and finish my degree. One reason was that Farron, who'd taken a job as a fitness trainer at a gym, would be there since he wasn't ready to leave his siblings behind yet. But I'd also wanted to keep playing with the Hawks. The sense of belonging I'd felt there was special, and it had only grown stronger after I'd been voted team captain my junior year.

My identity had been a bit of a public secret on campus. Every now and then, I'd get some remarks—some positive, some critical—but overall, people left me alone and accepted me as Tore Haakon rather than Prince Tore.

But now that I'd graduated, we had decided to spend at least two years in Norway. Farron's siblings would miss him, but I'd already promised they could come visit any time they wanted. Farron wanted to get to know my country—his future country as well because he'd get a Norwegian passport once we got married. The man needed to ask me first officially, but we both knew we wanted that down the line. My coming out had made the news in Europe, but it hadn't been a big issue. Thank goodness times had changed in that sense.

Farron had been terrified of how my fellow citizens would feel about him, especially since he didn't know much about Norway, but I'd assured him they'd love him. And, of course, we hadn't announced anything until after he'd gotten a crash course on our country, culture, and history and had started learning the language. A natural he wasn't, but people appreciated his efforts.

And my parents—a little apprehensive at first because he was an American—had come to love him as well. When my mom found out he'd supported his family all those years, she'd embraced him as her future son-in-law. My father had taken a little longer, but in the end, Farron's dedication to me had won him over.

As for my friends... well, they loved him. Of course, Nils, Floris, and Greg had given me endless grief for not only coming out as bi—both Greg and Floris had made some comments about being disappointed I hadn't been bicurious with them, the fuckers—but also for ending up with a Yank. But once they met him, they loved him.

Then again, those three had met some fascinating people themselves since then, so I'd been able to return the favor and tease them mercilessly... but that was not my story to tell.

I studied Farron as he stood there, one arm around Rowan—who was about to graduate from high school—and one arm around Calista. He was such a good brother to them. Would he want to have kids in the future? I could so easily see him as a dad, teaching our kids how to play football and dressing them in cute little football jerseys—Manchester City, obviously.

I wasn't sure where my journey with Farron would lead, but it didn't matter. Whether we ended up in Norway, the US, or even somewhere else, we'd be together, and in the end, that was all that mattered.

As long as I had Farron by my side, I had everything I needed for my happily ever after.

ACKNOWLEDGMENTS

I want to thank the team at Boldwood for the warm welcome they gave me, especially Megan Haslam. You believed in this series from the start, and it makes me so happy. The cover is amazing, and I'm so proud of this book.

A big thank you to Abbie and Vicki who caught stupid mistakes, fixed errors I missed, and did it all under a super tight deadline. You two are amazing, and I hope you know that.

But above all, a massive thank you to my amazing readers. Thank you for loving my men as much as I do. My heart is so full.

ABOUT THE AUTHOR

Nora Phoenix is a *USA Today* Bestselling author of over 60 MM/gay romances. When she's not writing or reading, she's spending time with her son, travelling, or gardening. Originally from The Netherlands, she currently resides in upstate New York.

Sign up to Nora Phoenix's mailing list here for news, competitions and updates on future books.

Visit Nora's website: www.noraphoenix.com

Follow Nora on social media:

- facebook.com/authornoraphoenix
- instagram.com/nora.phoenix
- bookbub.com/authors/nora-phoenix

Boldwood EVER AFTER

xoxo

JOIN BOLDWOOD'S **ROMANCE COMMUNITY** FOR SWEET AND SPICY BOOK RECS WITH ALL YOUR FAVOURITE TROPES!

SIGN UP TO OUR NEWSLETTER
HTTPS://BIT.LY/BOLDWOODEVERAFTER

Boldwood

Boldwood Books is an award-winning fiction publishing company seeking out the best stories from around the world.

Find out more at www.boldwoodbooks.com

Join our reader community for brilliant books, competitions and offers!

**Follow us
@BoldwoodBooks
@TheBoldBookClub**

Sign up to our weekly deals newsletter

https://bit.ly/BoldwoodBNewsletter

www.ingramcontent.com/pod-product-compliance
Ingram Content Group UK Ltd.
Pitfield, Milton Keynes, MK11 3LW, UK
UKHW020506110325
456073UK00001B/4